THE MOUNTAIN-SPRITE'S KINGDOM

The Mountain–Sprite's Kingdom

And Other Stories

By *Edward Knatchbull-Hugessen*
(Baron Brabourne)

1881

Black Rolf and Elfrida

CONTENTS

1

THE MOUNTAIN-SPRITE'S KINGODM

I T WAS A gorge-a very deep gorge in the side of a very large mountain, and it seemed for all the world as if some enormous giant–bigger than anybody has ever imagined, and more hungry than giants usually are—had mistaken the mountain for a gigantic plumcake, and cut out of it a tremendous hunch in order to satisfy his ravenous appetite. This, at least, was what it looked like when you first saw it from the waters of the lake below the mountain, and it was not until you got close to it that you found it was rather more than a slice which had been cut out, and that the giant must not only have been very hungry indeed, but must have cut his cake very oddly and very awkwardly. At the point where you would have expected to find the end of the slice, the gorge suddenly curved round to the right and left, and became two separate gorges, diving quite into the heart of the mountain, much further and much deeper than any giant would ever have been likely to cut.

So I do not believe the story of the giant at all, and I cannot advise the children to do so either. Perhaps the gorge was made by the waters of the blue lake below, only it does not seem as if they could ever have got high enough to make it : perhaps an avalanche of snow from the top of the higher mountains came down and cut out the gorge by the force of its weight; or perhaps the fairies and mountain-sprites did it all for their own amusement, some day when they had nothing better to do. After all, this is the most likely "perhaps," because those mountains were said to be full of sprites and fairies, and that is the reason why I am going to tell you something about them.

Some people, of course, will tell you that it is all nonsense, and that there are no such things as sprites and fairies, but then those are the people who do not like the children to make a noise, and are always grave and quiet and wise themselves, and to such people fairies do not care to come, and therefore, as they never see them, it is perhaps natural that they should not believe in their existence. But those who read this little story will see at once that there inst be fairies and sprites, because otherwise the things of which I am going to tell you could never really have happened. And if these things had never happened, how could old Karl the woodman have ever told them to me so that I could write them down for the children to read ? It was not so very long ago, either, though I forgot to ask the exact date, but I know it was in the days when England was an island, and English people could not come to the continent of Europe without crossing the sea in a ship or boat. So you see things have not changed so very greatly, and if we knew the whole truth, there may be fairies and all kinds of wonderful beings at this very moment in the place which was the scene of my story.

Old Karl was at work in the gorge, cutting wood to carry down to the big hotel at the foot of the mountain, as he had done for several years past; in fact, ever since the hotel had been built, to provide lodging for the travellers who had been coming, every year in greater numbers, to see the beautiful lake and the snow-crowned mountains which hovered over it like guardian spirits. In this particular year, more strangers than ever seemed to have arrived, and everything was bustle and confusion in the hotel and down by the shores of the lake, where several people had begun to build lodging-houses to attract the wanderers. But, higher up in the mountains, all was quiet enough. The magpies who frequented the woods on each side of the gorge, had it pretty much all to themselves, except when a journeying rook broke in upon their lazy chattering with his businesslike caw as he passed by; or a large hawk, on his search for prey, hovered over the ravine for an instant, and then soared away over the high mountains, with a haughty disdain for birds who could not fly as high as he himself could.

All, I say, was quiet, and old Karl went on chopping his wood and minding his own business, which is a very good thing for everybody to do, and generally prevents people from getting into trouble. Chop, chop, chop, went the old man, and was getting on capitally with his day's work, when he was suddenly interrupted by the sound of voices, which being a very unusual sound at that particular place, caused him to stop and listen in some surprise at the interruption. Yes, voices they undoubtedly were, and young voices, too; merry voices into the bargain; and with the voices came laughter, bright, pleasant laughter, such as comes from hearts upon which the cares of the world have not yet begun to press heavily. They came nearer and nearer, up the little path which Karl himself had followed to reach the spot where he was at work, and before he had time to wonder much longer at the unexpected sounds, the owners of the voices came in sight, close to him, walking along the path straight to the place where the old man stood.

They were two persons, a boy and a girl, and it was at once evident to Karl that they were strangers, no doubt the children of some of those travellers from distant lands of whom I have just spoken. The boy seemed to be about fourteen, tall and strong for his age, well-built, with an honest, open face, and a joyous expression upon it as if he had come out to be pleased with everything and meant to be so too. His sister—for such she evidently was—seemed to be about a year younger:—she was of a fair complexion, with light brown hair and blue eyes, and though she was unlike her brother in

11

features, there was the same joyous expression, which told of a guileless, happy nature, untainted by the coldness and hardness which advancing years too often bring with them. The brother and sister appeared to be on the best possible terms, and came laughing and singing along towards old Karl, whom they saw for the first time as they turned the corner of the path and came close upon him.

"Hurrah!" shouted the boy, as soon as he saw the old wood-cutter. "Here is an old man who will be able to tell us all we want to know, if we can only make him understand!" and forthwith the boy began to question Karl about the place they were in—where the path led to—how far it was to the top of the mountain—and whether there were not splendid views to be seen higher up?

Now all this was information very useful to a traveller, and very desirable to be acquired by such, but in this case there was a little difficulty in the matter, inasmuch as the young questioner spoke in a language which old Karl could by no means understand. Fortunately, however, the lady was (as ladies not unfrequently are) the means of making things go smoothly. Although Karl could not understand her language, she, having been a good girl, and always attentive to her governess (as good girls invariably are), knew some of his sufficiently to make him understand what her brother was asking him, and to interpret his reply.

This, it must be confessed, was not favourable to their further progress. The old woodcutter honestly told them that the path was steep and difficult, and moreover expressed his own belief that the side of the mountain was inhabited by so many wonderful and powerful spirits, of one kind or another, that it was by no means safe for mortals to travel upon it. But the children only laughed at these wise words, and said that they did so long to see the beautiful view which they knew there must be from the mountains that they were determined to go on. The old man shook his head gravely, but it was none of his business to stop them, and if he had wished to do so ever so much, I do not think he would have succeeded. This was probably his own opinion too, so after standing still for a few seconds, watching the two gay young creatures as they went on their way, he resumed his work, and went steadily on with it until it was time to go home.

I do not suppose he thought much more about the children after they had left him. When the proper time came he stopped work, shouldered his axe, left his faggots tied up according to his custom, and marched slowly down the mountain to his little cottage, where his old wife greeted him kindly, and they had their usual pleasant gossip over all that they had to gossip about, which was, after all, very little. The old man was not likely to have picked up much news upon the mountain-side, where there was nobody to talk to, and in listening to the scraps of information which his wife had gathered during her journey to the village below, where she had been, according to custom, to buy sundry household necessaries, he quite forgot to tell her of the only adventure which had actually happened to him, namely, his interview with the two young creatures.

So the evening passed away quietly enough, and the worthy couple retired to rest at their usual time, troubled by few cares, and having before them the calm prospect of a long succession of similarly tranquil and uneventful days. This prospect, however, was destined to be interrupted in a manner which neither of them could by any possibility have expected.

The morrow, indeed, dawned as fair as ever, the morning sun lighted up the woody sides of the mountain with his cheerful rays; the placid waters of the lake below reflected his grandeur in the heavens above; the fresh air filled every breathing creature with new life and vigour; and every human being capable of enjoying existence blessed in his heart the Creator who had made so glorious a world for His creatures to live in.

Old Karl was astir betimes, and, shouldering his axe, marched steadily up the hill to the place where his usual work was to be performed. Although his limbs were aged, his heart felt young and light and glad on that beautiful morning, and his strokes fell upon the trees like the strokes of a youthful and vigorous man, so inspiriting was the delicious air of his native mountains, and so invigorating the breath of the glorious morning. He worked on steadily till towards mid-day, and then, as upon the day before, he heard voices, but voices of less musical and pleasant tones than those which had then fallen upon his ears. They were the voices of men, of excited and angry men, speaking in loud and fierce accents, and at first he could not understand what they meant.

"Where is he?" cried one voice, "where is the murderer?" And another chimed in with words of the same sort, "Where is the old rascal who decoys and kills innocent children?"

Karl turned himself round as he heard these words, wondering what they could mean, and never for one moment suspecting that they were intended to apply to himself. He was, however, soon undeceived.

The speakers were rapidly approaching the spot on which he stood, and as he leaned upon his axe and faced the path which led from the village up the mountain, he saw some twenty peasants crowding together and hurrying up, and perceived at once that it was from them that had proceeded the words which he had heard. As to the person for whom they were intended, he was not long left in doubt, for, no sooner had they caught sight of the old woodcutter, than their *cries redoubled, and they rushed upon him with such haste and vehemence, that it seemed as if they were about to destroy him.

Meanwhile, as they all spoke at once, and in very loud tones, the old man found some difficulty at first in understanding what they meant. In fact, before he had discovered this, he was hustled this way and that, his hat knocked off, his axe taken from him, and such cuffs and shakings inficted upon him, that he began to think his neighbours had all suddenly gone mad. For they were his neighbours beyond all doubt. There was Pierre the cobbler, the greatest gossip of the village ; and Jacques the tailor; and Jean Baptiste the orange-seller ; and half-a-dozen more people with whom he had lived on friendly terms for the best part of his life, but who now seemed prompted by some strange and unaccountable desire to tear him to pieces. It was vain to struggle against such numbers, and the old man did not attempt it. But, after the first violence of his assailants had subsided, he managed with some difficulty to stammer forth the words—

"What have I done, my masters, that ye use me thus?"

Instantly they recommenced a babel of cries which were scarcely as yet intelligible to the ancient woodcutter, until at last he found that they resolved themselves principally into the question, which he could have answered much more readily if he had been allowed to hear it at first,

"Where are the strange children? What have you done with the little ones?"

When he comprehended that which was asked of him, Karl was none the less surprised at the personal attack to which he had been subjected, for as we know very well, though the simple peasants were ignorant of it, the old man had not only done the children no harm whatever, but had seen them but for a few moments, and held with them the most innocent and friendly conversation.

"The children!" he said, as soon as he could make his voice heard, "What children?"

The words were scarcely out of his mouth when his persecutors broke out again with their angry and incoherent cries.

"He pretends not to know, the old villain! Doubtless he has murdered the pretty innocents, and hidden away their bodies in some ravine! Pierre saw them going up the path towards the place where he was at work! They have never come down! What is clearer! What more certain! Oh! the old rascal, Karl, whom we all thought so quiet and respectable! Throw him down! Tear him in pieces! the child-slayer! the wretch!"

From these and similar exclamations, the woodcutter soon perceived that he was suspected of having decoyed away and murdered the two young people who had visited him upon the previous day, and, being perfectly innocent of any such offence, he felt at once indignant at being suspected thereof, and confident that his innocence could and would without difficulty be proved. If, however, the persons before him should proceed to inflict the summary punishment which they now threatened by voice and gesture, his innocence would avail him but little; therefore, being a man not devoid of common sense, he perceived that his first object must be to escape from the then present danger, and he forthwith proceeded to make the attempt.

"It is false!" he cried. "I am as innocent as any of you! Take me to the Maire!"

He could not have spoken more wisely for his own purposes. The people who threatened him were of an excitable race, whose passions were easily roused and who might commit excesses of violence in their exasperation. But they were not an unjust or cruel people, they loved fair play, and when reminded that there was a law by which the criminal, if criminal he were, could surely be punished, they gave up at once the idea of taking that law into their own hands.

"He speaks well!" they cried: "So be it—take him to the Maire. To the Maire with the old sinner!"—and without more ado Karl was hurried down the mountainside in the direction of the village.

Before he reached his destination, however, he had to encounter a worse ordeal than that which he had already passed through.

At the very entrance of the village a number of peasant women met him, whose violence, both of gesture and language was greater than that of the men. They called him every name they could lay their tongues to, accused him of the murder of the two children, and hinted this was by no means his first crime, whilst some went so far as to declare that his wife was probably as bad as he was, and that both of them ought to be made and end of at once.

To all this abuse Karl made no reply, and in due time the tongues of his revilers were hushed, and the old wood-cutter was ushered into the presence of the Maire, and for the first time learned the exact nature and full extent of the crime wit which he was charged.

It appeared that an English family had arrived, two days before, at one of the large hotels upon the edge of the lake, intending to remain there for some little time. The day after their arrival, the youthful son and daughter of the family, Lionel and Ethel Newton, had sallied forth to explore the mountains after the fashion, from time immemorial, of restless and curious English youth. They had been seen walking through the village, and Pierre, the cobbler, who had happened to have been that day higher up the mountain than usual, had met them, and declared that they were then going direct to the spot at which old Karl the woodcutter was working. Since that time they had disappeared, and no trace whatever could be found of them, although their disconsolate parents had made every inquiry.

In these circumstances, however, there was nothing so absolutely to attract suspicion to the old woodcutter as to justify the energetic and somewhat hasty proceedings of the villagers. Why, then, and at whose direction, had these proceedings been taken? This was the mysterious part of the story, and herein again was Pierre the cobbler one of the most important witnesses. This worthy man against whose character no one had ever averred aught save to the effect that he was a bit of a gossip, solemnly declared that at a later hour in the afternoon than that at which he had seen the two missing ones upon the mountain; in fact, when the shades of evening were first wrapping the hillside in obscurity, and objects could be only indistinctly seen, he had seen and heard that which filled him with alarm and dismay.

While sitting at his window, which commanded a view of the path from the village to the mountain, and musing, as he said, upon things in general, he had heard sounds of sobbing and weeping, which evidently proceeded from the hillside. Castin ghis eyes up, he perceived two shadowy, misty forms, flitting rather than walking through the fast-rising mist, and in another instant, as they passed close to his window, he distinctly recognized the figures of the very boy and girl whom he had met upon the mountainside. Pale they were, paler than when he had met them, but they wore precisely the same dresses, and were, beyond all doubt, the same brother and sister whom he had seen. And as they passed rapidly by, he heard them, as plainly as he had ever heard anybody in his life, lamenting and bewailing some misfortune of the nature and extent of which he would have been profoundly ignorant, had not the two figures stayed their course for one moment just when they had passed his

house, and uttered the following words on to the other in
mournful tones, which, as Pierre protested, seemed to pierce
down into his very heart:—

"Oh, brother dear, how wretched is our doom
To perish thus so far away from home!"

"Yes, sister, who so sad as you and I,
By axe of cruel woodcutter to die?"

On hearing these words and seeing the two figures,
Pierre was, as he said, overwhelmed with astonishment, but,
being sufficiently wise to know that if he were to disclose
what he had seen and heard without due caution, he might be
accused either of dealing with supernatural beings, as these
doubtless were, or of having had something to do with the
misfortune which had fallen upon the brother and sister, he
said nothing at the moment. This might perhaps have arisen
from another cause besides that of wisdom, for Pierre, being
a bachelor and living alone, had no one to whom he could
have spoken upon the matter, however much he might have
wished it, without leaving his house, and to do this he had
no inclination. But when, later on in the evening, word came
from the hotel that the two young people were missing, it
soon transpired that other persons beside Pierre had seen the
figures and heard something of the same sort as had come
to his ears, and thus it was that suspicion began to point
towards old Karl the woodcutter.

It was not, however, until the next morning that the
people began to lay their heads together and to compare
notes, and hence the delay which caused it to be well-nigh
mid-day before the old man was interrupted at his work, and
presently dragged down to the village and carried before the
Maire. By this functionary he was sternly questioned, and
told all he knew without any concealment. This, however,

had but little effect in calming the anger of the people or turning their suspicions in any other direction. To their minds the evidence was quite conclusive. The two lost children had been seen going to the place where Karl had been at work, —they had never been seen again—and the mysterious figures which had appeared in the village had beyond all doubt been the spirits of the brother and sister, who had been permitted to return to earth in order that their murderer might be discovered, and his abominable crime meet with well-merited punishment.

To the simple villagers the matter seemed to admit of no question whatever, and had their opinion been fully given and as freely taken, Karl would probably have been executed without delay. Fortunately for him, however, matters were ordered in a somewhat more regular form, and no such rough and ready proceeding was attempted. The Maire, indeed, frowned upon him a good deal, interrupted him a good deal more, when he tried to answer the questions which were asked him, one after the other, with great rapidity, and succeeded in frightening him not a little. But no bodily injury was inflicted upon him, and when the examination had been concluded, the old man was only told that he would in due time be tried for the offence of which he was accused, and that meanwhile he would be kept in safe custody.

Accordingly, he was hurried off, amid the hootings and revilings of those who had up to so recent a period been his friends and neighbours, and was taken down to the prison which was deemed the strongest and most secure for the safe keeping of so terrible a malefactor. In fact, it was the only prison which that neighbourhood possessed, for there were but few crimes committed there, and small necessity for making provision for the detention of criminals. An old, very old, castle stood actually in the lake, being connected with the mainland by an ancient drawbridge, and entered by means of huge, old-fashioned gates which might well be supposed by the simpleminded to be the production of some wizard or magician, so ponderous and strong did they appear, and with such strange and fantastic figures were they carved and ornamented.

Beneath this castle were strange old dungeons, concerning which many wonderful legends were told, and which were visited, many a time and oft, by the curious stranger, who generally appeared to think that he knew a great deal more about the place than the guide who conducted him. But the peasants and fishermen who lived on the borders of the lake seldom or never passed within the castle walls, and few of them would have cared to enter the dungeons, even in broad daylight. Old Karl had never done so, and he felt his blood run cold, first, when he was pushed along through the castle gates and heard the grating lock turned harshly behind him, and still more when he was roughly thrust into one of the aforesaid dungeons, a loaf of brown bread, and a stone pitcher, filled with water, placed in the corner thereof, and the door closed upon him by the hand of the keeper of the place. Left alone to his meditations, the old man felt at first quite bewildered and confused,—and whilst he is in this state it will be desirable that we should take this favourable opportunity of going back in our narration of this true and rational history, and endeavour to relate what had actually become of the two young persons of whose murder the old woodcutter had been accused.

When Lionel and Ethel Newton had left the old man, they marched gaily forward along the path which led up the mountain, talking and laughing as they went, and expecting soon to come upon some magnificent view which would amply repay them for the trouble of the ascent. But, as a matter of fact, the higher they climbed, the less view did they obtain. The reason of this was very clear. At the lower part of the mountain, as the path turned and wound along the hillside, there were certainly beautiful views to be had from time to time—you could peep through the trees, and here and there, looking back, you saw the lake lying far below you, in its silent majesty, the glorious mountains surrounding it on either side, and the white outlines of the large villages which had sprung up around it glistening in the sunshine and relieving the eye as it glanced from the deep blue waters of the lake to rest upon them and the vineyards beneath which they nestled, and which seemed to creep up the foot of the mountain like fortifications built there to defend the frontier against all comers.

But the higher you ascended the mountain, and the more turns of the path you followed, thicker of course grew the leafy screen which interposed itself between you and the view, and at last our two travellers arrived at a point from which there was very little to be seen except wood and mountain. Back, to their left hand, sank the gorge, thickly wooded, and with such tall trees that they could no longer see over them to the lake; immediately before them frowned the dark woods, which seemed to reach up to the very top of the hill, and that top, alas! appeared very little nearer than when they had first begun the ascent.

They stopped for a moment, and took counsel together what they should do. Immediately before them was the course of a mountain torrent which crossed the path. It was tolerably dry at that time of year, though no doubt after snow or heavy rain it would have been impossible to cross it. Beyond it, the path seemed to wind on just as it had hitherto done, and the woods to grow thicker, or at least to be no less thick, than those through which they had already passed. But immediately to their right there appeared to be a kind of half-path, which was neither more nor less than the dry bed of that self-same torrent, which, for reasons best known to itself, had at some time or other changed its course, or of some other equally respectable torrent, which had become tired of being a torrent, or had left that particular spot to go and be a torrent somewhere else. This dry bed was full of pebbles and stones, with big rocks here and there on one side of it, and here and there jagged roots of great trees, now a large patch of furze growing as happily as if it was in a quiet, peaceful English wood, now a large slope of moss, looking as soft and comfortable as moss does look sometimes; but, between moss and fern, roots, rocks, and trees, you could make out the bed of the torrent, which evidently came from some spot very near the top of the mountain, and which would consequently lead the traveller who followed it to that desirable place.

Lionel and Ethel had seated themselves upon the trunk of a fallen tree in order to look around them and decide what route they should take, and for a few moments neither of them spoke. It was a wild, romantic scene. The dark trees above and below, the torrent trickling carelessly down the mountainside, as if with a consciousness of innate strength, which it didn't care to use then, but which it could use if it liked, and would, too, if occasion should require it; the dry bed of the old torrent, reminding one of the strength which had once been exerted, but which was now past and gone, and had only left behind it the token and memory of what it was—a mute parody upon the might and strength of man—the deep, silent gorge at their feet—the wood-crowned heights above their head; all was calculated to strike with awe and reverence the heart of the mortal who found himself in such a wild and sublime spot.

I do not think, however, that either awe or reverence were precisely the feelings which affected our two travellers at this particular moment. They were both sufficiently tired to find a few minutes' rest the reverse of unpleasant, but neither of them had the slightest wish to abandon their project of reaching the top of the mountain and seeing the glorious view which they knew must be there to be seen. Still, the difficulties had proved greater than they had anticipated, and they felt less sure than when they started of being able to accomplish the task which they had set themselves to perform. Before they had sat still very long, they both came to the same conclusion, namely, that the regular path would never lead them to the top of the mountain, or at least not without such numerous turnings and windings as would very considerably lengthen the journey.

Then came the question—Would it be possible to make use of the dry bed of the torrent? It seemed steeper, to be sure, and would be less easy to climb than the regular path. Nevertheless, it could be climbed, and was not so very bad after all. Then, there were rocks and roots on which they could rest from time to time, and it certainly seemed to be a short cut to the top of the mountain. Indeed, when they looked up, they saw what appeared to be the top, and perceived also that the torrent-bed seemed to run exactly in the right direction to reach it. True, there was a dark bit of wood to pass through, so dark and thick that they could not make sure of its length. But there was one bit of green on the top above the wood, of green grass apparently, growing close to certain crags and rocks, and all this they could see beyond the wood. It was a feat to perform, but it was possible to perform it; and what a triumph to go home with the story that they had climbed to the very top, and had seen the grandest view that was to be seen from the mountain.

So, after a short consultation, they left their seat, quitted the main path, and resolutely began to ascend by the new way which they had chosen. Their progress, as may be supposed, was neither easy nor rapid. It would have been a steep ascent, even had it teen up a smooth and well-made path, and it was anything but that; the large pebbles had a knack of turning under the foot of the climber, as if specially bent on spraining his ankle; the larger pieces of rock were not always firm enough to be trodden on with safety, and the moss was uncommonly slippery, and must be dealt with cautiously. However, the brother and sister were not to be stopped by trifles; little by little they pushed their way on, higher and higher, encouraging each other as they went, and their hopes of eventual success rising rapidly each moment.

At one time the torrent-bed was quite open, with no trees within several yards of it, and exposed to the rays of the sun in a manner which made one wonder how it had ever been anything else than a dry bed; then it passed in under shelving banks, down under the very roots of the great trees by its side, and became quite an underground passage, just for all the world as if it had been excavated by human hands. Still Lionel and Ethel pushed bravely on, and presently approached the spot at which the wood appeared denser and thicker, and above which they had been able to see nothing from their resting-place below save the green and the rock on the crest of the hill far beyond.

The brother and sister had got within a few yards of this spot, when their attention was suddenly arrested by an unexpected sound. A low, curious chuckle it was, as if some-one had been intensely amused by a joke, or a funny thought, and was giving vent to his amusement in this not uncommon manner. At home, or at the hotel, or anywhere else among their companions and fellow creatures there would have been nothing extraordinary in the sound, but it was widely different when it was heard high up upon the mountains, and issued from woods which, without exaggeration, might be called gloomy. Beings who chuckle in such places do not always do it for amusement, and may be laughing at instead of with the traveller who hears them.

It is not, therefore, surprising that the sound which reached the ears of the brother and sister by no means tended to incline them to join in a similar sound of merriment. They stopped and looked at each other with a puzzled air for a moment, and each seemed to think that the noise must have proceeded from the other, when it was repeated, not from one but apparently from many throats, and it really appeared as if the wood was full of merry people whose profession was chuckling, and who thoroughly understood the business.

From every side, above, below, right and left, came the same sounds, and after the interval of a few seconds, during which Lionel and Ethel stared at each other with speechless astonishment, the chuckle changed into a laugh, and the whole mountain-side seemed to ring with peal upon peal of laughter; not pleasant, kindly, jovial laughter such as one hears round the fireside at Christmas time, or after dinner in a country-house with a cheery host who cracks his jokes with his filberts, but harsh, cruel, mocking, gibing laughter, as of someone with hard heart and savage eyes watching the sufferings of some other creature and gloating over them with malicious pleasure.

Such were the sounds which fell upon the ears of the now frightened pair, and Ethel nestled up as close as she could to Lionel, while they both peered eagerly round in the hope of discovering whence these strange sounds proceeded. The attempt, however, was vain, and still the sounds continued, and rather seemed to increase than to abate in volume and vehemence. This lasted for certainly more than a minute, perhaps for two, and then all of a sudden there occurred something of a still more extraordinary character. The shadows of the surrounding trees had so darkened the place where the children stood that it was nearly impossible to discover any object at a greater distance than a couple of yards or so. All in an instant the whole scenery around them was lighted up with a bright blue light, not unlike that which bursts forth after the celebrated game of snap-dragon, when the salt has been thrown into the burning raisins, and the red flame of the blazing brandy suddenly becomes blue, and turns everybody's face into a caricature by no means flattering to the personal vanity of those who undergo the operation.

In like manner to this was the mountain-side lighted up in the most extraordinary and unexpected manner, and the brother and sister beheld such a sight as they had never even pictured to themselves in the wildest dreams. The wood, no longer still and calm and silent in its sombre grandeur, was perfectly alive with creatures, and such creatures as you would never believe to have existed unless you had actually seen them with your own eyes. One had the large head of a goat upon the diminutive body of a man, another a woman's head upon a form which appeared to be that of a cat. One, apparently human, was all body, with a head no bigger than a marble ; another had a head rather larger than common, with a body only two or three inches in length, so that his beard draggled on the ground. One had legs like pins, a second had no legs at all, a third was noseless, and a fourth had his head on wrong side foremost.

Most of them squinted, none were anything near the ordinary height of even a short man, and upon the faces of all—that is of those who had faces sufficiently human to enable one to judge of the matter—was a weird, strange,

uncanny expression, whilst their eyes glistened and shone
like glowworms in a dark night, or a gleam of sunshine
through the chink of a door, or a red-hot coal in a glowing
fire, or like anything else which expresses a sharp, piercing,
twinkling eye, which, multiplied manyfold, and glaring upon
you unexpectedly from all sides, is not precisely calculated
to inspire the heart with confidence, the mouth with words,
or the spirit with joy. So indeed our young travellers found
it, and were astonished beyond measure, as well as to some
extent alarmed, at the curious company in which they found
themselves.

Lionel, however, threw his left arm round his sister's
waist, and drawing her to him, prepared to defend her, if
necessary, against any danger which might threaten. Then
again the loud, shrill, mocking laughter ran along the mountain-side, as if all the beings around the children, whoever or
whatever they were, were amazingly delighted at something
which had just happened, or was immediately about to happen. It died away presently, in a faint cadence, like the end

of a tune played by a particularly disagreeable organ in the streets, and for an instant all was again silent.

For an instant only, however, and then there came bounding into the bed of the torrent, and stood before the brother and sister, a figure more strange and marvellous than any they had yet seen. Its head was the head of a man, with frizzly and very bright red hair sticking up all round, as if its owner had just been awakened out of sleep by a dream or vision so terrible as to make his hair stand on end with affright. One of his eyes was apparently the eye of a boiled fish, at least it had exactly that white, dried-up look, which made it difficult to suppose that it could easily be of any use to him. The other eye seemed to be set sideways in its socket, and reached halfway down his cheek, presenting the most hideous and grotesque appearance. His nose was very wide and flat, his mouth remarkably broad, and the ears on either side of his head stood up as high, for all the world, as if they were the ears of a donkey. But, although it was. beyond all doubt the head of a man, the neck was as evidently the neck of a bird, being covered with feathers, as long again as a man's neck would have been, and connected with a body which it is almost impossible to describe. It was the body of an animal, and of an animal with a tail, too, but whether the scaly skin with which it was clothed might be more properly said to belong to a fish or a beast of the hippopotamus tribe was a question not to be easily solved. The tail would incline one to the beast theory, though it was certainly a strange kind of beast at best, and the legs which supported the body seemed of so flexible a nature, and endowed with such extraordinary powers of contraction or expansion according to the caprice of their owner, that they really seemed to be made of India-rubber. But the marvellous thing about the whole figure was that it was quite transparent. You could see through it—through head, neck, body, and legs; and yet you could perfectly well distinguish its outline, form, and features. All seemed shadowy, yet all was sufficiently clear to be seen, and the air of mingled subtlety and malignity which sat upon its features was but too perceptible to our hero and heroine.

Now, a wood on the side of a mountain is not of itself an unpleasant thing. There is much to admire in it, and whilst you can stretch your limbs as much as you like in attempting the ascent, you have the benefit and comfort of shade to protect you from the sun, and thick foliage to ward off the passing shower. But a wood on the side of a mountain is a very different thing when peopled by such creatures as those who surrounded our two travellers, in the manner in which I have described ; and both Lionel and Ethel would very much rather have been upon a flat plain, without any trees at all, if they could have been without these strange and undesirable companions. Where the figure had come from, which they now saw immediately before them, was known to neither of them. He or it, whichever you please to say, bounded down into the centre of the road, or rather the torrentbed, and stood regarding them for a moment without any word or gesture ; then, all of a sudden, he tossed his arms high above his head, and gave vent to a kind of sound between a whine, a laugh, a shriek, and a yell, evidently the sound of no human or ordinary being. Such arms as they were, too, which he tossed aloft! neither more nor less, as it appeared to the astonished children, than the huge claws of a lobster—at least they looked red, and the hands seemed as like to that which I have mentioned as one thing can well be to another.

After his first cry, he appeared to have come to the conclusion that it would be better to express himself in some more rational and intelligible manner; and accordingly, without more delay, the following words fell upon the ears of his disturbed and astonished hearers:—

"Who are ye who dare to scale
 Mountain-side and wooded glade ?
Bid your mortal hearts to quail !
 Here your progress must be stayed.
To the region ye have come
 Where I reign, by day and night,
And the voice of man is dumb
 At the bid of Mountain Sprite!"

The extraordinary Being uttered these words in a clear, shrill, ringing voice, and, drawing himself up at the same time to his full height, which might have been nearly three feet, looked sternly at those whom he addressed, and apparently paused for a reply. What that reply should be was a question not easily to be settled by the astonished children. The whole occurrence had been so sudden and unexpected that, to use a common expression, they hardly knew whether they were standing on their head or their heels.

But it was evident that some kind of an answer was expected; and Lionel, being an English boy, and consequently not given to being afraid, plucked up spirit and answered thus—

"Who are we? Why, Lionel and Ethel Newton, to be sure; and we didn't know we were doing any harm by climbing up here."

Scarcely were the words out of the boy's mouth, than again there broke forth an universal chorus of wild laughter all around, and the little figure in front leaped up at least a yard high in the air, kicked his legs right and left, after the most absurd and grotesque fashion, and, snapping his fingers madly above his head, cried out in loud tones—

"He has answered! he has answered! The mortal child has spoken to the Sprite King. He is ours—she is ours—they are both ours!"

And again the unearthly laughter rang along the mountain-side, and died away as before in mournful cadence. And then all the fantastic figures came crowding around the brother and sister, pressing up to them on every side, and making as if they would take hold of them, and they clung closer together, and were utterly at a loss what to do or say. Suddenly a loud sound like a thunderclap re-echoed through the woods; the earth seemed to open wide immediately before them, and almost without their knowing that they had moved, they found themselves insensibly carried forward, the earth seemed to close behind them, and they were inside the mountain, shut out from the sun, and air, and trees, and away from the sight of the beautiful world outside.

It was a strange place in which they found themselves. There was the same blue light which had appeared upon the mountainside, and it illuminated the vast space inside the mountain. Marvellous were the sights which it disclosed. Quantities of trees and shrubs there were, but they all seemed to be growing downwards, as if upon the earth turned upside down. Were they walking, then, on the sky? This was the first thought that passed through their brains, but it was not so by any means, or, if it was, the sky was of a novel and curious description. They trod upon a smooth and polished surface like marble, but so bright that they could see themselves in it, as in a looking-glass, and as far as they could see right and left, there seemed to be no end to it, and no valley or hill or anything to interrupt the perfect level of the marble plain. The same strange figures were capering and jabbering all around them, and the extraordinary Being, who had first accosted them, and to whom all the others appeared to pay great deference, came up and spoke to them in the same voice.

"Young mortals!" said he, "you are now in the kingdom of the Mountain Sprite, and, as you may perhaps have guessed, I myself am that fortunate individual. You will now be my slaves for a hundred years or so, and had better make yourselves at home without further delay. The sooner you forget your past life, the better for your future happiness. Meanwhile, lest you should not have done so already, but cherish as yet some slight remembrance of your friends on Man's Earth, let me set your minds at rest. They will soon forget you, for two of my most accomplished sprites, having for a time assumed your forms and appearance, have gone down to let it be generally known that you have been murdered by an old woodcutter. This is sure to be believed, and whilst it will put an end to any unpleasantness which you might feel from the belief that your friends would be uncertain as to your fate, it will also, in all probability, serve the useful purpose of getting rid of that abominable old man who is forever annoying us by chopping down trees on our outside playground. So cheer up, and be good slaves at once!"

There were many things in this speech which greatly afflicted both Lionel and Ethel. They didn't much like the idea of being slaves, having been educated in the popular belief that this is exactly what Britons never will be, and not knowing that this only holds good as long as Britons either remain in their own, or some other free country, or, being in a slave country, are stronger than the slave owners. No man, whether Briton or not, is ever a slave from choice, and when he has no choice, he is a slave, whether Briton or not, however much he may dislike it and deny it. And when people are captured by mountain sprites they are in an awkward position, and as likely to become slaves as anything else.

But there were other things which were decidedly unpleasant in the speech to which the children had just listened. A hundred years is a long time under any circumstances, and a very long time to be shut up inside a mountain. Besides, they had a certain amount of affection for their parents and family, and did not relish the prospect of being soon forgotten by them, or of their being distressed by false accounts of their murder. As soon, therefore, as the mountain sprite had concluded his speech, both the children, struck with the same thought, gave vent to the same exclamation with one voice—

"We won't be slaves! Let us out!" and boldly looked the transparent monarch in the face.

The sprite, however, by no means angry or annoyed at this reply, burst into an immoderate fit of laughter, turning several times head over heels as he did so, as if to quiet himself by the exertion. His laughter was as usual re-echoed by his surrounding subjects, and when it had in some measure subsided, he again accosted the brother and sister in the following words:—

"You must be slaves, and you can't get out; so pray don't be troublesome, my young friends. Here, Mufflehausen, show these mortals the ways of the place, and let them rest a while before we give them work to do."

Thus summoned, a spirit of a peculiarly repulsive aspect approached the children, having the head of a .weasel, the body of a large snake, and the legs of a bird. His voice was like the shrill whistle of an engine, and pierced through the ears of those who heard him in a most painful manner.

Impelled by some resistless impulse, the brother and sister followed this strange creature, and soon found that they had by no means seen all the wonders which existed upon the smooth marble plain on which they were standing. They moved very fast, and presently they came to a number of small, low cots, nicely done up, after the fashion of mortal cots, and evidently intended for people to sleep in.

"Here,' said, or rather whistled, Mufflehausen, "you can sleep in any of these, and the sooner you get your rest the better, for our king makes the new slaves work pretty hard, I can tell you."

This was no good news to his hearers, but they were both tolerably tired, and the cots looked comfortable. So, without more ado, they each got into one, and determined that the best thing they could do would be to go to sleep. No sooner, however, had they laid themselves down with this resolution, than the cots instantly set off as hard as they could go in different directions.

Lionel heard his sister call out his name, and springing up was about to jump out and see what she wanted, when he was prevented by the extreme velocity with which his cot darted off, and he could only lie down again and wonder.

The cot was apparently upon wheels, or else was so

constructed as to run easily upon the smooth marble; but whether it was propelled by an invisible hand, or by secret machinery, Lionel had no means of ascertaining, nor did he very much care. He felt that he was "in for it," and must bear it as best he could. Neither he nor his sister had exactly such a night's rest as they could have wished. There was a good deal of noise—shrieks, laughter, howls, and sounds more or less discordant through the night, and the cots kept moving about continually as if they were alive.

At last Lionel could stand it no longer, and sat up in his cot to look around him.

There, close to him, was Ethel's cot perfectly still, whilst his was just passing it; and as he went by, she had just time to say to him—

"Charlemagne!"

And then he was past.

The natural thing for him to do was to say immediately to himself—

"Charlemagne! What does she say that for?"

And hardly were the words out of his mouth, when his cot came to a dead stop, some few yards behind that of his sister.

Lionel at once got out and stood by his sister's side.

"What on earth made you say that?" he asked; "and what a curious thing that it should have stopped the cots!"

"Yes," replied Ethel, "very curious indeed! The reason I said it was that somebody whispered it to me."

"Whispered it to you!" exclaimed Lionel. "When and where; and who was it?"

"Whilst my cot was going on quite fast," replied his sister, "I felt something like a bird pecking my cheek; and opening my eyes, which I had closed from sheer weariness, I saw a tiny bird, like a golden-crested wren. It had such a pretty little head, and such a pleasant look about it; and it whispered quite low to me, 'Say Charlemagne when you want to stop; and ask the King for a lemon drop!' and then it was gone in a moment."

"What a very funny bird!" said Lionel, "and what a queer thing to want you to say. But I don't see what you want with a lemon drop, and I daresay it was only chaff!"

"But," returned Ethel, "it couldn't be only 'chaff,' or else why did the cot stop at the word the wren told me to say? But perhaps it only said that about a lemon drop for the rhyme, and at all events I don't want one just now."

"Neither do I," responded the brother, "but all the same, I should like some breakfast."

True enough, it was time for breakfast, but here were our two young friends in the inside of the mountain, with no apparent prospect of getting anything to eat, as far as they could see. They looked wistfully at each other, and hesitated as to what they should do. They had not long to wait, however, for several creatures of extraordinary shape and form came rushing up to them with orders that they were to come to the king. As they had evidently no choice in the matter, they at once obeyed, and on approaching the curious Being who had announced to them, on the evening before, their future fate, he at once elevated his arms and snapped his fingers in the same manner. Then he made some curious passes and signs with his arms, twisted his legs about in a ridiculously absurd manner, and pronounced some words which neither Lionel nor Ethel could in the least understand. But as soon as the words were spoken, they felt all hunger pass away from them, nor did they feel hungry or thirsty again whilst they were inside the mountain.

The King of the Mountain Sprites called to some of his attendants, directed brooms to be brought, and addressing the two children by the playful appellation of "Slavekins," ordered them to sweep the marble floor, a proceeding all the more irksome because wholly unnecessary, there being apparently not one scrap of dust upon it from one end to the other. Some mysterious power, however, compelled them to obey, and thus began a life of servitude which, as far as they knew, might really continue for the time during which the Mountain Sprite had told them they should continue his slaves.

But it is time to inquire after the fate of the innocent woodcutter. Thrust roughly into the dungeon of the old castle, he was shut out from all communication with living beings. There was a quantity of straw in one corner of his prison, and upon this the old man threw himself in utter despair. It seemed hard—very hard—that so cruel a fate should have overtaken him without any fault of his own. Still, on the whole, he thought (and thought rightly) that it was better so than if there had been fault on his part, for in that case he should have lacked the comfort which he derived from his own consciousness of being innocent. This, however, did not furnish him with any means of escape from the danger in which he perceived himself to be. There could be no doubt that the people of the place were generally convinced of his guilt : that was hard too, for they were his neighbours, who had long known him, and ought not to have been so ready to think evil of him. But so it was, and as far as he could see before him, the prospect was very dark. He would probably be dragged before the magistrate—perhaps again and again ; what would be done to him he knew not, but if he escaped with his life it would be by something little short of a miracle.

As he lay upon the straw, musing over all that had happened, and still almost stunned by the suddenness and severity of the misfortune which had fallen upon him, the old man cast up his eyes, and perceived that his dungeon was lighted up by a soft light, produced by the rays of the moon piercing through a slit in the wall, high above his head. This was better, anyhow, than being entirely in the dark, and although the silence was rather dull than otherwise, it was relieved by the sound of the water gurgling round the old castle walls, and seeming as if it was exploring every hole and crevice to find its way in, and murmuring gently to itself as it found the task too hard for it.

So there the old man lay, quiet enough, thinking and listening, listening and thinking, until his thoughts and attention were both turned in another direction by a very singular occurrence. In the embrasure of the wall in which was the slit. which admitted the light, there suddenly appeared something which for an instant obscured the rays of the moon. Only for an instant, however, and then it leapt lightly from its place down on to the floor of the dungeon and stood exactly in front of the prisoner. It was the figure of a woman—a little woman—a very little woman—ard she was dressed in feathers from top to toe—in soft brown feathers, intermixed with plumage of a brighter and variegated character which relieved the brown, and gave to her whole costume a rich and gay appearance. In height she could scarcely have reached two feet—the symmetry of her form was perfection itself—her face, shadowy and indistinct, had yet something at once sweet and noble in its expression which you could easily enough discern—her hands and feet were the smallest you can imagine, and there was something about her altogether so royal and queenlike that the old woodcutter felt certain that he was in the presence of a very noble and exalted personage. She stood before him for a moment without uttering a syllable, and then, gracefully waving her hand, thus accosted the wondering old man:—

"Karl!" she said, and her voice rang through the dungeon clear and sweet, and at the same time soft and soothing like the chimes of a church bell heard across the water upon a calm summer's evening, "Karl! Cheer up! You have friends at hand!"

The old woodcutter was so astonished at the sight he saw and the words he heard that he could at first make no reply to his gracious speech, but, recovering himself in a few moments, he sat up upon his straw bed, and, reverently bowing his head to his visitor, responded to her salutation in the following manner:— "Friends! and need enough poor old Karl has of friends, please your gracious Highness's greatness's Majesty! To think of such as your Royalty's graciousness coming to the likes of I! But how the friends will get me out of this terrible place is more than I can guess, being but an ignorant old woodcutter."

The strange visitor smiled at these words. does not know one's friends always in this world, good Karl," she said, "nor, for the matter of that, one's enemies either—nevertheless, be assured that I speak the truth to you, and that you most certainly have friends, and powerful friends too, and such as will not rest satisfied until you are not only delivered from this hateful dungeon, but your innocence of the foul crime imputed to you established beyond the possibility of doubt in the open light of day."

"Ah me!" sighed old Karl as he heard this pleasant speech. "No doubt, no doubt, it can be proved if the folk will listen, but who is to prove it? and will they believe it, since they were so ready to believe against me? Is your ladyship's High Mightiness able to make the neighbours believe me innocent?"

"We shall see," replied the lady, with another sweet smile; and then she added, "Lest you should doubt my power, good Karl, I will tell you who and what I am, and why it is that I am here to befriend you today. Do you remember last spring, when you drove away the boys who were going to take the golden-crested wren's nest ? Twice you drove them away, and the little bird hatched her young in safety. Little did you think that the good deed, which your kind heart prompted you to do, would be so soon repaid to you. Be it known to you, Karl, that upon these mountains there are two sorts of spirits. The Mountain-Sprite claims the whole dominion, and indeed he is almost all-powerful in the interior of the mountains. Outside, however, it is very different, and the Bird-Fairies dispute the supremacy with this mischievous elf. I am the Wren-queen, and of all the bird-fairies none are so mighty as I in these parts. Now Wrens never forget a kindness, and you may be sure that your kindness will not be unrewarded, therefore do not despair. Keep a light heart in your honest bosom, and before three days have passed over your head you shall be again a free and happy man."

So saying, and without giving the old man time to reply, the Wren-queen lightly sprang upon the embrasure, passed through into the silent night, and left the old wood-cutter alone in his dungeon-alone, but no longer in the sad and despondent state in which she had found him. Hope, the brightest companion of the human heart, had newly sprung up in his breast, and although the way and time of his escape were still unknown to him, somehow or other he had the most implicit faith in the promise which had been given him by this strange visitor.

So, being a man of a practical turn of mind, and more-over rather tired with the labour and excitement of the day, he turned over upon his straw bed, and fell fast asleep.

In this state of blissful repose we will leave our old friend, in order to inquire into the state of things which had all this time prevailed in the village. During the whole of that day the place had been in a state of ferment and excitement, to which it was usually a stranger. People talked and gossiped, and stared and wondered, and stood about in groups, and asked one another questions, everybody earnestly seeking to obtain some scrap of information about the matter which nobody was able to afford them, because nobody knew any-thing about the two lost children except themselves and the Mountain Sprite, or some other supernatural beings.

But, after all, the people really to be pitied were two individuals to whom I have scarcely yet alluded, namely, the unfortunate parents of the two lost children. Mr. and Mrs.

Newton were extremely fond of their two treasures, which is not an uncommon thing with fathers and mothers, and is in fact their natural condition, unless some extraordinary reason exists for a different state of feeling. They had, therefore, been deeply distressed at the disappearance of Lionel and Ethel, and had passed an exceedingly miserable time ever since it occurred. As hour after hour passed on, and still no tidings came of the missing wanderers, the misery of the parents became almost unendurable. A thousand times they bemoaned their hard fate; a thousand times they repented the love of mountain and lake scenery which had tempted them from their native land, and avowed in their inmost souls that if they were but permitted to take their beloved children home again, they would never quit the safe shores of old England.

Such thoughts, such regrets, such repentance, such vows were but idle and useless efforts of the perturbed mind and troubled spirit of the worthy couple, and the cause of their anguish remained unremoved and untouched. The day after their loss drew sadly to its close, and whilst the old woodcutter was sleeping calmly upon his prison bed, the unhappy Newtons knew no rest, and scarcely sought it indeed, so oppressed were they with the bitterness of their heavy grief.

The next day dawned fair and mild—the sun lighted up the mountainside with his glorious rays—the birds twittered—the flowers up-raised their heads newly washed and still heavy with the morning dew—the lake reflected back the sun's image from its smooth surface, and lay there calm and still in its mighty silence-and all creation appeared to rejoice and revel in the fresh strength and life of a newly born day. With slow steps and heavy hearts the poor parents walked out into the little garden between their hotel and the lake, and looked with mournful eyes upon the peaceful, happy scene before them. All was joyous—all tranquil—all lovely—but to their eyes the loveliness had lost its charm—tranquillity was banished from their hearts, and joy seemed to have fled forever. Slowly and sadly they walked down to the edge of the lake; their hearts were too full for words, and they sighed deeply as they stood there together.

Suddenly a sound struck upon their ears which caused them the utmost surprise, and after an instant turned the whole current of their thoughts. A clear, sweet, bell-like voice came to them, whether from lake or land they could scarcely tell, but it was easy enough to hear, and they could distinguish every syllable as distinctly as if the speaker had been one of themselves : and these were the words they heard:—

> "Over the mountains by day and by night
> Roameth the restless Mountain Sprite,
> Woe to the maiden and woe to the child
> That meeteth, unaided, that spirit wild!
> Yet, though his might may be strange and great,
> Oft is he checked ere he works his ends,
> Oft has the mortal escaped his fate,
> Spirit-foes quelling by spirit-friends!
> Cheer the sad spirit and banish fear,
> (Ill root to rest in the heart of men,)
> And when ye welcome your children dear,
> Bless the kind birds and the queenly wren!"

The voice ceased as suddenly as it had begun, and the listeners looked at each other in the greatest astonishment. Although they could not understand the exact meaning of the words, and could see nothing of the speaker, it was evident that allusion was intended to the fate of their children, and that the meaning conveyed was by no means one of an unfavourable nature. Hope revived in their breasts at once, and, moving eagerly forward in the direction from which the voice appeared to proceed, they addressed the unseen speaker in earnest accents, imploring him to tell them something more, and to disclose himself that they might thank him for the comfort which he had given them in their distress.

But they might as well have spoken to the trees or stones. No one appeared—no one replied. Not a word more did they hear; and had it been only one of them who had heard the first words the other would certainly have fancied that it was only a delusion or a dream. This, however, was an idea which never entered their heads for an instant. Both had heard the voice, both had eagerly drunk in every word, and both were prepared to swear solemnly to the fact of the unseen speaker having spoken in the above manner. They felt, therefore, in spite of the silence which followed, that they had grounds for hope which they had not previously entertained, and were immeasurably relieved accordingly.

Mr. Newton began to recollect all the tales which he had heard of sprites and fairies possessing power in those wild mountain regions which was denied to them in more civilised parts of the world ; and although he had always been accustomed to reject such tales as idle delusions, the product of highly-wrought imaginations and fanciful brains, he now began to hope eagerly that they might be true after all, and that in their truth he and his wife might find the solution of their present troubles.

Cheered by the new hope which had been thus strangely awakened in their breasts the parents passed that day with somewhat less of misery than they had previously felt since their affliction had befallen them. They sorrowed indeed, and still almost doubted the reality of the scene which had occurred at the edge of the lake, but hope, stronger than doubt, buoyed them up, and they strove to encourage each other by recalling the words which they had heard, and the confident as well as friendly tone in which they had been uttered. The day wore slowly on, and as the shades of evening began again to fall upon the shores of the lake, and still no tidings of the lost ones had arrived, hope once more grew fainter, and doubts and fears again arose with redoubled strength.

Mr. Newton had inquired high and low, and had offered rewards of sufficient amount to have tempted any one in that poor neighbourhood who had news to tell or information to afford. But all was useless, and when night had nearly closed in nothing had been heard of the brother and sister, to whom it is but proper that we should now return.

They had been ordered, we know, to sweep the floor of the Mountain Sprites' Palace (if thus should be called the inside of the mountain), and felt themselves compelled to obey by some mysterious power. On and on they swept, not at all liking the work, and wishing over and over again that they were well out of the place. The matter was not improved, either, by the conduct of the strange inhabitants of the place, who kept dancing about, grinning at the children, jeering, laughing, and making remarks which were anything but polite or agreeable. There was no help for it, however; they felt themselves obliged to work on, and their only comfort was that they could do so together.

But even this consolation was not long left to them. A being with a cod's head and shoulders and the body of a tortoise upon the legs of a Cochin-China fowl stalked up to the two children and conveyed the king's orders that the boy slavekin should immediately clean his boots, whilst the girl was to come and comb his hair. As the strange creature spoke he tossed the boots to Lionel, and a curious pair of boots they were, and apparently made of eel-skin, and so wonderfully slippery that he had the greatest difficulty in holding them, whilst how to clean such things he had not the least idea.

So there he stood, fumbling about with the boots, not knowing what to do next, whilst his sister was led to the

king, a large gold comb put into her hand, and bidden to
begin to comb his hair immediately. The hair did not seem
to want combing at all, and stood up so straight and stiff
all round his majesty's head that under no circumstances
could much have been done with it in the way of combing.
Still less when the head was never for a moment still; first
it bobbed up and then it bobbed down, at one moment it
nodded violently, at the next threw itself back as if intent
upon breaking its neck, then it wagged vehemently from one

side to the other, and all the time the face made the most extraordinary grimaces, and the eyes squinted and winked and leered in a manner perfectly outrageous.

Poor Ethel could make nothing of the job, do what she would, and the attendant sprites and wonderfully-shaped creatures around hooted and laughed and yelled in great amusement. At last the king jumped up, bounded away, turned head over heels, threw up his legs and cracked his fingers as usual, and declared he would have no more of it till next time. To this poor Ethel had not the slightest objection, and was beginning to move quietly away, although hardly knowing where to go to or what to do, when the king suddenly appeared to have changed his mind, for rushing back again he begun to tumble about in his usual fantastic manner, and then planting himself before the child made several miraculously ugly faces in quick succession, and informed her that her next duty would be to tickle his ears with a feather.

This task appeared likely to be even less easy of accomplishment than the last, unless his majesty would keep his royal head rather more still than before; but Ethel felt some power which compelled her to attempt it, and accordingly commenced, using a feather which was handed to her by one of the attendant sprites. Vainly, however, did she strive to keep the feather on or near the king's ear. The head, as before, was never still for an instant, and, what was worse, the mountain-sprite began to get cross and to abuse her for not doing her work properly.

"Slavekin!" he cried, "vile mortal slavekin, you are useless and idle. Take more pains, little earth-child, or you must be punished."

This rather frightened Ethel, and produced no improvement in the tickling. So the king became more and more cross, and threatened her again. It was by this time late in the afternoon, and the children had now been more than a whole day and night in the heart of the mountain. Ethel looked round for her brother with some vain idea that he might come and help her, but she saw no help, and at that moment the king called out—

"Bring the other slavekin and whip him well, that will punish her," and two or three sprites immediately hurried off.

Just then something lightly touched Ethel's ear, and she heard a little low, chirping whisper, which said quite clearly and quite close to her—

" If he threaten but one more time
Ask as I told you—but ask in rhyme."

Until that moment the child had quite forgotten what had happened in the morning when her cot stopped at the mystic word, but she remembered directly she heard this voice, and determined at once to do as she was told. She had not much time to think, before she saw Lionel coming on, apparently pushed by several creatures who were crowding round behind him and urging him forward until he came close to where the king was. When he was quite near, the monarch threw up his legs and arms after his own peculiar fashion, and then said in a loud voice:—

"Since we can make so little of the sister,
Upon the brother's back we'll raise a blister—
So, no delay, my sprites, the hours are jogging,
Give the male slavekin a tremendous flogging!"

He cracked his fingers as he spoke, and in an instant the sprites around seemed ready to obey his commands, for several of them drew from their sides whips which appeared to be nothing less than live snakes, whirled them aloft in the air, and to all appearance were about to lay them smartly upon poor Lionel's back.

But before a single blow could fall, Ethel interposed in great haste with a rhyme which she had been busily making ever since she had heard the voice:—

"Stay, sir! before my brother thus you whop
I'll trouble you for just one lemon drop."

The words were scarcely out of her mouth, when a piercing shriek issued from the mouth of the king, which was immediately re-echoed by all the strange beings around him. One united, simultaneous, awful yell, and the next moment all was silence. Nor did the marvel stop here. The

light suddenly disappeared, and the whole interior of the
mountain was plunged in darkness the most profound. At
the same time the children insensibly drew close together
and joined hand in hand. As they did so, they heard the
gentle rustling of wings near them, and a voice whispered
once more in their ears:—

"The spell is broken for a while;
        The mystic words of magic art
Have freed ye from the spirit's guile;
        Then haste, oh, haste ye, to depart."

This time the voice was easily heard by both brother
and sister, and they were quite ready to profit by the advice
which it gave. It is difficult, however, to walk in the dark,
and they would hardly have known what to do, if an invisible
hand had not laid hold of each of them and guided them
forward. They had not far to go, and in one moment, when
they least expected it, a door seemed to open before them,
and they stepped out upon the side of the mountain. Ah,

what a glorious, happy change from that terrible and wonderful place from which they had just emerged! The pure air of heaven kissed their cheeks, the beautiful green trees waved over their heads, the blue sky hung in serene majesty overhead, and they realised in that one moment how lovely and marvellous is the world in which the Great Creator has placed his mortal children.

There was something unusual, too, on the mountainside. Above, around, on each side, everywhere, were myriads of wrens, chirping and singing joyously, and flying from bush to bush with evident delight. It was impossible to mistake their carol of joy, and still more so when amongst them appeared a figure which I need scarcely describe to any one who remembers the little lady who visited old Karl in his lonely dungeon. She it was, and she sweetly smiled on Lionel and Ethel as she spoke to them in the following words:

> "By fairy will and wrennish might
> Have ye escaped the Mountain Sprite.
> Now bide no longer on the hill
> Where such have power to work you ill.
> Haste to your parents! Tarry not,
> Nor let old Karl be quite forgot!"

She spoke, and as she did so, pointed to the path which led down the mountainside, which the brother and sister began immediately to descend. Before they had gone two steps, however, the same thought struck both of them at the same time, and they turned round together, saying, "Oh, lady, how shall we ever thank you enough for—" But here they suddenly stopped, for they were speaking to empty space. In one second, lady, wrens, and every living creature had disappeared, and all seemed as quiet and natural as if such things as wrens and mountain-sprites had never existed.

Much surprised, and not without a certain amount of dread, the children delayed no longer, but hurried as fast as they could down the mountain to the village. Curiously enough, they thought they had only been one day and one night in the interior of the mountain, but we who know what had happened since their disappearance are aware that they must have been there more than double that time. For, as far as I can make out (though people differ so in their account of the same things that it is almost impossible to discover the real truth about them), Mr. and Mrs. Newton must have been at least two nights without news of their children, including that which preceded the afternoon of their disappearance; and old Karl, as we know, having been arrested on the day after, had passed the second night in his dungeon. Therefore, as near as I can tell, Lionel and Ethel must have been, say from Monday evening until Wednesday evening in the kingdom of the MountainSprite, and I am not quite sure whether it was really Wednesday or Thursday upon which they got out. I like to be particular, but after all it does not much signify now that we know they did get out, and what is more, that they got safely down from the mountain into the village.

Their appearance there created the greatest surprise. Some people screamed—some fainted—some ran away—but the greater part surrounded them with shouts of joy and eager inquiries as to where they had been and what had been the cause of their absence. Being but imperfectly acquainted with the language of the country, neither Lionel nor Ethel was able to satisfy their questions, but, surrounded by the eager crowd, they made the best of their way to the hotel at which their parents were staying, and arrived there just as the latter, having partaken of a melancholy dinner, were standing upon the balcony, and looking with sad and wistful gaze towards the mountains which seemed to have swallowed up their treasures.

They heard the loud shouts of the approaching villagers, and although the night was closing in too fast to allow of the objects before them being distinctly visible, the mother's instinct soon told her the truth, and in a very few moments a meeting took place which can be better imagined than described. Neither is it necessary to relate the particulars of the scene which followed, though you may be sure it was one of general rejoicing, who is by far the best general I know. Both Lionel and Ethel had, as you may suppose, much to tell, although with all that they could relate they were unable to satisfy the curiosity of their parents.

There was something else to think of, however, besides curiosity. As soon as the first feeling of joy at the children's return had begun to subside in the bosoms of the honest villagers, there came upon them a deep and just feeling of shame at their abominable behaviour to poor old Karl. Nor were they slow to act upon their changed disposition. They hurried off to the Maire to obtain the requisite authority, and then descended in a body to the lake, and crowded up to the gates of the old castle. When the keeper knew their errand, and was assured of the entire innocence of his prisoner, he very soon admitted them to the dungeon in which the old woodcutter was confined. With cries of joy and enthusiasm, they dragged the good man from his couch of straw, and conducted him to the open air, everybody telling him the good news at the same time, and nearly deafening his venerable ears with their clamour and confusion. He bore it all with great tranquillity, and evinced but little gratitude for the kindness of those who had been so ready to desert and even to assail him when he had most wanted their aid. But he was truly glad when they brought him to his cottage, and his true old wife met him with open arms and streaming eyes, and the villagers had the good sense and good taste to leave the worthy old couple alone, to enjoy their newly-recovered happiness.

Next day, too, brought an addition to their contentment, for Mr. and Mrs. Newton paid their cottage a visit, accompanied by Lionel and Ethel. They spoke kindly to the old woodcutter and his wife, told them how grieved they were at the trouble which had so undeservedly fallen upon them, and made them such a handsome present that Karl declared he thought he should never need to go woodcutting again.

I do not think, however, that he kept to this resolution, for I heard of an old man very like him who was engaged in the same business the last time I was in that neighbourhood, and a man who has been used to hard work and plenty of exercise all his life is not wise to give it up all at once, even if he be able to do so. So perhaps Karl still works on that mountain, though Ethel Newton (who told me the story) did not know for certain. She did know, though, that she and her brother and father and mother came safely home, and that they have never visited the same place again. But ever since that time, the wren has been a sacred bird in the Newton family-if a wren was to come and ask for her most precious possession, says Ethel, she would give it directly, and she is quite safe in saying so, since there is not the smallest probability that a wren would ever do anything of the sort. Still, Ethel and all the family are quite right to be grateful to the Wren-queen, and to be partial to wrens in general, and I can only hope that if any of my readers get into such difficulties as those which befell Lionel and his sister, they may find as powerful a friend to aid them as the brother and sister found when in the Kingdom of the Mountain-Sprite.

2

BLACK ROLF OF ROOKSTONE

CHAPTER I.

THE BARON Fitzuron had gone to his lordly couch. It was late, very late. He had sat deep into the night, alone in the circular tower, deeply engrossed in his own thoughts.

It was cold, bitterly cold. Although there was no wind outside the castle walls, the Baron's room was draughty, and the heavy, dark curtains waved to and fro around his bed. It was a ghostly room, and ever and anon the dead stillness of night was broken by sharp, sudden, unaccountable creakings of the ancient chests and cumbrous chairs with which the apartment was filled.

It was late, I say, very late, and the Baron was weary in body and mind. Yet no sleep came to close his heavy eyelids in the repose he so much needed. Restlessly he tossed upon his pillow. With fingers stiffened by cold he strove to pull the scanty covering higher and higher over his chest. No fire smouldered upon the hearth. That hearth had known no fire for all the years during which the Baron had slept in the tower, and when at home he had occupied the same room every night of his life.

He was getting to be an old man now, and the end of that life could not be far distant. He might as well have made himself warm and comfortable for his few remaining years. But it was not cold that kept sleep from those aged eyelids. It was not suffering. It was not sorrow. It was joy. A joy so strange and so unusual to his bosom that he could not feel at home with it. He could not rest. All his life long had been spent in the steady, unwavering, determined pursuit of one object. After many years of doubt and difficulty, of anticipation of success and intense bitterness of failure, that object had been at last attained.

In the days long gone by, when the Baron Fitzuron was very young, a babe too young, one would have thought, to have understood such things, he first was told that a title should by rights have been his, and that the name by which he was then known was but the family name of the ancient Barons Fitzuron. By dark deeds of treason against the reigning king, an ancestor had forfeited the name and rank which had come down to him through long centuries, come down to him from those who had won and kept both name and rank with their own true hearts and sharp swords. Nor was this all. The greater part of the vast estates belonging to that ancient family had been confiscated, and the infant Rolf inherited but a few barren acres beyond the castle walls.

He was but a child indeed when this was told him, but he was no common child. There was more of force and stern resolve in that tiny heart, more determination expressed in those sharply-chiselled baby lips, more thought beneath that infant brow, than many a grown man has possessed through life. In his childish heart the boy registered two solemn vows. One that he would recover every inch of land that had formerly belonged to his family; the other, that he would regain the old title, and once more should the representative of his ancient house take place among the nobility of his native land. Cost what it might this vow should be kept. From that time he began to save and to scheme, to plot and to work, for the accomplishment of these two purposes.

It has been said that the boy's inheritance had been

small, yet before he had reached middle age, little by little he had regained every rood of land which had been owned by the Barons Fitzuron in the old times. Strange to say, these lands had all come for sale within that time, and he had never failed to obtain them. He had done even more ; much more. He had greatly added to the former possessions of his race. Far and wide he could gaze from the battlements of his castle upon high mountains and pleasant valleys, and feel with internal satisfaction that all was his own, his very own.

He could have taken his place with the richest of the land; but he did no such thing. He lived in utter solitude in his mountain fastness, and still he saved and saved, ground down his vassals, and screwed the last farthing out of the poor tenants of his domain. The gold he had accumulated was said to be of fabulous amount. No man knew how he could have gathered such treasures together, although of course the proceeds of his estates were vast as the latter increased in extent. But other means of gaining wealth were attributed to him by common report, and some such he must certainly have employed. Men spoke of his hardness and cruelty as equalling his avarice and parsimony. Even in days when lawlessness was the rule rather than the exception, and when dark deeds too often disgraced the land, people stood aghast at the tales of terror which were rumoured concerning Black Rolf of Rookstone.

Many a poor and ruined family had been driven from their humble homes to seek refuge where they could, in order to make way for men better able to pay the extortionate demands of the lord of the land. Nay, there were even whispers of wickedness still greater. It was said that people had been missing—people who were in debt to the Baron— and that their fate was still worse than that of the outcasts I have named, for that they had been sold as slaves in foreign lands It was muttered in fearful but angry tones that the dark dungeons beneath the rocks on which the castle stood could have told fearful tales of anguish and despair.

It was known that a secret communication existed between these horrible places and the sea, and that twice or thrice in the year strange vessels were seen hovering about that coast. At these times dark rough men of foreign appearance were noticed about the castle. They spoke in a strange tongue, and none but the master of the castle could hold converse with them, but it was strongly suspected that it was by their agency that refractory vassals were disposed of, and the coffers of Black Rolf more rapidly filled than would otherwise have been the case.

But whatever reports were set afloat respecting him, the master of Rookstone, even if he heard of them, cared not one jot. With unaltered resolution and with untiring energy he followed out the second great design of his life. As yet the title was not his, but his it should be, and nothing should turn him from his purpose. Saving, penury, and cruelty had become such habits of his existence that he continued to practise them long after the need to do so had ceased to exist. As time progressed he even increased the care with which he constantly added to his hoarded wealth. Old retainers died; their places were not filled up, and so the expense of their maintenance was spared. Anything like new furniture or new curtains or carpets had long been unknown in the old castle, and for some years before the accomplishment of the second part of Rolf's cherished design he had lived with but a very scanty establishment around him, at the head of which presided his old nurse, Elfrida, who had ever been deeply attached to him and to his fortunes.

Years and years had passed away before the fulfilment of his second wish, and his rugged temper had not been softened by the delay. His hope had ever been that the rank and title of his forefathers would have been bestowed upon him, either on account of his great wealth and power, or by the judicious employment of that wealth at some time when the king, perchance in distress for money wherewith to pursue his pleasures or prosecute his wars, might be willing to grant an empty title in exchange for solid gold.

At last the thing really had come to pass. From the day he had come of age, and had taken possession of the property which he had afterwards so greatly increased, the young man had never ceased to importune his sovereign for the boon he so eagerly craved. By every conceivable method he had petitioned and implored; every possible influence had been set to work in his behalf, but hitherto always in vain. With a wise and righteous king Rolf's character had of itself been a fatal bar to his success. But now a young, needy, and thoughtless monarch had ascended the throne, and the request having been urged at a fortunate moment, the bauble of an empty title was flung, not unwillingly, to the eager applicant in exchange for a portion— "alack," thought he, "a large portion" of his hoarded gold.

Had the young king known how boundless was the wealth from which that portion was drawn, he would surely have required more. As it was, he was pleased and satisfied with the price paid, and laughed with his courtiers at the folly of the old man who had been willing to pay so much for a mere title, remarking that, after all, the Black Rook of Rookstone had employed his gold better in giving it to his sovereign than if he had kept it buried and hidden away in his mountain home.

Black Rolf was well content that the king should believe that he had drawn heavily upon his resources, for he desired that men should think him less wealthy than he really was. But, in reality, he would have paid a far higher price sooner than have failed in the great object which he had so long desired, and he chuckled within himself as he thought of the mighty treasures he still possessed. He chuckled, deeply and grimly, as he lay that night upon his sleepless couch—that night which followed the day on which the formal deeds which confirmed him in his new title had come down by a special messenger from his royal master: that night of the day on which his retainers had called him "my lord" for the first time, every such appellation reminding him of the success of his life-long struggle. Still he tossed restlessly upon his bed. Would that night never end? Would it never be day, when he might sally forth to hear again the new title which tickled his ears so mightily, and feel that he really occupied the position which he had so long coveted?

Ha! what sound is that? Day cannot be far distant now, for he can faintly hear the low, regular, continued caw of the rooks in the old rookery close to the tower. He knows that sound well : he has known it all his life: it has been the accompaniment to many a meditation of dark and evil deeds; to many a bitter hour of disappointed hopes in his eager pursuit of that which he had won at last; to many an anxious thought about the future of the house whose power he had so ardently laboured to restore. He chuckled again to himself as he recognized that familiar sound, and at last he dozed off in an uneasy sleep.

Those rooks had long been considered as household birds by the family of which Baron Fitzuron was now the head. If the old legends which tradition had handed down were to be believed, and if the records in the pages of the great red velvet book, with massive iron clasps, which lay in the old oak-panelled library deserved any credit, it was these birds who had been the cause of the building of Rookstone Castle and from whom its name was taken.

It was told in that book that in the far past the fair heiress of the broad lands of Fitzuron used to meet her favoured lover, in spite of her father's disapproval of his suit. He was a foreigner, dark, handsome, accomplished, but with neither wealth nor lineage to recommend him. His ship was moored off the shore near the Fitzuron lands, and it was by the hands of his followers that the passage beneath the rocks was made. By this passage the lover was wont to come to the rookery, where the fair damsel met him, and more than once they interchanged their vows. One day, said the legend, they were surprised by her father, who had received notice from a traitor of their meeting and fully intended to put a summary end to his daughter's engagement by destroying her lover. But the rooks, flying down in large numbers, not only warned the foreigners to stand on the defence, but so flurried and annoyed the attacking party with beak and wing that in the end they were routed, and the cruel father himself perished in the brawl. Afterwards, when the heiress married her affianced suitor, they built a castle on the site of the present building, and named it Rookstone in honour of their brave and friendly birds.

Since that time there had always been an appointed hour in each day when golden grain was spread in the great court of the castle for the rooks, and oftentimes the lady of the house, and sometimes the Baron himself, had attended the repast. But Black Rolf would have none of this folly. The grain was costly, and the expense must be stopped. So stopped it was.

The Baron slept: but it was not for long. The cawing grew louder and louder, until at last it became a volume of sound which startled the owner of the castle from his coveted rest. What was it? Where was he? In vain he strove to collect his scattered thoughts; for several seconds he could remember nothing, and all reasoning power seemed to have left him. Then, by a mighty effort of the mind, he brought himself to know who, what, and where he was; the mists cleared away from his mental perception, and he recognized again that he was the Baron Fitzuron, and in the tower bedchamber of his mansion.

But he was no longer alone. There was a Presence with him in the room a Something which seemed to oppress his senses and to make him doubt the reality of the scene that was passing before his eyes. He seemed to see a mass of black, glossy, shining feathers, as if he were gazing upon a vast concourse of rooks with their breasts all towards him, whilst at the same time their loud, angry cawing rent the very drums of his ears with its sound. It was as if the castle walls were opened and the rooks advancing in battle array against him. Then, gradually, the cawing grew fainter and fainter, until at last it ceased entirely; the wall seemed to have closed again, and returned to its natural condition, the windows were still fastened and the door locked, and there was no visible way in which an intruder could have entered, unless he had tumbled down the chimney, the passage by which, moreover, was rendered more than commonly difficult by huge bars of iron which traversed it from side to side with but narrow space between.

Still, the Presence was there, and as soon as he was thoroughly awake and found himself able to collect his senses and try to realize the situation, the Baron perceived that upon the wooden framework which passed from bedpost to bedpost at the foot of his old-fashioned bed, there was seated no less an intruder than a rook. Yes, an undoubted rook; a large rook; an enormous rook; a glossy rook; a particularly glossy rook; an old, nay, a venerable, rook, and doubtless also a respectable, influential, perhaps even a generally, meritorious rook, but for all that, to the best of the Baron's understanding, only a rook after all, and that, too, seated in a position which no bird had, in his opinion, the slightest right to occupy.

"Halloo!" cried the Baron, as soon as he had sufficiently recovered from his surprise to speak.

"Halloo!" retorted the rook in a perfectly natural voice, and without in the smallest degree shifting his position.

"What! you speak man's language, bird?" asked the astonished Baron.

Certainly, when necessary," responded the other, and
then, after giving vent to a sound which partook partly of the
nature of a caw and partly of a cough, but which was evidently

intended as a clearing of the throat before he commenced his
speech, thus addressed the owner of Rookstone Towers:—

"For years you have laboured, Black Baron Fitzuron,
Your title to gain and your seat to sit sure on.
But now that your ends you've accomplished and carried,
I'll tell you some news; 'tis for this I have tarried.
Before to this site the house-builders e'er took stone
The rooks were established as owners of Rookstone;
They loved it; and thought it the dearest of places;
And men who the same thought stood high in their graces:
Your ancestors, Rolf, the rooks loved and respected;
By you the same birds have been foully neglected,
And therefore, although 'tis an issue distressing,
Their curse is upon you, instead of their blessing.
To what I now tell you attentively listen,
'Twill make your heart stop, blood run cold, and eyes glisten
With tears which you'll shed when you see that it's true in
My words 'twill be told your unspeakable ruin.
Don't doubt what I say, for the proof is quite handy:
Your mother had twins—but the eldest was bandy—
And therefore your sire said, 'Away with this baby!
His better-shaped brother my eldest thus may be.'
He spoke: no one thought of his word disobeying,
For what he'd have done if they had, there's no saying!
But they threw the poor baby as food to the fishes,
And told him they'd fully accomplished his wishes.
The 'better-shaped brother' was you, you old tyrant,
(In badness you very unlike your old sire an't,)
And thenceforth all trouble, they fancied, surmounted,
As eldest and heir you were always accounted,
But now comes the wonderful part of the story,
Related to me by a worthy John Dorey,
From whom, Baron Rolf, you need never expect lie;

He will tell the truth—should you boil him directly!
That baby was scarce the deep waters thrown then in
When by came a boat with a number of men in,
Who, seeing the child, whilst all up and down bobbing,
Secured him at once, though the fish they were robbing.
They went not ashore, for they didn't require to,
And no one was ever desired by your sire to,
And so he ne'er knew what had chanced on that morning,
And you never knew till this same hour of warning.
The child was conveyed to a land at a distance,
Too young, had he wished, to make any resistance.
He grew up—got married—had daughters and sons too,
And died—but now, Rolf, you may see what this runs to,
Your brother's first son, a lad full of ambition,
Has lately been told of his father's position.
He ne'er would have known he'd been shamefully cheated,
Had you treated rooks as they ought to be treated.
Your conduct as that of your fathers the same an't,
And therefore we rooks have gone in for the Claimant.
Till fortune and title were safe we have waited,
But now, to lose both you are certainly fated.
Our grain you denied us. So now, Rolf, you may know
Your fate—and may trust what I say—not cum grano,
But fully, entirely. The warning pray book it—
Your nephew's at hand, and you'll soon have to 'hook it!'"

Whilst the rook repeated the above statement in calm, slow, and measured accents, the Baron lay still and listened as if bound by some mighty spell. The story was of course entirely new to him. He had, it is true, been told that he once had a brother who died in early childhood, but, with all his cares and hopes concentrated on the future, wherein lay the task which he had projected for himself, the past had but: little interest for him, and he had scarce remembered the fact. As the words of the rook, however, fell upon his ears, he could not but feel the possibility of their truth, and that very possibility, remote though it might be, chilled his heart with horror.

What! was it then possible that his life-long toil should have been in vain! Much, indeed, of the land which he had acquired could hardly be wrested from him, but the title, having been restored to him as the rightful heir of the old family, and not given as a new creation, of which he had made, in his blindness as he thought now, a particular point, would probably, nay, certainly, have to be relinquished, whilst beyond all doubt the castle itself and its immediate surroundings would pass from him into the hands of the legitimate heir. What he would have left would be but the wreck; that which he might save from the bulk which he now possessed, and even that might be sadly diminished if the men of the law were once called in upon the business. All these thoughts passed through the Baron's brain whilst the rook sat solemnly at the foot of his bed, reciting his unpleasant communication, and doing it, moreover, as if he rather liked it than not.

By the time he had finished, however, rage and indignation had conquered every other feeling in the mind of his hearer: rage, that such a statement should be made to him at all : indignation, that the creature, whoever or whatever he might be when at home, should coolly force himself into a man's own bedroom in order to tell him, with infinite glee, of his coming ruin. So the rook had scarcely concluded his narrative before the Baron hurled the pillow at his head, with all his force, accompanying it with an exclamation couched in somewhat strong language, and following it up, at excessively short intervals, with one of his slippers and the bootjack, which happened to be at the side of his bed, and within reach. This action, however, produced no other result than, in the case of the last-mentioned article, to knock a china-cup, which the Baron rather valued, off the mantel-piece and break it into a thousand pieces. As far as the rook was concerned, he took not the slightest notice whatever of the incident, but merely shook his feathers after the manner of rooks, ruffling them all up with one tremulous motion of his body, and smoothing them all down by another, and having done this, he put his head slyly on one side, winked knowingly at the irate Baron, and remarking in a somewhat comical tone, "We shall see, old fellow, we shall see," flew, apparently, straight through the wall as if there had been no wall at all, and in another moment had entirely vanished from the sight and hearing of the perturbed owner of Rookstone.

For a time Baron Fitzuron lay as one bereft of sense and reason, so stupefied was he by the extraordinary nature of the vision which he had just seen. He had fallen back upon his bed utterly amazed and bewildered at seeing the various objects which he had hurled at his visitor apparently pass through him as if he was air, without affecting his composure in the slightest degree. There lay the Baron, I repeat, for a time, and there ran through his body a tremor of a cold and shivering character, such as might seize upon a man who had been greatly alarmed and terrified.

But fear was a sensation which had no abidingplace in the bosom of Black Rolf of Rookstone. Presently with a mighty effort he recovered himself, and sat upright in his bed, gazing before him at the wall through which his uninvited guest had come and gone. It presented no unusual appearance to his keen eye; everything was the same as it ever was, and he could have fancied the whole scene a dream, if he had not been perfectly well aware that it was a frightful reality.

CHAPTER II.

He, the Lord of Rookstone, the Baron Fitzuron, the richest and most powerful person in the country round, had been bearded in his own bedroom by a common—or rather a most uncommon—rook, and had been denounced to his face as the wrongful possessor of the title and estates which were so dear to him as the reward of a life's work. It was not to be endured for a moment. Gradually, every other sensation which had agitated his breast gave way to rage: deep, dire, grim rage at the rook, at his threats, and at the world in general, for when a man once gives way to his anger, nothing appears. pleasant or agreeable, and he feels a disposition to quarrel with everything he sees and everybody he chances to meet. As soon as he had a little recovered his composure and collected his thoughts, the Baron rose and performed a hasty toilet, during which operation he frequently gnashed his teeth and uttered imprecations of a nature more decided than polite.

Since the departure of the foreboder of evil he had formed a portentous resolution, upon the carrying out of which he became more determined every moment. He would destroy the rookery! His mind was quite made up upon the subject. No more should those birds be harboured around the mansion against whose owner they had rebelled. Even supposing that every word uttered by the rook had been true as gospel, there was something to be said upon the other side. True, he had treated the birds somewhat differently from his ancestors, in that he had denied them their daily feast of grain.

But what of that? Had he not still permitted them to inhabit the lofty elms and limes which they had so long occupied, and from whence they could swoop down at will and gather food for themselves like other rooks? Why, forsooth,

were they to fare better than other birds of their own species? What had they done to maintain the ancient power
and prosperity of the House of Rolf? And in what was he
beholden to them for his present position? He had achieved
it for himself by the might of his own right hand and the
work of his own brain. Why had he denied them their old
meal of grain? It was because he was bound to practise every
economy in order to build up the fortunes of his fallen house.
Had the rooks done so for him, economy would have been
unnecessary, and they might have eaten grain till they burst
for all he cared.

Thus did the Baron argue with himself as he dressed,
and soon came to the conclusion that he was a wronged and
injured man, that the rooks had behaved infamously to him
and his, and that the sooner they were got rid of the better.
When, therefore, he left his room and proceeded to the old
oak parlour, in which he always ate his morning meal, his
first care was to summon the old Elfrida 'to his presence.
She came, surprised indeed at the message, but anxious to
know what service she could do to the being she loved best
on earth.

In a few curt words the Baron informed her that the
woodmen and foresters who still remained attached to the
castle must be summoned forthwith, for that he had resolved
to cut down the rookery.

On hearing this, the old woman threw up her arms with
a despairing cry! "Oh sir—master—my lord," she exclaimed,
"surely my ears are deaf with age and I cannot have heard
rightly. Destroy the rookery? Goodlack, but I must be mad
to think thou saidst such a thing."

The Baron frowned darkly. "Didst ever know me trifle?"
said he sternly. "The rookery falls: every tree, lime and elm,
comes down. They have harboured a nest of black feathered
traitors, and I will none of either."

Again the old woman wrung her hands in anguish as

she renewed her appeal. "Bethink ye, good my lord," she urged in sad hut earnest tones; "bethink thee, 'tis easy to destroy; but hard to build again. These trees have seen generations of thy noble family spring, flourish, and pass away. The rooks have ever been accounted friendly unto thine house: to fell the one and banish the other! Can it be right? Can it be prudent? Alas and alack, I fear me terribly there will be evil days if it is to be so!"

Black Rolf struck his fist fiercely upon the table.

"Begone, woman!" he cried, in a loud voice, "and execute my orders. Hadst thou not carried me on thy knee when I was a puny child I had not brooked to hear so much from thee. Begone, I say!"

Alarmed at his words and threatening manner, old Elfrida withdrew, weeping bitterly, for although she knew that her master must have some hidden reason for what he did, she felt sure that evil would follow, and felt sad at heart for the nursling she had watched from childhood to youth, from youth to middle age, and from middle age until his head had begun to whiten and age to creep slowly on. She was herself very aged, but the feelings of her heart were warm as ever towards the child she had nursed, and bitterly did she grieve over the thought that of a surety misfortune was at hand.

Under any circumstances this would not have been a very unnatural thing to suppose, for when a man directs his home rookery to be cut down he must either be mad, in considerable difficulty with regard to his money affairs, or remarkably badly off for timber, in either of which cases there is a great probability of misfortune being nearer than his friends could wish.

However, the Baron's orders had been so peremptory that Elfrida could do nothing else than carry them out. Accordingly she gave directions that all the woodmen and foresters about the place should be summoned, and directed to bring axes, hatchets, and saws, in order that the work of destruction might be begun that very afternoon. There were not many people to send, and not many people to be sent for, since the Baron had been constantly reducing the number of his servants and dependants for many years past. However, some fourteen or fifteen men were got together by two o'clock in the afternoon, and the Baron was duly informed that they were ready.

Accordingly, he strode forth from his room and stood upon the sloping lawn in front of the castle, close by the ancient terrace walk. Immediately upon his right hand stood an oak of enormous girth, said. to be the largest for many miles round. It was probably the oldest without doubt, and was hollow within from age, but still of grand and noble appearance, and likely to see out several more generations of the house of Rolf. On the Baron's left hand, at the end of the lawn, stood that noble grove of elms and limes, part of which formed an avenue by which the castle was approached on that side, and which, together, constituted the rookery which the owner had doomed to destruction. It was a magnificent sight, and beautiful also was the view upon which the Baron gazed as he stood upon his lawn.

At that moment the ancient Elfrida came out again and threw herself upon her knees before him. "Oh, good my lord!" she cried, as the tears coursed down her aged cheeks, and her whole frame quivered with fear and excitement, "Think what you do! You may bring a curse upon the place and upon yourself. Oh, pause before it be too late, my dear, dear lord!"

But Rolf spurned her roughly from him. "Up!" he cried in anger. "Up and begone! This is no place for crones and aged drivellers. I tell thee, Black Rolf will no more be moved from his purpose than yon oak from its place!"

Wonder upon wonders! Scarcely had these words left the lips of the Baron, than the venerable and gigantic tree to which he had alluded gave a creak from top to bottom, and a groan as if struck by heavy wind, although there was not a breath stirring in the heavens: and then, its mighty roots seemed all at once to fail it, and without any perceptible cause it toppled over, and fell with a terrific crash upon the ground.

With a shriek of terror the ancient dame fled into the house, and the workmen who were assembled at the end of the walk nearest the rookery, stared in horror-struck amazement at the extraordinary occurrence. But the Baron was only moved to wrath.

"Fool that I was to speak!" muttered he to himself, "as if my speech could have had anything to do with the fall of that tree. It was as old as the hills, and the only wonder is that it did not fall long before." So saying he turned his back upon the fallen monarch of the forest, and approached his men with the intention of cheering them up by his presence, and encouraging them to begin their work at once.

All this time the rooks, evidently aware of the measures about to be taken against them, were wheeling about overhead, describing rapid circles in the air, which they darkened with their number as with a cloud, and giving continual vent to a loud and indignant cawing.

This, however, caused the Baron rather satisfaction than otherwise, since he interpreted it to mean that they recognized his power to dispossess them of their homes, and did not like it at all. He grimly smiled, therefore, as he bade his men approach the rookery and begin their work upon a large elm that stood near, which, but for the season of the year, would have been full of new nests, but as it was winter, had of course nothing but old ones. Hardly, however, had the party got within a few yards of the tree, when the whole aspect of the heavens changed, and a storm began of which the like had never been seen or heard within the memory of man. The peals of thunder rolled like the roar of twenty thousand cannons fired all at once, so that every window in the castle was either broken or cracked by the vibration.

The lightning darted with such vivid and awful flashes that it lighted up the whole country for the moment that it lasted, and made it seem dark as pitch by contrast when it ceased. Large, heavy drops of rain began to fall; the wind rose, and it first wailed mournfully through the tops of the elms and limes as if it was the spirit of the trees moaning and sighing over their approaching downfall. Then all of a sudden it changed its tone, and began to roar. And it did roar, louder than wind had ever been heard to roar there before. Out at sea it lashed the waves until they danced about like mad things, and hurled huge white flakes of foam and froth high into the air, and tossed the ships and boats about as if they were so many straws, and then came rushing and dashing against the rocks as if they had made up their minds to sweep them right away once for all.

Yet none of the elms or limes blew down, and the trees round the castle stood firm, although they groaned and bent before the fury of the. blast. And then the wind partially lulled, but with no apparent intention of making matters better, for it only did so sufficiently to permit a hailstorm to sweep over the earth without blowing the hailstones away. Such hailstones were never seen. Their average size was that of a blackbird's egg, and they came down with such force and rapidity that nothing could stand against them. This settled the question of the rookery for that afternoon, at least, for as soon as the woodmen and foresters felt the hailstones, they turned to a man and ran away as fast as they could to find shelter.

The Baron left the place last; but he, too, was driven off by the violence of the storm. Still he turned slowly and sullenly round, as a stag driven to bay by hounds, and scarce felt the hailstones as they pattered against him, so consumed was he by the flame of anger which burned within him. Drenched to the skin with hail and rain, dazzled by the lightning and deafened by the thunder and wind, he re-entered the castle a different man from him who had so recently quitted it, so far at least as personal appearance was concerned.

But the proud spirit was still unquelled: the stubborn disposition was unchanged, and the firm determination with which he had set out remained the same as ever. What! the fall of an oak, a clap or two of thunder, a gale of wind and a hailstorm! Were these things to change the purpose of a Rolf of Rookstone?

He was more than ever determined that the rookery should be destroyed. That night the Baron drank deep, but his nerves were of iron and his constitution too hardy to be affected by a chance carousal. Yet his potations, instead of cheering him, only darkened the cloud which hung over him, intensified his anger and hardened his inflexible purpose. He was later than usual in retiring to rest, and again lie tossed upon a sleepless couch. Do what he would, the words of the rook kept ringing in his ears in the most unpleasant manner, especially those concluding lines in which the bird stated that his nephew was near, and intimated, in coarse and vulgar phraseology, that he would shortly be called upon to relinquish his hereditary possessions and quit the castle of his ancestors.

He half expected that his unwelcome visitor would reappear: there was no reason why he should not, for if he could come through a thick wall at one time, the Baron supposed he could do so with equal ease at another. Moreover, he thought that the bird would probably wish to say something disagreeable about his day's expedition, and indulge in a little chaff at his expense in consequence of its failure. But nothing of the sort occurred. After he had lain awake rather longer than he liked, he dropped off to sleep, and slept till morn.

His dreams, to be sure, were not of the most pleasant nature, being composed of a medley of strange things, storms, thunder, trees falling, rooks cawing, and a number of other things wrought into curious, fantastic, and horrible images by the magic power of dreaming But at last morning came, and Baron Fitzuron arose as calmly as if nothing particular had happened, and on looking out of the window, perceived that the day was fine and the sky clear overhead. His first act was to repeat his yesterday's orders, and direct the woodmen and foresters to be summoned as before. Once more did old Elfrida endeavour to restrain him, but he rebuked her more sternly than on the previous day, vowing that but for the peculiar relations in which she stood to him, she should be consigned to the dungeons for daring for the third time to cross the will of a Fitzuron. Thus silenced, the ancient crone forbore to reply, and abandoned every hope of turning her whilom nursling from his infatuated course. Again he stepped forward on the lawn, called to his people, and approached the rookery. At a short distance from the first tree he paused and spoke to the men.

"Now," said he, "ye know that I am a man of my word. I will have these foul birds here no more, destroying the whole place, and preventing sleep with their abominable and eternal cawing. The only way to drive them hence is to fell the trees which harbour them. I have said it shall be done, and what I say I mean. Go therefore to work with a will, and ye shall have double pay if within six days the last tree falls."

"But when will the first fall?" asked a voice in defiant tones, as the Baron finished his speech.

He looked around, but could see no one. It seemed to come from above his head, but when he looked up he could only see a quantity of rooks flying to and fro, and he preferred not to look up any longer.

"Onward!" he shouted, and the woodmen and foresters, who had not previously appeared very eager to commence the work, advanced with some readiness under the prospect of the double pay to which their master had alluded.

No sooner, however, had the first axe been raised to strike the old elm at the head of the avenue, than a novel and extraordinary scene occurred. From every side the rooks swooped down boldly upon the men, uttering a loud, constant, and fearful cawing, and attacking with beak and claws the would-be destroyers of their homes. The workmen were so taken by surprise that they hardly knew what to do. Accustomed to consider rooks as quiet birds, of a domestic turn of mind and of peaceable habits generally, they were completely astonished to witness the warlike demeanour which was now assumed by their feathered foes, and the pertinacious valour with which they did battle for their hearths and homes, if indeed a rook's nest can by any poetic license be called a hearth. The men struck wildly and blindly at the birds, and speedily knocked over a number of them. But more and more came swooping down, and so many attacked each man at one and the same moment, that defence was almost impossible against such overwhelming odds.

The Baron, who had stood aghast at the sudden and unexpected nature of this new obstacle to the accomplishment of his designs, now thought it high time to interfere. Waving over his head his favourite spud, with which he usually walked about the park and grounds of the castle, he uttered a loud and indignant shout, and with one blow knocked down half a dozen of the birds who were assailing his dependants in so strange and violent a manner. What effect might have been produced by this active and timely interposition on the Baron's. part can hardly be guessed, for at this identical instant the horn which hung at the outer castle gate was sounded loudly, in a manner which showed that some one required admittance who deemed his business important and pressing.

The Baron paused for a moment, unwilling to relinquish the combat, and yet startled by the suddenness and vehemence of the ringing at the bell. But even whilst he paused the ringing recommenced, and it was evident that his presence was necessary to receive the visitor who demanded

The Attaci of the Rooks

entrance with so much urgency. Casting a look of fury at the rooks, who appeared to be gathering for another attack upon him, he strode hastily towards the castle, whilst a loud and triumphant cawing told the defeat of his servants, who as soon as his back was turned, dropped axe and hatchet and fled in dismay from the wrath of the furious birds.

Before the owner of the castle could reach the gate. it had been thrown open by the hand of the aged Elfrida, and the clamorous visitor admitted. He proved to be a messenger from the Baron's agent for law matters, who lived in the nearest town, some ten miles distant from the castle. The messenger carried a scroll which, with a lowly obeisance, he presented to the Baron, and said that he was to wait for a reply.

Upon the outside of this scroll was written in large, sprawling characters, "For the hands of the noble Baron Fitzuron of Rookstone Towers. Haste—Post-haste. These with speed. Ride—Ride—Ride."

CHAPTER III.

Now the messenger certainly had ridden with a vengeance, to judge by the appearance of his horse, which was covered with white flakes of foam, whilst the blood upon its sides and flanks showed the frequent application of whip and spur. The Baron took the scroll from the hands of him who bore it, and turned it over and over in his hands. The only thing which prevented him from opening it at once was the unfortunate circumstance of his being unable to read. In those days few save monks and holy clerks, or wily men of law, could read or write, and the Baron was no exception to the general rule. So he turned the scroll in his hands, held it up to the light, looked at it again and again, and then bade the bearer return whence he came, and take back word that the Lord of Rookstone would send back an answer in due season.

The varlet departed, right glad to be dismissed from the presence of one so feared as Black Rolf, and in spite of his jaded horse, and his own fatigue after so hasty a ride, set off home without delay.

Then the Baron gazed long on the scroll, and for the first time regretted the priest who in old times had his allotted room in the castle, wherein he dwelt, and who could now have expounded the document, which might perchance be of such great importance. But some years before, the holy man had quitted the castle in disgust, partly on account of the general bad character of its owner, and partly because the latter had kicked him down-stairs for some trifling cause, and further insulted religion in his person by filling his bed with black beetles. So now, in his hour of need, no priest was at hand to unravel the mystery which might be hidden in the missive of the man of law. Rolf bit his lips, as he pondered thoughtfully over the circumstances in which he was placed. So deeply was he impressed with the probable importance of the contents of the scroll that he entirely forgot for the time his projected destruction of the rookery, or if he remembered it, put it aside as something which might be postponed for the present.

So the day wore on, and the Baron worried himself a good deal about the matter, without being able to make up his mind what would be the best course to pursue. The shades of night stole over the castle whilst he was yet undetermined, and after another evening during which his potations were again more deep than was his wont, he retired to his bed full of restless and uneasy thoughts. He slept: but the thoughts were only changed to dreams, and after the fitful slumber of scarce an hour, he started up in bed as suddenly as if a pail of water had been thrown in his face, or the gout had given him one of those terrible twinges with which it knows

Black Rolf Inspects the Scroll

so well the way to rouse its unhappy victims. It was neither cold water, nor the gout, however, which had awakened the Baron, but a visitor still stranger and more unwelcome than either. There, in the old place, sat the detested Rook, as composedly as if he were a pet dove, or a parrot, or any other well-conducted bird which is frequently admitted to the homes and houses of mankind. It sat there, I say, as happily as possible, and winked knowingly at the Baron as soon as it saw that he had discovered its presence.

Nor did the bird long delay to declare the object of its coming. "Now then!" it called out in a hard, disagreeable tone of voice.

"Now then!" responded the Baron moodily, who had nothing else to say, and knew that it was perfectly useless to be silent and sulky in dealing with a creature against whom slippers and bootjacks were nothing, and who could come and go through thick walls without effort or inconvenience.

The bird then proceeded to elevate his right claw and place it confidentially against his beak, whilst he thus addressed the individual whose privacy he had so unceremoniously invaded:—

"Your conduct, Black Rolf, since I paid my last visit,
Is hardly deserving of pardon—now is it?
I told you some truths which were possibly ugly,
But Truth in a Well doesn't always quite snug lie,
And when it is told, unless mad as a hatter,
A person will just make the best of the matter.
You, Rolf, all the rights of our Rookdom invading,
'Gainst old limes and elms have gone wildly crusading,
Because you've been told you've a nephew surviving.
The fact is quite true—there's no plot or contriving,
And you, if you're wise, your bad conduct regretting,
No longer will follow this fuming and fretting,

But search out your nephew—your title abandon
To him, and this bargain I'll give you my hand on,
That if you'll withdraw all your claims—which are rotten,
Your many misdeeds shall be wholly forgotten,
And you, who now frowned on by angels on high are,
Shall wander a while as a mendicant friar,
And then, when your sand to the last grain is driven,
Shall peacefully die with your crimes all forgiven!"

Whilst the rook chaunted forth these lines in a monotonous tone of voice, the Baron listened somewhat more composedly than he had done upon the first occasion. As the concluding words fell upon his ear, a grim sense of humour crept into his rugged breast, partly at the idea of a rook being selected as a messenger to reclaim the sinner from his evil ways, and partly at the fanciful thought that he, Black Rolf, of Rookstone Towers, could under any circumstances become a priest of any sort or kind. This latter point so tickled him, that for the first and last time in his life he felt stimulated to endeavour to pay back his visitor in his own coin, and answer him in rhyme. So looking the bird steadily in the face, and speaking in a gruff, but withal a somewhat comic voice, he thus addressed him:—

"Rook ! you are nothing but a daw!
You give your hand ? you mean your claw!
And though you sing so high a note,
Your bargain isn't worth a groat.
Whoe'er you be, where'er you live,
You've got no warrant to forgive ;
And all you say, a man of sense
Will count as sheer impertinence.
Think you Black Rolf to fright and funk
Until he turn a canting monk?

Before he'd live one hour as such
He'd rather be a monkey-much.
So hence, foul bird, you've said your say,
And now had better go away!"

A scornful laugh ended Rolf's address to the bird, who now stood upon his other leg, and acted with his left claw in the same manner as he had previously done with his right, whilst he again accosted the Baron. This time, however, he abandoned rhyming, either because his versifying powers failed him, or perhaps because he had had enough of it.

"Fool!" he exclaimed at which word the Baron started, and hastily stretched out his hand for his bootjack, but recollecting his previous failure, subsided quietly). "Fool! thou hast had thy chance, and hast rejected it. Now listen once more. Thou doubtest my power, and perchance thou doubtest my story. I will give thee such proof that thou shalt doubt no longer. In the old chest in the dark recess of the oak library there is a secret place which thou hast never yet found. Open the farthest drawer at either end. At the back of each drawer is a brass knob. Press each at the same moment, and at the same time pull out the middle drawer. Behind the latter the woodwork will then open and disclose a recess which holds the secret. Attempt to destroy it, and the everlasting caw of the Rooks of Rookstone shall sound your doom for ever." So saying the Rook turned round, and flew straight through the wall with the most provoking coolness, leaving the Baron in a state of alarm and vexation such as it would be difficult to describe.

No more sleep had he that night, and on the morrow he arose gloomy and dejected, with forebodings of evil heavy upon his wicked soul. He determined that he would search the chest named by the rook without any unnecessary delay. At any rate, he might as well know whether there was a secret, and, if so, what it was, for it would be safe in his keeping, especially if the disclosure would in any way affect his own interests. So he dragged one of the heavy, oldfashioned library chairs opposite the chest, and sat down to look more carefully than ever into the same. The drawers were of ebony, black and shining, and without difficulty he pulled out those on the right and left, and at once perceived the brass knob at the back of each. These he pressed as the bird had directed, but as it took both his hands to do so, he found he could not conveniently pull out the middle drawer at the same time.

A third person was required for this process, and his old nurse appeared to be the most suitable member of his establishment to be trusted in the matter. So he summoned Elfrida to his presence, and acquainted her with his desire. Anxious to do anything her beloved nursling wished, the old woman readily undertook to draw out the middle drawer sharply, whilst he pressed the brass knobs on either side. She did so, and sure enough, the woodwork behind opened and out dropped a miniature and a piece of old parchment, yellow and shrivelled with age. The Baron eagerly seized the former, and opening the case, beheld the portrait of a child with dark and unlovely features, but bearing upon them the unmistakeable impress of the Rolf family.

Was this then the baby brother of whom the Rook had spoken? And what said the parchment? That, indeed, Rolf could no more discover for himself than he could decipher the contents of the scroll sent by the man of law. He felt, however, that it could be nothing favourable to himself, and the thought crossed his mind that his best plan would be to destroy both miniature and parchment then and there. Seizing the two, therefore, in his hand, he held them in the flaring light of the pine torch which he had brought with him, the better to examine the dark recesses of that ancient chest. Wonder of wonders! they burned not: the flame flared steadily enough, but the fire appeared to have no effect whatever upon either parchment or picture.

Astonished at his action, the old nurse hastily interposed. "What would'st thou, good my lord !" she cried in alarm. "Perchance these contain some rare treasure, or disclose some secret which it were ill to destroy."

"Secret!" returned the Baron, with a sound between a growl and a sneer. "Secret indeed! it is some jugglery of that vile Rook, and nothing else."

"What rook, my dear lord?" quoth the old dame, and forthwith in a few words the Baron told her all, though he had meant to have buried the story of the Rook's double visit deep within his own breast.

Elfrida wrung her hands in dire dismay as she heard the tale. " Alas and alack aday, my lord," she said, sobbing bitterly as she spoke, "these are evil tidings. Hast thou never heard the old saying of thine ancient family, darkly spoken ages since?

'He who sees by night the rook,
For his sins is brought to book.'"

"Fool and dotard!" cried the Baron, "prate not of such folly to me! The bird has never yet been hatched that shall frighten Black Rolf of Rookstone. Yet since these things will not be burned, I will e'en place them in safety till I can know more." With these words Baron Fitzuron carefully picked up the miniature and the parchment, looked once again at each, and then left the room, muttering words which I fear me were scarce a blessing.

No interruption of his rest took place that night, and early on the following morning the Baron ordered his favourite black charger, Belial, to be saddled for his use. He had resolved to do that which he had never done since he was quite a boy, namely, to ride over to the famous abbey which stood some five miles from his castle, there to obtain the assistance of some learned monk to unfold to him the contents of the scroll and parchment which had not unnaturally excited his curiosity.

At the appointed time the steed was brought round, but ere he mounted old Elfrida sought his chamber, and begged him to observe that since yesterday not a rook had been seen about the place. An unusual bustle had been observed among the birds during the previous afternoon, after which they seemed all to have taken their departure. "A malison light upon them!" cried the Baron in reply. "I think they have left their cawing behind them, for since the time we stood together by yonder chest, I seem to hear it constantly in mine ears."

The old crone shuddered as her master spoke, for although he had not told her the threat which the Rook had made, if he should attempt to destroy the secret which he should find in the old chest, yet she well remembered another old distich respecting the House of Rolf—

> "Whose ears the rooks with ceaseless caw shall greet
> Is nigh the time when he his doom must meet,
> And when the caw shall cease, the doom's complete!

As she called these words to mind, the old woman burst into tears, and sobbed bitterly.

But the Baron laughed lightly, and springing into his saddle with an agility which belied his years, galloped off in the direction of the abbey. As his gallant steed carried him quickly over the ground, thoughts ran with even greater rapidity through his brain, and he felt perturbed and unquiet in his mind to a greater degree than had been the case for many a long year. He could not but feel that he bore upon him documents which might exercise a wonderful influence over his future fate, and a burning desire to know their contents raged within his bosom. So the distance was traversed in little more than half the usual time, and the Baron Fitzuron found himself at his destination, and loudly rang the bell which hung at the ancient gateway.

The abbey was a venerable pile of buildings, erected many years before, and bearing a great reputation as a holy place. It was long, indeed, since Black Rolf of Rookstone had been near it, but the monks received him none the less gladly, hoping perchance that he had come to avow his repentance for many bad deeds in the past, and perhaps even to make some atonement for sins against Mother Church by adding somewhat to the endowments of their beloved House. No such motive, however, had Rolf for his ride, and his intention in coming was made known to the brotherhood with but little delay. One of their number, old Brother Peter, took in hand the scroll of the man of law, and forthwith proceeded to acquaint the Baron with its contents. It told him that he must prepare to defend his claim to house, lands, and title, and that both law and arms might possibly be employed against him. The new claimant had, by hook or by crook (verily, by rook, thought the Baron), obtained access to the young king, and by all accounts had interested him in his cause. At all events, said the man of law, the matter is too serious to be neglected. The appearance of the stranger was reported to be in his favour, and to bear a marked resemblance to the family of which he claimed to be a member. He had documents, it was said, and other proofs that he was what he asserted himself to be, and he had avowed a steadfast determination to fight to the last for what he termed his rights. As the Baron heard these words, which the old monk mumbled over with great deliberation, his brow knitted and a fierce look of dogged determination came over his countenance.

He muttered a low but deep oath when the good brother

had concluded, and gnashed his teeth in bitterness of spirit. Then he stamped his foot hard upon the ground and spake out his mind more boldly than befitted that holy place. "Beshrew me!" he cried, "but the knaves are malapert! But think they that Black Rolf of Rookstone can be driven from house and home like a vassal who has failed to pay his dues? By the claws of Lucifer they shall learn a different tale ere long!"

"Oh hush, my son!" exclaimed Brother Peter, terrified at the violence of the Baron. "Speak not such evil words, but put thy trust in the Powers on High to guard thee—"

"Hush thyself, prating priest," roughly interrupted the Baron, "thou hast but half performed thy task. I have here another puzzle for thy clerkly skill, and see that it bear better news than the last." With these words he drew from his vest the parchment which he had found in the old chest, and handed it to the trembling monk, again bidding him to make haste, and not to stand there chattering like an old woman.

But Rolf had used at random a word which was literally true, the parchment was a complete puzzle to the old man. He turned it upside down ; held it up to the light, first in one hand and then in the other and finally confessed that he could make neither head nor tail of it. The crooked characters, written in a crabbed handwriting, in ink which had long since turned yellow from age, could be mastered by none save those of knowledge and experience more vast and wondrous than that of Brother Peter. Such a man was to be found, however, in the person of the Lord Abbot, a man whose age was very, very great, so that no one knew the date of his birth, though it was said that the deeds which he could recall as an eyewitness proved that he had long passed his hundreth year.

It was not upon every day, not at every hour, that an audience could be had of this venerable man. In the present instance the Baron was forced to wait, and although he ill brooked the delay, he had no remedy but patience. At last he was ushered into the Abbot's room, which was a low, vaulted chamber, thickly strewn with rushes, and hung round with the skins of wild animals on three sides, the forth having a sable curtain hanging before it, behind which were many holy relics and emblems only to be looked upon by pious eyes.

The Abbot sat in a low chair, nigh to the hearth, on which a large log was smouldering, the dying embers casting a fitful and uncertain light upon the objects around. He half-inclined his head as the Baron bowed before him, overcome for the moment by the appearance of the man and the sanctity of the place. Then he took the parchment from the hands of his visitor, and read every word carefully from beginning to end without uttering a syllable. When his task was completed, he slowly lifted his hoary head and regarded the Baron steadfastly with his filmy eyes. Presently he spoke in the feeble accents of extreme old age.

"What knowest thou, my son, of these documents?" he asked.

"Not a jot," replied the Baron, "seeing that never a word of writing can I read, be it fair as it may. I found the rubbish in the old black chest at Rookstone, Holy Father, and fain would I know the import thereof."

The aged eye wandered from the Baron's face back to the parchment again, and Black Rolf began to fear he had come too late: the intellect was waning. Not so. In another moment a light beamed over the face, wrinkled and seamed by the cares of more than a century, and again the old man spake:

"This is a wondrous page, my son. It carries me back many, many years, even to the time when I played, a white-headed boy, beneath the ancient chestnuts of my father's park. I well remember thy mother, the writer of this scroll, though she must have been dead these sixty years or more. Ah" me, ah's me! she was a winsome lass a while since. It seems but yesterday she was bright, and blithe, and bonnie —ay, and I could hold my own with the best of them then, too! That was before I came here at all. Long ago—yes—long, long ago."

During this discourse, the Baron became half wild with impatience. He had already got over his respect for the presence in which he stood, and nought but his eager and passionate desire to learn the contents of the parchment restrained him from breaking out into some act of violent anger. It was maddening to be kept from the desired knowledge by the garrulity of old age, but inasmuch as that knowledge could only be obtained through the aged man before him, he restrained his impatience by a gigantic effort, and compelled himself to listen whilst the Lord Abbot prated on about a childhood which no living creature but himself could remember, and the details of which had long ceased to interest any one. At last, however, the Baron found an opportunity of interposing a word, and accordingly asked,

"But what of the scroll, Lord Abbot, what of the wondrous page thou hast just read through?"

"It is indeed a wondrous page," replied the old man in the same tremulous tones, "and thou hast done full well to bring it here, albeit it may not be to thine own worldly advantage. Yet perchance it may be so, it may be so indeed, noble sir, for as I have heard, thou hast no heir to thy title and broad lands, and it were well to yield them to one of thine own blood during life, rather than know that thy race would end with thine own breath."

At these words the Baron gave vent to his feelings in a deep groan, for they seemed to confirm the statement of the foul Rook, and were of evil augury towards himself. The Abbot slowly lifted the parchment in his hand, and as he began to read it, the cawing in the Baron's ears sounded louder and louder, as if the rooks were rejoicing over the news which was about to be told. And thus read the Lord Abbot—

"This is by mee writ. Joan, wife of James, rightful

Baron Fitzuron of Rookstone Towers, tho' deprived of the rank which is truly his. This year my eldest sonne Egbert, being of such foul shape and small that my Lord and I do judge him unfit to hold after us these lands and castle, was by my Lord doomed to be drowned so that my litt sonne Bertram being stronger and better favoured, should inherit. But by trusty hand I procured that the childe should be saved, and carried to the fair land of Provence. There he dwelleth and will dwell, and there are wrytings with him withal which shall this tale prove true. And further to prevent ill-doing, I have this parchment steeped in distillerys of herbes which shall garde it safe from fire.

"Signed by mee Joan, wife of the said James."

Black Rolf listened to these words in horror-struck rage. Then the bird had spoken true. There could be no doubt of it. It was more than sixty years ago that his mother had died. Supposing his brother to have married abroad, say at the age of thirty, he might well have a surviving son old enough to do manful battle for his rights. If it were so, and if the young man should be able to prove himself the lawful heir, there would be nothing for it but either to yield him peaceful possession, or strive by force of arms to hold the position which he had struggled so long to obtain. It was a terrible alternative, and the very thought of what was before him nearly drove the dark, stern man distracted. Snatching the parchment rudely from the hands of the Lord Abbot, and thereby causing dire amazement to that saintly man, he strode hastily from the apartment. There was no need to tarry longer in the abbey. Little had he sought from the holy men who dwelt there, and little had they had from him during his long life of crime and recklessness. He had this day learned from their chief tidings which boded him no good, and he hastened to leave them and their dwelling behind. So he flung himself quickly on his black steed, and rode off at best pace on his homeward journey. As he rode, he muttered curses loud and deep against the fate which seemed to pursue him, against the claimant who dared to appear against him, ay, even against the mother, whose lingering affection for her puny child had prevented its destruction, and preserved the life which was about to prove so troublesome and dangerous to her second son.

The Baron ground his teeth savagely, and dug the spurs cruelly into the flanks of his faithful steed, as he pressed madly forward towards the home which might haply be his but for a short time longer. And ever and anon, as he rode, there sounded in his ears that fearful, mysterious cawing, now low and faint like the distant noise of the waves rippling on to the beach on a calm summer's evening, now loud and angry, like the sound of the same waves lashed into fury by the wild winds of heaven. In vain he strove to think it was but fancy; it was something more; some dread reality which perforce he must carry about with him, and which even his iron nerves could scarce endure forever. He neared the ascent to his castle, and as he looked on the strength and position of Rookstone, he smiled proudly in his confidence that the foe, be he who he might, who should dare to attack so fine a fortress, would have a hard nut to crack ere he won his venture. What figure is that ascending the hill and nearing the castle-gate? Figure, nay, there are two —one, his old nurse Elfrida, and the other, one of those prying monks whom he had long since forbade the castle, and for whose canting and praying he had no forbearance. He urged his steed forward still, and shouted for the pair to stop. Yet they glided on from tree to tree, and at first seemed to take no heed of his summons. But as he roared out his commands a second time, being now close upon them, the monk and the woman stayed their upward course, and awaited his approached.

"What dost thou here, Elfrida?" asked the Baron, in angry tone.

"And thou, caitiff, with thy head shaven and shorn, as bare, methinks, of hair as thy heart of aught brave and manly. What seekest thou at Rookstone? 'Tis no place for such as thou—hence—begone!"

The monk made no reply, but the old woman faltered out in trembling accents:—

"Oh, good my lord, chide not, I pray thee, neither this holy man nor thy poor old servant. It is long since I have had ghostly counsel and comfort, and my age is so great I know not how long I may be able to receive it. So while wandering forth to watch for thy return, when I met this holy man I persuaded him to turn back to the castle, and—"

"Peace, fool!" growled the Baron, "cease thy prating, and let thy holy man take his holiness off without further delay. I like not such cattle, and would have him wait next time until the master sends for him before he visits my castle. Hence, sirrah! Be off, and thank thy stars thou dost so with a whole skin! We have a rough way of treating trespassers here!"

The person thus addressed drew himself up to his full height, and looked the Baron full in the face. As he did so his eyes seemed to glare from beneath his cowl like live coals, and the Baron felt less easy than he could have imagined possible when confronting a mere lazy priest, such as he imagined the stranger to be. The monk gazed upon the Baron for a moment in silence, and then laughed aloud.

"I go!" he cried, "but, thou man of foul tongue, and heart still more foul, beware thou of our next meeting!"

With these words, before the incensed Baron could either make reply or take such summary steps towards his apprehension as he might possibly have felt inclined to do, the monk stepped hastily into the adjoining thicket and disappeared among the trees. Then the Baron turned to Elfrida, and sternly upbraided her with negligence, if no worse, on having been about to introduce into the castle one who was evidently no friend to its master. The old woman, however, protested her innocence of any evil intention, and vowed that she had only acted from an intense and increasing desire to obtain that spiritual consolation of which she had so long been deprived. Forced to be content with this explanation, the Baron rode moodily into the court-yard, dismounted from his steed, and entered the castle. All that evening he brooded gloomily over the events of the last few days, and strove by deep potations to drive away, or at least deaden, the perpetual cawing which sounded in his restless ears. This, however, was beyond his power, and although he obtained some fitful snatches of sleep during the night, the morning found him but little refreshed in body, whilst his soul was filled with gloomy thoughts and melancholy forebodings as to coming events.

The next morning dawned dull and lowering. Black, brooding shadows seemed to rest upon the lawn and shrubberies near the castle, the sky was heavy with leaden clouds, which like a vast sable shroud swept slowly over the face of the heavens, and the sun only relieved the darkness of the day with a fitful, lurid light, as if unable to penetrate through the mists and vapours which wrapped the world in their murky folds. The Baron's mind was a faithful reflection of the outward world. Clouds of doubts, distrust, uncertainty, and uneasiness possessed his soul. A stranger to bodily fear, still. a dread feeling, which he could not have defined, stole gradually over him, and he experienced sensations more nearly akin to terror than had ever hitherto fallen upon him during his reckless life. The prescience of coming evil seemed to be with him, and he vainly strove to shake off the heaviness which oppressed him, whilst ever and anon that unearthly cawing continued.

In such a state of mind and body anything was more tolerable than inaction. Something he must do. He roamed over his castle like one distraught, stood gazing from the battlements at one moment, and at the next hurried from room to room, as if in search of something, he knew not what. At last a thought suddenly struck him : he would go forthwith to the man of law and learn from him, face to face, what was likely to be the issue of this affair. No sooner had the idea come into his head than he proceeded to put it into execution, and at once ordered his horse. But was it safe to leave the castle with such few retainers as were still in his service? Thrift, avarice, and the long years of saving which had passed over his head, had left him with but a scanty garrison in case the castle should be attacked in his absence. True, this might scarce be likely, before other and more peaceful means had been tried by the claimant of his title and estates, but the risk was too great to be run. He sat down in the old library and thought silently for a few moments. Then he started up, having fully determined upon the best course to pursue.

Before proceeding to the town where dwelt the man of law, he would betake him to the Towers of Barnascran, where dwelt that stout old knight, Sir Hugh de Montenoy: Although the Baron had never been intimate with his neighbours, and had indeed but few with whom he could have associated had such been his wish, yet he had always managed to preserve friendly relations with the owner of Barnascran. Perchance this had resulted partly from the fact that the lands of the latter, commencing some ten miles off, ran in a direction so far away from those of the Baron that none of those jealousies had arisen which have at all times been apt to prevail between the owners of neighbouring estates, and partly from the fact that Sir Hugh, being a noted warrior and one who kept a large band of retainers about him, was a person with whom no one was likely to be desirous of picking a quarrel.

CHAPTER IV.

FROM whatever cause, however, the Baron had acted, it is certain that during all his career of reckless proAligacy and crime he had never been otherwise than friendly with the old knight, and to him he now turned in the hour of his distress. He rode forth with to the Towers of Barnascran, and, having been at once admitted to the presence of their owner, lost no time in making known his request.

"I am harassed, good neighbour," said the wily Baron, "with evil reports, the which, whilst they were yet but reports, I cast aside, as idle fables unworthy the attention of a man and a warrior. But I can treat them so no longer, since from safe channels I learn that there is a false knave abroad pretending to have descended from an elder branch of my family, and to have a claim upon my lands and title."

Sir Hugh smiled grimly. "Methinks, neighbour," said he, "it must be a bold man indeed, and foolishly reckless withal, who shall think to oust Black Rolf of Rookstone from his ancient halls. But hath the knave thy blood in his veins?"

"Not a drop hath he," promptly returned the Baron, "but hath somehow or other got possession of some old legend of our family, out of which he has coined a tale to win over idle fools, and hath thus gotten to himself friends by whose aid he threateneth to despoil me of mine own."

"Beshrew the knave!" returned the good knight. "It grieveth me deeply that such men should exist. But say, neighbour mine, how can I serve thee in this matter, and by my halidome it shall be done. No De Montenoy will see a friend and neighbour wronged an he have power to shield him."

"Thanks, kind and true friend," replied the Baron: "thou canst mightily aid me, since thou art so well inclined. Thou knowest full well that, for one cause or another, I have disbanded the followers who once filled my halls, and the

Towers of Rookstone are now but feebly defended. I must needs go to the town to seek from my man at law certain deeds, and to hear more certainly the doings and plottings of this evil foe. It may be one day, two, or even three that I shall be away. Should the enemy hear of my absence, he may take that moment to fall upon my castle, and with so small a force as I have to defend it mischief may follow. But if thou wouldst take some small portion of thy followers, and occupy the castle until I return, the danger would be avoided, and I should speedily be with thee again to pledge thee in red wine and drink confusion to all who war against thee and me."

Sir Hugh de Montenoy willingly listened to the proposal of the Black Rook of Rookstone, and readily agreed to ride forthwith to Rookstone with five-and-twenty men, and hold the place in safety during the absence of its owner. His preparations were not long to make, and that same evening the Baron returned with his friend and his friend's followers, and confided them all to the care of old Elfrida, who was somewhat astonished at the number of visitors, and the change which appeared to have come over her master, who for so long a time had scarcely admitted a single stranger within his walls.

Being now well satisfied of the security of his castle against a surprise, Black Rolf mounted his horse betimes next morning and set off for the town, determined to find out all that could be discovered about the person of whom the man of law had written. He rode moodily on, still accompanied by the ceaseless cawing which would have driven an ordinary man mad, but which merely had the effect of making the Baron more savage than usual. Still he rode not with the headlong haste which had marked his ride to the abbey. The intense excitement he had then felt seemed to have passed away, and to have given place to a deep, sullen feeling of resentment, and a sense of injury which was none the less keen because it was hardly justified by the circumstances.

In truth it was the new claimant to his property who had been really injured, and cruelly injured, in the past, but this mattered little to the Baron. He had been in possession of the old castle so long, and had (though by means which would not bear inquiry) so added to the family estates and position, that the bare thought of being dispossessed was like gall and wormwood to his haughty soul.

He could not—he would not—believe the tale of his brother's wrongs. Yet there was it written in black and white: there could be no doubt that the ancient Abbot had rightly read the scroll and interpreted its meaning, and the disbelief, real or pretended, of the person whose property was affected by its contents would weigh but little with others who might be made acquainted with the same. The evidence was strong—too strong—and if the brotherhood at the abbey should make the facts known, and give their endorsement to them, it is certain that many would accept these facts as true, and the new claimant would find a host of friends among those to whom the name of Black Rolf was already sufficiently obnoxious to render it certain that they would gladly join his foes. All these thoughts passed through the Baron's mind, and did not tend to lessen the gloom which overshadowed him. He gnashed his teeth savagely as he rode onward, and muttered low, but deep, imprecations upon the head of his enemy, as he deemed the stripling to be who had come to claim his own from the hand of him who had so long withheld it from its rightful owner. The sun was high in the heavens when the Baron Fitzuron rode into the town and followed the twistings and turnings of the narrow streets which led to the abode of him whom he sought. The man of law dwelt in an ancient house, in a quiet part of the town, away from the main thoroughfare, the noise and bustle of which might have interfered with the work which doubtless fell to his lot in the study of old deeds, the disentangling of matters clogged by the intricacies of the law, and the settlement of questions which people might have settled for themselves less expensively but less securely than by his legal craft. He was a man well advanced in years, one who had long followed his profession in that place, and who bore withal a name respected among his fellow-men. From him the Baron felt sure that he should obtain a just and true opinion upon the matter which lay so near his heart, and whatever that opinion might be, as far as the merits of the case were concerned, he trusted that the man of law, who had served him so long, would do so still, and would by his subtle craft postpone, even if he could not altogether avert, the evil with which he was threatened.

As he neared the door of the abode he sought, he perceived a horse standing near it, held by a boy. It was a magnificent roan, fit for a prince to ride, and perfect in shape and strength, as the Baron could tell at a glance. He had, however, neither time nor inclination to gaze long upon the animal, for he was in haste about the business which caused him so much anxiety. So he hastily sprang from his own horse and sounded so loud a peal upon the bell, that there was little delay before his summons was answered. To the page who opened the door he carelessly flung his rein, scarcely asking whether his master was at home as he strode rudely into the house.

"My lord, iny lord!" called the youth, who had seen the baron before and knew him at once, "my master cannot see thee at this moment. He is engaged in converse with a gentleman—he will see no other now—and I was bid to deny admittance to all."

But the lad might as well have spoken to the winds, for Black Rolf merely swore a deep oath, and strode forward to the office-room, which he knew full well. Without knock or call, or warning of any kind, he opened the door, and burst roughly and suddenly into the room, to the great apparent surprise and discomfiture of two persons who were seated therein and who instantly and at the same moment rose from their seats. The one was the man of law; the Baron knew him well, and recognized at a glance the old-fashioned office-table at which he sat, with deeds and papers scattered all around, doubtless containing the secret records of many an ancient and noble family. But who was the person with whom the man of law had been closeted? Tall and dark, a goodly and well-proportioned frame, sinewy limbs, finely-cut features, and hair of the raven hue, he was a man of mark beyond all doubt, and of this the man who beheld him was well assured at the first glance. But there was something more. That face brought back memories to the proud Baron which had long slumbered in his brain, or if they had ever arisen had been speedily stifled or banished: that eagle look, that keen, flashing eye, those lineaments that so vividly recalled the features of the dead—all told Black Rolf a tale which he doubted not for an instant, and it required not the words of a witness to convince him that he stood in the presence of one of his own race and blood.

Forthwith the man of law interposed with trembling accents, stammering in his haste and fear, and scarce knowing how to excuse himself to his own patron and employer for the circumstance of being found in consultation with his relative and rival.

"My lord," he said, "this is sudden—this is unexpected—this honour—your lordship's visit—had I but known—your lordship's goodness will understand 'twere difficult to have refused the interview I hold with this noble gentleman—your lordship will believe me—I know not—I fear me I may not rightly explain—your lordship's nephew—"

During this somewhat unconnected harangue the Baron had stood still, gazing with lowering brow from one to the other of his two companions and biting his lip as if to control some intense feeling; but at this point he broke out with a furious oath.

"Treacherous hound!" he yelled, rather than shouted, "art thou also in league with mine enemies? Nephew, sayest thou, thou plotting rascal—what knowest thou of nephews, thou foul quill-driver? And how darest thou prate thus to me whom thou hast betrayed?"

The Baron's rage prevented his further speech, and the man at law, overwhelmed with mingled fear, anger, and confusion, could only stammer forth in trembling accents—

"My lord, my lord—I cannot—I do not—I did not —I could not—," and then broke down entirely and stood speechless. But the third person present at this strange interview now took up the conversation. One step forward he took and laid his hand firmly upon the desk of the man at law as he thus gave utterance to his feelings:—

"The man hath done no wrong," he said in a calm, clear tone of voice, which seemed to strike like a chill upon the heart of him who listened; "he hath but heard what he could scarce avoid hearing—a tale of woe and wrong—of woe suffered and of wrong to be redressed. And thou be'st mine uncle, noble sir, I would have thee listen too, and deem him not thine enemy who seek but mine own. I am the son of thine elder brother, as I can verily and surely prove, and I come to claim the name and inheritance which neither force nor fraud shall withhold from me. But I seek no family quarrel, nor would I willingly injure my father's brother. Yield the place which by right belongeth to thine elder brother's son, and all may yet be well. Thou hast wealth enough beside, men say, and why shouldst thou grudge thy kinsman that which is his own?"

The Baron ground his teeth savagely at these words. "Kinsman!" he shouted, "no kinsman thou of mine. Bastard! Caitiff! Pretender! I own thee not—I know thee not. Thou hast neither part nor lot with the Rolfs of Rookstonet;" and he glared furiously at the other as he spoke.

It was a strange sight to see the two men at this moment.

The elder, mad with rage, every muscle in his aged frame quivering with excitement, regarded his disowned kinsman with a withering glance of concentrated wrath and hatred, which the young man returned with equal pride and indignation. And, in that instant, anyone who had looked upon the twain must have been struck by their wondrous resemblance in form, figure, and features, ay, even to the keen, dark, wild eyes from which flashed those hostile glances from one to the other. Incensed beyond measure at the last words of the Baron, the other laid his hand upon his sword, and was about to stride hastily and angrily forward, when the man of law, having somewhat recovered his courage, interposed his venerable form between the two.

"Stay, noble sirs, stay, I pray you, by the holy rood," he cried in trembling and anxious tones. "Break not the peace, nor brawl in any unseemly fashion as drunken churls might do; such conduct beseemeth not noble persons, nor is there any occasion for this outbreak. The law will see right done if nothing else can settle matters between ye. Noble lord, I pray you stand back—brave youth, raise not thine hand against thy father's brother."

"What!" thundered the Baron, on hearing the last word. "Sayest thou this to my face? Art thou no traitor, who ownest this false knave before my very eyes? The foul fiend seize thee and him together, for thou art assuredly in league with him, and shalt feel my vengeance accordingly. This is not place for honest men who wish to keep the estates they have fairly won with their own right arms. I go, ye thieving villains, but beware ye of the wrath of Black Rolf of Rookstone!"

So saying the Baron turned upon his heel without another word, and left the room in a state of mind bordering upon frenzy. He passed down the passage to the door at which he had left his steed, which was still held by the servant of the man of law, on whom he scarcely bestowed a glance, as he sprang hastily into the saddle and rushed down the street, hardly knowing which road he took, so vehemently did the wrathful tempest rage in his soul.

Down the streets his horse's hoofs clattered anon, through the marketplace and past the outskirts of the town into the open country beyond. Away, away over the open downs he sped, the fresh breeze of heaven scarcely cooling his heated brow, his teeth clenched with rage and his whole frame quivering with excitement. Away, away! And still there sounded in his ears that ceaseless cawing, now low, now loud, but ever the same wearisome, dull, continuous sound that marked but too surely that Black Rolf of Rookstone was under the ban of the sacred birds he had so boldly defied. Away, and still away, and in his frenzy he spared neither whip nor spur, but goaded on his already weary horse, as if in the pursuit of some object still far off, and only to be reached by frantic haste.

Away! Off the downs and into the great ravine, and over the ford and through the wood, all at the same headlong speed, though his brave horse was well nigh spent, and his flanks were covered with blood and foam, and he laboured heavily over the soft ground of the valley, as they came nearer the seashore, and the castle stood but a short two miles before them.

The day was wearing fast, and the Baron spurred on, making but little of his steed's distress, and consumed by the force of his own internal fury. Onward, still onward; but the two miles are all too long for the brave horse. Poor Belial! He had carried his master well through many a long day's ride, and borne him safely out of many a fray when brave and strong men had been left behind: nay, save the old Elfrida, there was perhaps no living thing that loved the Baron more than his faithful charger; he would start round and neigh at the sound of his voice, would prick up his ears and come to meet him in the paddock, and by arched neck and stately step showed the pride with which he carried the master whom

Death of the Black Steed

he had served so long. But neither his love nor his length of service availed him aught today. Forgetful alike of one and the other the Baron had urged the noble animal on beyond his strength, until the chords of the brave heart snapped asunder in the struggle. The black steed stumbled—once—twice—blundered forward upon his head, rolled over, and with one convulsive sob which quivered through his whole frame, lay dying at his master's feet.

The Baron, an expert horseman, quickly extricated himself as the horse fell, and stood still for an instant, calmed, and sobered by the occurrence. The filmy eyes of his faithful steed seemed for one instant to be turned upon him with looks of reproachful anguish —the next they were glazed in death. It was done. No more would that pleasant neigh welcome his approach to stable or paddock—no more would those strong limbs bear him abroad or that high courage support his own in the battle. It was over; and he had lost a trusty servant—ay, a friend. For one moment softness came over that hard heart, and remorse entered that stubborn breast.

Not long, however, did such unwonted guests remain. The Baron swore a deep oath and stamped savagely on the ground. The castle was still near half a mile off—curses on the ill-luck that had followed him of late—curses on the fate that had robbed him of his best horse when the latter would have had rest and food within five minutes—double, treble curses upon the foul birds who had worked him all this evil. He turned from the carcase of poor Black Belial! and strode forward towards the castle. All was as it should be. The rays of the setting sun fell full upon the old tower, upon which floated the banner of Sir Hugh de Montenoy, side by side with his own. The brave old knight sat carousing in his neighbour's hall, and Rolf heard the sound of laughter and revelry as he entered by the postern gate. He ground his teeth savagely; for such sounds ill-suited with his humour at that moment, and turning into a side passage sought the private way into the oak library. There he threw himself into a huge old-fashioned arm-chair that seemed as if it had been made in the age of giants, to suit the requirements of their mighty frames, and for a while remained there, wrapt in thought. Then again starting from his seat and striding hastily to the hall, he joined Sir Hugh, who received him with a loud greeting of welcome. For a short time the Baron shared with his guest in his carousal, but ere long he pleaded fatigue, and quitting the hall again, once more betook himself to the oak library, and summoned old Elfrida to his presence. She obeyed, though not without some misgiving, for she feared that the prospect of losing that for which he had worked so long might have tempted her master to plot some dark and deadly deed against him whom she somehow knew to be the rightful owner.

Black Rolf, however, said nothing of such matters, he did but require her assistance to obtain again from the chest in which he had replaced them after his visit to the abbey, the scroll and miniature which had caused him so much trouble. He had a project in his mind, upon the accomplishment of which he was now entirely bent. The secret way communicating with the passage which led from the castle to the sea-shore was known to few—to no one, as Rolf believed, but to Elfrida and himself, nor, indeed, to her in any such practical way as that in which he knew and had long known it. For the old dame, though she knew the existence of the secret way and the entrance thereto, had never had occasion to explore it.

The Baron had long turned it to account as a hiding-place for his treasures, and the thought which was now in his mind was neither more nor less than the getting rid of the chief evidence against his title to Rookstone by placing the miniature and scroll in some inner recess of the rocks through which wound the passage, where in all human probability the eye of mortal would never see them. Thus secured he thought he could defy his adversary in spite of all the rooks that had ever cawed. With this intention he claimed the assistance of old Elfrida, and having obtained the articles he desired, dismissed her again from his presence, answering with rough words her earnest prayers that he would not attempt to sin against the unseen powers by destroying those things which were forbidden to be destroyed. He bade her begone in a manner which showed her that further entreaty would be useless, and as soon as she had left the room threw himself once more into the same arm-chair and pondered deeply. The fiends take that cawing! How it bothered him! He could not collect his thoughts—that dull, heavy, monotonous, wearisome sound was beginning to wear out his patience and to prevent the free exercise of his thinking powers. Presently he arose and passed out of the oak library into the passage, from which a small spiral staircase led to some of the upper chambers of the castle. This he ascended, and passing through several large rooms, almost wholly empty of furniture, and bearing the desolate appearance which characterised the greater part of the interior of his dwelling, he paused for a moment before an old and curiously carved door at the far end of one of these chambers.

For a little while he stood silent as if doubtful of his purpose, and then, as if his mind was finally made up, he seized the handle of the door with a sudden grasp, and entered that which was known as the tapestried room. It was hung all round with very ancient tapestry, mouldy and moth-eaten in many places from age and want of care, but still presenting an imposing appearance as it hung heavily upon the walls, imparting a dark and sombre aspect to the room. Towards the corner to his left the Baron directed his steps, and drawing aside the tapestry, was about to stoop down to a panel in the wall, when a low sigh suddenly arrested his attention.

He started and turned round. "Whom have we here?" he angrily asked, but there was no reply. Muttering an oath, he stood for a moment irresolute, and then, striding to the other side of the room, from whence the sound had appeared to come, hastily tore away the tapestry, and disclosed the form of the old Elfrida cowering in a recess.

"Old beldame!" he shouted, "what dost thou here, and how darest thou play the spy upon thy master's doings?" With these words he seized the aged woman by the shoulder and shook her roughly.

In trembling accents she endeavoured to excuse herself. "Oh, my lord, my dear lord," she cried, whilst sobs and fear almost choked her voice, "what is it that thou seekest to do? Thou wouldst enter that awesome place. I pray thee hold back. The power thou defiest is too strong for thee—it is for thee I fear—."

Black Rolf swore a fearful oath. Her words showed that she had not forgotten, as he had hoped, the secret ways of the castle, known only to her besides himself, and this knowledge on her part, coupled with her evident fear of, if not friendship for, those who were opposed to him, betokened evil to his cause.

"Thou besotted old harridan!" he shouted, "thou pratest of that of which thou knowest nought. What place? What power? Hence at once, or it will be the worse for thee!" As he spake, he stamped violently on the ground, whilst the cawing in his ears became so loud and harsh that he was nearly driven wild.

"Oh, my lord," responded the terrified old woman, "I meant not thy mortal enemies, though they, Heaven knows, are mighty enough. But mightier still is the curse of the ancient rook, and much I fear me thou art lost if thou strive not to avert it. Oh, think whilst yet there is time, my nursling! Submit to the doom, yield thy goods to save thy precious soul, forsake thine evil life, give up thy present plan of wrong, and make friends with thy nephew before—"

She spoke no more—incensed beyond measure at her

words, Black Rolf seized her by the throat with another fearful imprecation, and drawing the dagger which ever hung by his side, would in another second have plunged it into her heart, when a hand, laid heavily upon his shoulder, caused him to drop the senseless frame of the old woman, and start hastily upon one side.

There, boldly confronting him, stood the monk whom he had angrily dismissed but two days before. His eyes flashed fiercely beneath his cowl, and his hand was still upraised in menace against the Lord of Rookstone. For an instant the latter was paralyzed between rage, shame, and surprise, and staggered back uncertain whether to believe the eyes which beheld a stranger, and evidently an enemy, in one of the most secret parts of his castle.

But during that instant something occurred to excite still more strongly his surprise and wrath. Stooping down, the monk lifted the form of Elfrida as if it had been that of a child, and stepping back to the opposite side of the room, lifted the tapestry; at the same moment, in a low, stern voice he addressed the astounded Baron.

"Doomed wretch!" he exclaimed. "Go to thy fate unpitied and unwept. I bade thee beware of our next meeting—we meet no more." And with these words he passed rapidly behind the tapestry with his burden, and disappeared from the eyes of the person he addressed.

The latter could scarcely yet recover himself from his astonishment, but as soon as he did so, he rushed furiously to the spot where the monk had stood, lifted the tapestry, and, dagger in hand, sought everywhere for his enemy. In vain. The monk had apparently vanished into thin air, and his disappearance opened up a new source of anxiety to the perplexed Baron. One secret passage from that apartment he knew well. To prevent its existence coming to the knowledge of others, he had been ready to slay even the old servant who had served him so long and loved him so well. But could there be another outlet, and unknown to him? The thought was indeed alarming, and such as would at another time have induced him to postpone or abandon the work on hand until he had carefully sought out the truth of the matter.

But his nerves were at this moment in a state of tension which forbade calm consideration, and the still increasing sound in his ears almost maddened him by its continuance. Only for a few seconds he sought, and then, doubtful whether he had not seen a vision, and the old woman had not been bodily carried off by the powers of darkness, he returned to the 'corner to which he had first advanced upon entering the room. Stooping down, he touched a spring, and at the same time pushing against a panel in the wainscoting, it flew back and revealed a door in the wall behind. This the Baron opened and passed through, carefully closing it behind him. He now stood in a small vestibule, at the further side of which was a flight of stone steps. It was near the outside wall of the castle, and the only light in the vestibule proceeded from a slit in the massive stonework above, which, however, was sufficient to enable the owner of the castle to find his way to the stairs, which he forthwith descended. The way, indeed, was well known to him, for the staircase led, by a long descent, to secret vaults and rooms below, in which he had from time to time stored such portions of his accumulated treasures as could not be readily converted into money. The first of these was entered by means of a massive iron door, of which Rolf carried the ponderous key in his girdle.

Before, however, he attempted to open it, he turned to a deep recess in the wall, wherein stood a silver lamp with a glass cover, and by its side an appliance for lighting it. He carefully struck a light, adjusted the glass firmly upon the lamp, and then, having opened the door, entered the first vault. Within it, scattered here and there around, lay a varied and considerable treasure, rich bales of merchandise, the produce of piratical expeditions upon the coast, costly suits of armour, bars of gold, jewelry, garments of rich texture; all mixed together and thrown carelessly upon the floor, as from time to time the robber Baron had found it convenient to bring them to his secret hiding-place. Amid these he passed with cautious steps, and opened the door of a vault, somewhat similar to the first, in which lay gold and silver coin in no trifling quantity. Those were not the days of banks, and Black Rolf's coined treasure being too vast for ordinary money chests to contain, he kept much of it in these secret vaults.

In this second chamber he paused, doubtful for a moment whether a safe place could be found in which to deposit the miniature and the parchment. Little did he know how much depended upon his decision. Why should he not hide them there? No human eye was likely to penetrate to the place where he stood, no stranger hand to drag forth the fatal things he bore from a hiding-place in the earth of the vault. Yet it might be that if ill-health fell upon him, or increased age forced him, however unwillingly, to trust the secrets of the castle to others, that the necessity of employing some of his treasure might, one day or another, oblige him to send some one to that place. However trustworthy that some one might be, better that a secret the discovery of which would be fraught with such alarming consequences, should be beyond the possibility of falling into his hands. Yes, assuredly it would be better to make matters safe once for all, and to hide the things he carried in a place still more secure and inaccessible. Of all men living, Black Rolf of Rookstone, as he believed, was the only one who knew the secrets of that place.

CHAPTER V.

FROM the vault in which he stood, a secret passage led to the sea-shore—that passage by which, in his earlier days of wickedness, he had held communication with those pirate voyagers who had aided him to amass his wealth. For years past the passage had been disused, and as its outlet to the sea was carefully concealed, few persons knew of its existence, and none could have found it from the sea-side. At the end of the second vault were three stone steps, at the bottom of which was a low door. Here Rolf stopped once more and drew from his girdle a small case, containing several wing-feathers of a rook. Carefully passing his hand over the surface of the door, and holding his lamp close, he perceived a small hole, into which he softly and cautiously thrust one of the feathers ich he had taken from his case. By this means a spring was touched which held the door-one push—and it swung heavily open. By three more steps the Baron descended, pushing the door to behind him, and he now found himself in a room so low that he could hardly stand upright. It was rather a small room of irregular shape, and its walls on either side were formed entirely of the rough rock out of which it had been cut, and upon which the castle was built. At its further extremity was another low door which led directly into the passage to the sea, and upon the floor of the room were more bags of coin, and sundry precious jewels fit for titled and court-bred dames, but lying there rusty and unused. It was Rolt's intention to secrete the miniature and the parchment in some crevice of the rock within that room, where he felt certain they would remain undiscovered until the end of the world. These once destroyed, he feared no legal proof that his nephew—if such really was his opponent—could bring in support of his claim, and, old as he was, he was determined to do battle to the last for the possessions which he had gained by the toil, the arts, the wickedness of a life.

Full of these ideas, he advanced to the middle of the room and stood for an instant peering round to discover the best place for concealment of the objects he bore. At that moment the cawing in his ears seemed to get more violent and furious than ever. It even seemed to shape itself into words, dire, fierce, threatening words, and presently there seemed to ring through his very brain this fearful sentence—

"Ne'er shalt thou quit this fatal room,
Black Rolf! The rook decrees thy doom!"

So vividly, so clearly, so loudly did the notes ring through his head, that in spite of all his fortitude, the Baron started violently. It was indeed enough to carry terror to the stoutest heart. Save for the light of his own lamp, all was dark as night around him, and such words, spoken in a tone so strangely unnatural, between the voice of a man and the caw of a bird, chilled his blood and sent to his heart a sensation as near to fear as he had ever experienced. The doom foretold was an awesome doom indeed, and the prophecy, like some others, aided to fulfil itself. For in the violent start which the Baron gave, he struck his foot against a loose fragment of rock which lay upon the floor, involuntarily stretched forth his hand to recover himself, failed to do so, and in another instant tumbled forward and fell upon the ground, fell too, terrible to tell, upon his lamp, which was extinguished and crushed beneath his body. A thrill of despair ran through the heart of the unhappy man as, in an instant, he realized his position. He raised himself to his knees and clasped one hand over his forehead, whilst the other still grasped the miniature and parchment, which he thrust into his breast as he staggered to his feet.

Stay! there was yet hope: the door by which he had
entered was but half closed; could he regain it the appliance
for lighting the lamp would not be hard to find, and but little
light would be needful to retrace his steps, if he could once
regain the larger, upper vaults in which his treasure lay. At
that moment he would have given half that treasure for one
inch of lighted candle! Slowly he rose to his feet and trem-
blingly felt his way back, his knees knocking together, and
his teeth chattering with the real, the dreadful fear which
was now upon him. Is he going straight to the door? He had
never before known how difficult it was to walk straight in
entire darkness. Yet it must be done—he must find his way:
those nerves, once of iron, must be firmly set once more,
and the egress from his self-made prison must be secured.

But, low and deep, constant, hoarse, awful in its depth
and intensity, ever there rang in his ears and through his
brain that terrible cawing, paralysing his brain, and adding
in a wonderful degree to the terrors of the darkness, and the
confusion of his ideas. And now it seemed to speak to the
luckless victim of its wrath, and again it shaped itself into
words, and it seemed like the tolling of the passing-bell, and
to clang out in harsh and discordant sounds the dreadful
words—"Never—never—hence thou passest never." The sound
was maddening, but with a mighty effort the Baron girded
himself to the task before him, and advancing to the wall,
stifled every feeling of doubt or fear whilst he felt steadily
along it until he found the steps. An involuntary cry of joy
escaped from his lips as he raised himself upon them, and
eagerly put forward his hand to find the handle of the door.
At that moment the cawing seemed to be redoubled, and in
his confusion and hurry he miscalculated the distance, his
hand came against the door, whilst he thought he was yet
several inches from it, and that so sharply that the door closed
with a spring and a snap, and Black Rolf of Rookstone had
shut himself into his living tomb with his own hand. With

one loud frantic yell of despair he fell down upon the stone steps and lay there as one dead. Presently he rose again to his feet and dashed himself against the door. It was in vain : the massive work could have resisted the strength of a hundred men, and he sank again, with hands torn and bleeding, upon the steps, and gave vent to such a groan as only the agony of despair could have wrung from his soul.

Then occurred a strange and wondrous thing The cawing which had tormented him incessantly for so long a time ceased completely and at once. He heard again as clearly and well as ever. Alas! what was there to hear? No human voice might ever sound upon his ears again—no music of birds, no noise of martial array, no, nor even the dull, heavy sound of the waves beating against the rocks as he knew they must be doing not fifty yards from where he lay. No such sounds could reach him, for the thickness of his rocky prison shut them all out, and when he listened with an intensity of nervousness of which he would have thought himself incapable a few minutes before, he could hear nothing but the slow, steady, continuous dripping of water from the roof at one corner of the dungeon. Why had the cawing ceased? Horrible thought it was the old prophecy of which Elfrida had told him—"And when the caw shall cease, the Doom's complete."

His doom then was at hand. What doom? He had fought in many a desperate fight, hand to hand with brave foes, and risked his life full oft in many a daring deed—it had sometimes been his thought that thus it behooved a soldier to die, and had fancied that he would meet his fate, when it came, as bravely as any of the puling monks over there at the Monastery. But to die like a trapped wolf left to starve in a pit, or worse, for the wolf would have light from above, but to him all was darkness—to die thus was a fate too awful to realize; in his own castle, too, almost within hail of his own people—almost! curses on it, that "almost" would kill him—why not quite? Oh! the curses of a dying man upon those who had made such an infernal dungeon and those who had not destroyed it as unfit to be a part of a noble's castle—stay! whom was he cursing? Himself!—yes! had he lived an honest life, he had wanted no secret vaults and passages, and had done away with them long since. Oh, the horrible folly of which he had been guilty! What was all his treasure to him now? of what good was his castle—his lands—his long-coveted and hardly-earned title?

Such thoughts as these coursed through his brain, one after another, and then came an almost worse state of mind. Bright and clear and vivid arose the memory of many a dark and evil deed, done during his wicked life, and never yet repented of until repentance was too late, atonement impossible. The smaller sins of his life, such as he had never recognised as sins, came crowding together upon him, bearing to his awakened mind a different and darker appearance than they had ever done before, while the deeper crimes of which he had cast away the remembrance whenever it arose, came back now with terrible, probing memories and flung down his guilty soul into the lowest depths of despair.

Once more he raised himself and staggered towards one side of his prison: again he stopped and listened, but there was nought to hear: he peered into the darkness with eyeballs starting from his head: there was nothing to see! Shut out alike from light—from fresh air—from hope itself—the full consciousness of his position came with crushing force upon the unhappy Baron, and with one more yell of mingled agony, fury, and despair, he fell prone among the treasures which seemed to mock him as he touched them, and felt how useless they were to aid him in his hour of need.

Elfrida, Elfrida, where art thou now? thy nursling for whom thou hast sinned and suffered, whom thou lovest as if he were thine own child—thy nursling, whose life thou hast watched over so long, needs thee sorely now. Wilt thou not come to his aid? Can none help him? Ah me! what is the strength of man, of what avail his treasure, his skill, his wrath? In his own castle—near his own people—the mighty Baron raves out his soul in cries useless, impotent, unheard.

When Sir Hugh de Montenoy arose next morning, he marvelled what had become of his host, and was at first disposed to resent his absence from the morning meal. But, remembering the cares and anxieties of the Baron's present position, and being himself of a good-natured and easy disposition, he betook himself to his breakfast without troubling himself greatly about the matter, and doubted not that Black Rolf would show himself at his own time.

An hour or so had rolled away, and the Knight of Barnascon might have thought more of the strange proceedings of the Baron, had not his attention been called to other and more pressing considerations. The sentinels upon the walls announced the approach of a large body of men, advancing with intentions evidently hostile to those who held the castle. As soon as this seemed to have been ascertained, Sir Hugh ordered every preparation for defence to be immediately made. The drawbridge was drawn up, the great gates of the court-yard closed, every weak point strengthened, and cross-bow men posted at every loop-hole whence they might annoy the enemy. About a quarter of a mile from the castle, the advancing force halted, and presently there rode out a horseman bearing a spear with a white handkerchief tied thereupon, in token that he demanded a parley. The old Knight of Montenoy forthwith proceeded to the postern gate and sallied forth with two retainers to meet the herald. He halted at a short distance, and lowering his spear, saluted the Lord of Barnascon as became his dignity. Sir Hugh returned the salutation, and proceeded to demand the errand of the other and the meaning of the appearance of the body of men from whom he had come.

"These," quoth the herald, "be the men-at-arms of Rolf

of Rookstone, the rightful owner of this castle and domain, and the lawful claimant to the ancient Barony of Fitzurse. By fraud and violence he hath been despoiled of his due inheritance, and by the strength of his right arm and the edge of his good sword he cometh to win back his own. Wherefore I summon this castle on his behalf. I summon thee, noble Sir, to surrender the castle to its rightful owner, and to quit it, thou and thine, peacefully and of good will."

Sir Hugh de Montenoy drew himself up proudly as these words were spoken, and then made reply forthwith. "Go back to those who sent thee," he said sternly, "and tell them that De Montenoy yields not at the first blast of the trumpet nor to the summons of those he knows not. All the world knows that Black Rolf of Rookstone—I would say the noble Baron Fitzurse—is the Lord of Rookstone Towers and the fair lands around. I know no other lord save my friend and neighbour, and until he bids me surrender, I may not quit my trust."

The herald bowed low as he heard these words and then raising his voice, aloud exclaimed, "Take notice, all whom it may concern, that I summon this castle, and demand its surrender to its rightful owner, my worshipful master, Egbert Rolf of Rookstone, by his right and due Baron Fitzurse! Resist him at your peril!"

With these words he turned his steed and forthwith galloped back to his master's host. There was a pause for some minutes after the herald had returned to his friends and the Lord of Barnascon had reentered the castle. He inquired at once whether the Baron Fitzurse had yet made his appearance, and marvelled much at receiving a reply in the negative.

There was, however, no time for further inquiry or search: the enemy were advancing, and seemed to have at least four or five hundred men, whilst scarce one hundred and twenty, all told, were within the castle walls. Yet such was the natural

The Herald's Parley

strength of the fortress, that Sir Hugh felt certain of being able to hold his own, so long as the supply of food lasted and no treachery was at work. His own flag swung proudly upon the towers, side by side with that of Fitzurse, and never yet had that flag swung over men unwilling or fearful to defend it. On came the foe, and presently a shower of stones and arrows, from slings and bows in skilled hands, rained upon the walls so fast and thick that scarce a man could show him. self with safety. Under cover of this shower the men advanced to whom had been confided the task of scaling the walls, and whilst the archers and slingers took advantage of every tree and bush, and poured forth their volleys with unceasing energy, these advanced with ladders, quickly and stealthily, and drew gradually nearer and nearer the castle. Every now and then came an arrow from the latter, aimed with good aim at the scaling party, several of whom were wounded in their advance, but the main body pressed on, and presently arose a loud shout as they dashed themselves against the wall which surrounded the courtyard, and under cover of which they were protected from shots aimed from the main building.

"A Rolf! a Rolf!" they shouted, whilst some cried. "An Egbert! an Egbert!" and from the castle came back in deep stern tones, "A Fitzurse! a Fitzurse!" and still more loudly and cheerily (for the Barnascon men much outnumbered their allies), "Montenoy, , Montenoy!"

Against the gates of the court-yard a resolute attack was made, headed by a tall figure in black armour, who was evidently in authority, and who fought with a courage and vigour which betokened him a brave warrior. He animated his followers by loud shouts, and with a ponderous battle-axe struck such blows against the gates as before long told with great effect, and at last with a crash they gave way, and the. assailants of the castle rushed forward with renewed ardour. But they were now more exposed than before to the aim of the defenders of the fortress, and several more were struck down as they pressed on, whilst at the same time a deep voice from the walls shouted loudly,

"Stand firm, men, and yield not an inch, on your lives. Strike for Montenoy!"

The issue of the day might indeed have been doubtful, so great was the courage and determination of either side, when an incident occurred which had a visible effect upon the combatants. Suddenly, and without any previous warning, the air became black with rooks, whose loud cawing filled the air, and, even at that moment of excitement, attracted general attention. They wheeled in circles over the heads of the attacking force, apparently encouraging them to fresh exertions, and anon flew with evidently hostile screams right into the faces of the garrison.

Both sides paused as if by mutual consent, and presently the Knight in black armour stepped boldly forward and raised his voice, the accents of which were scarcely heard, when the rooks ceased cawing as if by magic, and a dead silence ensued, which enabled every word to be distinctly heard.

"A parley!" he cried. "I crave a parley, and speech with him who commands the garrison." Forth stood the old Knight of Barnascon at once.

"Here I stand," answered he, "Sir Hugh de Montenoy, who never yet turned his back upon friend or foe. I hold this castle for mine ancient neighbour, and yield it not till summoned by one of better right than he."

The Knight bowed with stately courtesy. "Sir Hugh," said he, "none can doubt the skill and valour of which you have given fresh proof today. But where is mine uncle, Black Rolf? He was not wont to shun the fray. Let him stand forth and deny me for his nephew if he dare?" As he spoke, the young man unclosed his visor, and displayed features which bore so startling a resemblance to those of the Baron Fitzurse that the Knight of Barnascon stepped back in amazement.

"Sir Knight," he exclaimed after the pause of a few seconds—"thy face doth wonderfully confirm thy tale—but for thine uncle, if uncle he be, I have not seen him since yesterday, and know not why he is not here to speak for himself. But my word is plighted to hold the castle for him, and of a surety he will not be long away."

At this speech the leader of the attacking party seemed somewhat surprised. "By my faith!" he cried. This is passing strange. We know that mine uncle returned hither yesterday, and he could scarce have gone hence, save by sea, without some of our people having seen him, since they have been out on all sides. But was there ever such a thing heard of as a neighbour keeping a castle for one who cares not to hold it for himself? If my uncle be within, let him come and face the matter out. But if, as I begin to think, he has fled secretly by sea, knowing my claim to be just, why should De Montenoy fight with one against whom he has no quarrel ? Why should innocent men be killing each other for a cause which does not exist, and for a man who has already confessed himself wrong by his flight?"

"Boy!" returned the grim old warrior whom he addressed, "thou reasonest well, but yet I cannot yield the castle till I know more of the cause of my neighbour's absence. My word has been given to defend it, and so I will."

"But," resumed the other, "does such a pledge last forever? Hear me for a moment. I will draw off my men for four-and-twenty hours, and during that time, no man shall lift a hand or shoot a bolt against the castle. If he who calls himself Baron Fitzurse shall appear before that time, thou shalt hear my statement and his answer, and judge whether thou wilt longer defend him: if he appear not, thou shalt withdraw to thine own place, and leave me to hold the towers of my ancestors until a better claimant show himself." Sir

Hugh de Montenoy listened attentively to this proposal. He could not imagine what had become of the Baron, whose room was empty, and his bed evidently had not been slept in during the previous night, and who really seemed to have vanished altogether. It seemed an absurd thing to fight for a man who did not seem inclined to fight for himself, and moreover it certainly appeared unreasonable to expose his own followers to the assaults of an enemy against whom neither they nor their master had any cause of complaint. Truly he had undertaken to defend Rookstone Towers if it should be attacked during the absence of the Baron, but the Baron had certainly returned, and in any case such a pledge could not be interpreted to bind one for ever, nor to prevent th acceptance of any proposal so reasonable as that to which he had just listened, by which the new claimant of the castle offered to submit in a manner to his judgment upon the merits of his case.

Still, so leal and loyal was the old Knight, that he would not run the risk of being accused of treating his pledge lightly. So after a pause of several seconds, he thus replied to the proposal of the Knight in black armour.

"Sir Knight, be thou Black Rolf's kinsman or not, thou speakest fairly, nor do I care to adventure more than my word binds me to do in a quarrel which may be doubtful. But twenty-four hours is too short a space. My old neighbour may have been suddenly called away, or even may have been captured by some enemy. But double the time thou namest, and I agree to thine offer. If he be not here when forty-eight hours have passed, I will quit the castle with my men, and leave thee to hold it an thou list, for no man can be bound to fight in another's quarrel forever, nor did I ever engage to do so."

Thus spoke Sir Hugh de Montenoy, and the person whom he addressed promptly accepted his proposition.

"For," said he, "thou and I may hereafter be friends,

and my cause is too good to be injured by the few hours' delay which, for thy friend's sake, thou seekest."

Accordingly the retreat was at once sounded, and the attacking force withdrew to a distance from the castle, where they set about preparing their encampment. The garrison were by no means sorry for this arrangement, and, having posted his sentinels to guard against any possible surprise (though he apprehended no real attempt) the Knight of Barnascon proceeded to make further search for his host. All, however, was in vain, and he had to take his solitary meal, enlivened by the presence of such of his retainers as he chose to summon, and the night once more closed in upon Rookstone Towers. The next day passed away in a listless, easy manner, the garrison quietly keeping their places, and the forces which had lately attacked them making no attempt to approach the castle. Another night came and went, and the appointed forty-eight hours passed without any news of the Baron Fitzurse. Then the Knight of Barnascon ordered the two flags to be lowered from the tower in token that he surrendered the castle, and rode out to meet him who was about to become the Rolf of Rookstone. The latter shook him warmly by the hand, and they congratulated each other upon the peaceful termination of that which might have ended in a far more disastrous manner. Egbert Rolf, for so he dubbed himself, declared that, since he was now going to take possession of his ancestral towers, his neighbour and friend, he hoped, that would be, must not leave them without tasting his hospitality.

Provision there was in larder and in the camp of his people, and the castle wine should be broached, in order that his accession to the home of his forefathers should at once be celebrated, and the soldiers who had so lately met face to face in battle should now sit side by side in joyful feastings and council. This proposal suited with the temper of the Knight and the humour of the times, and so it fell out that those who had recently been foes, now became to each other good fellows and boon companions, and the late strife was succeeded by words of revelry and mirth which lasted throughout the evening. Whilst the feast was yet in progress, and the wine-cup and aleflagon quickly passing round, a loud knocking at the doors arrested the attention of the revellers, and presently a new-comer was ushered into the presence of Sir Hugh de Montenoy and his host, who sat side by side at the head of the table. It was a monk from the neighbouring monastery, who forthwith explained his errand. Two nights before, he said, a brother who had been accustomed to visit the castle to afford spiritual aid to such of its inmates as were desirous to avail themselves of his services, had returned, bearing with him, more dead than alive, an ancient domestic of the house of Rolf. In consequence of the hostility which Black Rolf of Rookstone entertained towards the priests, the visits of this brother had always been made stealthily, and without the Baron's knowledge.

Latterly his ministrations had been specially sought by the domestic in question, whose name was Elfrida, and in order that he might come and go safely, she had revealed to him a secret way, unknown to the Baron himself, which led from the tapestry chamber to the postern gate of the castle. By this way he had often passed, and on the occasion of his last visit had been able thereby to preserve old Elfrida and to convey her to the monastery upon the mule which had brought him to the castle. Once safe within the sacred walls, the old woman had rallied sufficiently to open her whole soul in that confession of past misdeeds which she trusted would procure her the consolations of the Church and forgiveness for an ill-spent life.

She had told of much evil done by Black Rolf, to which she had been privy, and which weighed deeply upon her guilty soul. But, freed at last from the trammels in which she had been doubly bound both by her feudal feeling towards her lord and her affection for her nursling—freed because she felt her end was nigh, and that in the eternity before her no such feeling could avail her aught if she left behind her unrevealed wickedness, she had confessed other matters which had greatly moved the holy men at the Monastery.

She had fully confirmed the testimony in the parchment read by the Abbot to Baron Fitzurse, and had added sundry particulars which left no doubt on the minds of those who heard her that every word of the story was true, and that he who called himself Egbert Rolf had a full right to that name, and was the lawful nephew of Black Rolf of Rookstone.

Only on the morning of that day old Elfrida had breathed her last. Her confession had been, at her own request, duly written down and attested by witnesses. Then came the question, what should be done with it? After a short consultation, it occurred to the good monks that, as rumours had reached them that an attack was even then being made upon Rookstone Towers by him whom they were now assured was the rightful owner, the sooner that their newly-acquired knowledge was made known to the combatants, the better chance would there be of putting an end to strife and bloodshed.

Therefore the monk had been sent off to Rookstone, and had arrived to find the strife indeed over, but his tidings nevertheless welcome to those to whom he brought them. They did not stop the feasting and merriment, which continued all that night and so far into the next morning that it was thought well that the visitors should stay one more day before leaving the castle, in order to recruit their energies and perhaps cement their new alliance by a final carouse. But the course of events was ordered in such a manner as to prevent the latter occurrence.

It had been observed that the rooks had not again departed from the grounds of the castle. As soon as the terms of surrender had been settled, they had apparently ceased to care about the matter, and had occupied themselves, with loud and satisfied cawings, in taking possession of their former habitations. About mid-day, however, of the following day, there was visible uneasiness among them : they flew round and round, cawing hoarsely, and evidently fearful of some impending misfortune. At the same time the sky grew unnaturally dark, the wind rose and moaned from the sea in a melancholy and portentous manner, the waves roared as if excited by some unseen cause, and everything seemed to presage a coming storm. And as the evening closed in, the storm came—a storm never forgotten upon that coast. The wind blew with a vehemence which was perfectly horrific, tearing up large trees by the roots as if they were small sticks, whirling haystacks, cottages, and even animals along with it in its fury, and suffering nothing to stand which was not well and firmly built. The thunder rolled terribly, vivid flashes of lightning illuminated the night, torrents of rain succeeded the wind, and the sea roared against the rocks as the din of constant and heavy artillery. Moreover the earth heaved as if with an earthquake, walls fell, houses rocked, women fled shrieking into safe corners, and men crossed themselves with fear and doubt lest the end of the world had come upon them all unprepared. The inmates of the castle had no thought of carousing that night. The stoutest heart quailed, and the proudest spirit owned that there was a power in creation beyond that of mortal man.

The omnipotence of Heaven was recognised and the voice of God heard in the crash of the elements. The night passed away at last, and morning dawned, so brightly and peacefully, that it was difficult to believe that so short a time had gone by since the storm had raged so furiously. Sir Hugh de Montenoy and the young Egbert walked forth together to look at the desolation which had been wrought. It was great indeed. The rookery had been much damaged, and there was a plaintive sadness in the cawing of the birds as they busily employed themselves in repairing the mischief which had fallen upon their homes. The two men strolled onward towards the sea, and found that here, too, the ruin had been great. The rocks upon which the castle stood had been rent asunder in places, and huge boulders of stone, displaced from their former position, lay upon the shore.

As they approached, their attention was attracted to a group of children playing on the rocks, and even as they drew near, they perceived some of the children calling the others and pointing at some object in the rocks.

"It moves! it moves!" they cried. "It is a ghost coming after us!" and fled shrieking away. Sir Hugh called the biggest boy back, and walked with his companion to see what it was that had scared the party. He looked at first in vain, until the boy pointed to a hole in the rock, recently rent by the convulsions of nature in the storm. He knelt down and peered in, at first he could see nothing but something white which seemed to wave to and fro, presently he started back: that something was waved by a human hand—what could it be? what could it mean?

Forthwith they sent for workmen and tools, the hole was hewn open wider, and a sight presented itself which filled them all with horror. The hole opened into a vaulted chamber, low and long, the door from which to the sea could now be discovered, but the passage therefrom to the castle had been completely blocked by the fallen masses of rock. Upon that floor lay scattered gold and jewels and precious stones—but there lay something more.

Flat upon his back, with eyes wide open and staring hideously, with his under lip bitten through by his own teeth in his agony, and his knees gathered up, stiff, stark, and stone dead lay Black Rolf, the Baron Fitzurse. His left arm was beneath his body, his right, outstretched to its full length, still held in its death-grasp the miniature and parchment, and it was the fluttering of the latter in the current of air

THE MOUNTAIN SPRITE'S KINGDOM

through the cleft rocks that had attracted the attention of the children and had appeared as if waved by the dead man. Yes: dead—and dead in the very midst of those treasures for the sake of which he had wrought so much evil against his fellow-men and against his own soul. Dead—and gone where those treasures could not be taken with him, and where the title for which he had laboured so long and so hard would be his no more. That must fall to the nephew whom he had striven to keep from his inheritance, and all the labours of his long life had but served to amass riches for the son of the brother who had been so cruelly wronged. Ay, well, he was dead—and with that word ends all that this world can tell of any of us. They lifted him up—gently and reverently—though the bearers shuddered to look upon his ghastly and distorted face—and as they bore him away until he should be laid in the resting-place of his race, large flocks of rooks came eddying round their heads, and cawed in solemn tones the requiem of the Baron Fitzurse.

The rooks are cawing peacefully enough today around the ruins of the old castle, whilome known as Rookstone Towers. I wandered out into the old churchyard hard by, and sat me down on the low wall, and bethought me of the old legend. Close to me was a new grave, wherein had lately been laid a little maiden, but fourteen years of age, to whom the world could hardly have begun to be wearisome. I wondered if she, too, knew of the legend, and had ever heard of the Bad Baron and his wicked deeds in the ancient time. They say his spirit still haunts the place. But I wot the little maiden will sleep none the less soundly in her quiet nook in the old churchyard, and nought of evil will come nigh the resting-place of the young and pure. Then I wondered if there were many who wept for her and mourned that she should have been taken so early, and then again I thought how they might be consoled by comparing her short fourteen years with the long life of the old Baron, how the length of time that each passed on earth was as nothing in the unreckoned ages of eternity; and the shortness of time here in the one case was also the shortness of trial and the safeguard of innocence to the soul, while the length of years in the other had been but more and more opportunity for evil, so that it had been better, far better, for the aged sinner to have died in his childhood. And so I went on my way still deeply pondering on these matters, and feeling more than ever that the ways of Heaven are marvellous, and beyond the searching out of man.

3

THE HERMIT

CHAPTER I.

THERE was once a cave in the very midst of a forest. The forest was very large and very thick, and had by no means a good reputation. It was said to be full of wild beasts, robbers, witches, evil spirits, and whatever other creatures are likely to make a place disagreeable to live in. But the cave was the abode of a hermit, who did not care sixpence for any of these terrible things, but lived on very comfortably without being troubled by them.

The cave was in the side of a huge rock, and a stream of water trickled at the foot of the rock on its way through the forest, so near the entrance of the cave that the Hermit could sit with his feet in it if he pleased. He never did please, however, for reasons of his own, into which we need not inquire, although I have no doubt that the principal one was a dislike to wet feet, and the uncomfortable position which he would have been obliged to occupy, in consequence of the edges of the rock at the mouth of the cave being sharp and jagged. So he preferred to step gently down and stride across the stream (which was narrow at that part), whenever he wished to go forth into the forest.

He was a curious fellow to look at, that Hermit. Tall, gaunt, with dark hair matted over his brows, and long rugged beard falling down his breast, he looked like some malefactor who had escaped from prison and sought refuge in the woods, or like some wild man who had never known the comforts and habits of civilized life. His frame indicated vast strength, his arms, longer than those of most men, displayed muscular development of no ordinary character, which his sinewy legs well matched : and his whole appearance was such as made you feel at the very first sight of him that he was a man whom you would rather have upon your side than against you in the event of a scrimmage.

There was no chance, however, of having to take sides in a scrimmage of any kind at the time my story begins, for, so far as one could see, nobody seemed likely to come near the cave with intentions either friendly or the reverse. In spite of all that had been said or could be said about the forest, it appeared as if anybody who chose to be a hermit therein might play the hermit to his heart's content without any interference. My Hermit certainly did so for some time, and but for one circumstance might have done so to the end of his days without anybody being a bit the wiser for it. What do you think that circumstance was? Well, it is no use trying to guess, because you would never do so if you tried until a week of Sundays came together, and we all know that su happy and delightful event as that is entirely out of the question.

The circumstance was one which has probably never been mentioned before in the various histories of hermits which have been told or written. Still it is a true circumstance, as is also the fact that this particular hermit was in most respects very like other men in his tastes and habits, thereby differing greatly from the popular idea of hermits as gathered from, and related in, the histories to which I have alluded.

These other hermits were all extraordinary men ; they fasted frequently, which my hermit never did when there was anything to be had to eat; they spent long time in meditation and holy thoughts, in which respect my hero had but little in common with them, being altogether of a different temperament; they drank nothing but water from the brook, he never drank water at all when he could get anything better; finally, they frequently scourged and tormented themselves by way of penance, whereas the individual of whom I write always made himself as comfortable as he possibly could. And one thing he did, which leads me directly to the circumstance upon the occurrence of which the whole of this touching story is founded.

He smoked. Yes, he did. He smoked a pipe, and he wouldn't have given up that pipe for anything that you might have offered him. He thought—and there may have been reason for it—that there was to be found in his pipe a solace, a calming-down of troublesome thoughts, and a sweet forgetfulness of sorrow, which were to be found in nothing else.

Seated within the secret recesses of his cave, or reclining against the trunk of some ancient monarch of the forest, he would often sit for hours together with no other company than his pipe, musing over the past, and turning over in his mind many curious thoughts about men and things, which perchance would never have occurred to him but for that faithful friend.

A listless, dreamy existence you may deem it, and think that he was scarcely employing his time as usefully as he ought to have done. That may very likely be true, but the fact remains the same, and two closer friends never existed than my hermit and his pipe. It was indeed his only friend.

Some hermits, disgusted with mankind, have fled to dark woods and gloomy caves, and when there, finding it absolutely impossible to live quite alone, have chosen to associate upon intimate terms with some member or other of the brute creation. One has had a dog, another a cat, and I remember reading of one who made friends with a bear, though this intimacy, if I recollect right, terminated rather unfortunately, owing to the animal mistaking a bluebottle fly which settled upon the sleeping hermit's nose for a bee, and smashing in his friend's head with his paw in the kindly endeavour to prevent his being stung. But no animal could ever have been to my hermit what his pipe was. It soothed and consoled him, it was never cross to him, never answered him angrily, never teased and wearied him with conversation when he wanted silence, and never interfered with him when he desired to be left alone. It was his child-his own—his beloved—was this pipe to my hermit.

Unfortunately, however, pipes, being but mortal, I was going to say, but I suppose it would hardly be correct; pipes, then, being, like mortals, generally dependent upon somebody or something else to keep them as they should be, this particular pipe became entirely useless one day on account of its owner having come to the end of his tobacco.

This was the circumstance to which I have already referred, and it certainly was a circumstance with a vengeance. A pipe without tobacco is like an umbrella without any covering to its skeleton frame, or like a woman without a tongue (even worse, some wicked folk might say), or like a house without windows, or like a bird without wings, or like a purse without money, or like anything else you please to mention, without that which constitutes its chief perfection or which alone makes it useful and pleasant.

How the misfortune happened I can briefly tell you, without going into a narration of the events of the early life of our hermit, which I am at present bound not to disclose.

It happened in a very natural way. It was not that he dropped his tobacco pouch into the stream-he was far too careful of the precious article for that-it was not that any robber of the woods had taken it from him by force, or any nightly thief had crept in while he slept and carried off the precious article ; no, it was simply that he had not brought to the cave a sufficient quantity to last out, either because he had miscalculated the amount he had brought, or had not expected to stay so long ; and the consequence was that one fine morning, immediately after breakfast, when he went to his store to get out sufficient tobacco for the day's consumption, he found that he had only enough left to last him for another week.

This was, as I have remarked before, a circumstance with a vengeance. To do without his pipe, or without that which made his pipe valuable, was an utter impossibility. To get a new supply in the forest was equally out of the question. There remained, then, nothing for it but to return to the abodes of men in order to obtain that which was to him an absolute necessary of life.

But a man who has quitted society, given up the habit of associating with his kind, and adopted the life and assumed the character of a hermit, cannot easily retrace his steps. There are occasionally practical difficulties in the way. If he has not actually destroyed those garments which are deemed essential to persons entering or dwelling in a civilised community, he probably only possesses them in a state much worse than when he last wore them, entirely out of fashion, and not unlikely in an unwearable condition. Apart, moreover, from these technical considerations, the whole current of a man's thoughts when in such a position, his whole habit of life and the way of living into which he has fallen, render his return to civilised life extremely difficult.

Our Hermit felt all this, and felt it deeply. During the whole of that week he thought, and thought, and thought again, but with no other result than that to which he had come at first, namely, that the article he required must, somehow or other, be obtained. So determined was he upon this point, and so very difficult withal did the accomplishment of his determination appear, that I verily believe he would have turned robber forthwith, provided that the persons to be robbed had happened to be tobacco-merchants, or, at all events, persons well supplied with the article in question.

No such opportunity, however, offered; no such temptation was thrown in his way, and all his musing and thinking brought him to the conclusion that there was nothing for it but to sally forth into the world in order to get that which he wanted. As day after day of that week slipped away, the thing appeared more and more difficult, and the thought of giving up smoking once actually crossed his mind, though only to be banished the next moment with the contempt it deserved.

The week at last was nearly out, and so was the Hermit's tobacco. Then he took up his big staff, which was so heavy at one end as to give rise to dark suspicion that it was loaded with lead; he put on the old brown wide-awake which he constantly wore when he wore anything at all upon his head; he wrapped round his manly frame a cloak of skins which would serve equally well for a coat by day and a blanket by night; he fastened on his sandals with due care, and stepped boldly out of his cave across the stream. Then, taking off his wide-awake, he stooped down dipped his hand in the water, and passed it across his brow by way of refreshment, after which he rose, cast one look of fond and lingering regret upon the place which had been his home for many months past, and strode forward upon his journey.

Dense and dark was the forest for the most part, but the Hermit had started with sunrise, and the rays of the great luminary streamed in at intervals through the trees, and wherever they were less thickly planted he filled the forest with his glorious light, revealing a thousand woodland beauties and gladdening the eyes of him who beheld them. The way was in itself not without difficulties. Brakes and briars, tangled bushes, thorn-trees overcome by time which had bowed them to the ground, and seemingly resolved to vent their spleen upon the passing traveller by trailing their hidden branches, well studded with sharp spikes, upon the ground; fragments of rocks half concealed by the luxuriant growth of fern and brambles—a sharp ascent here, there a fall in the ground so sudden as to be near akin to a precipice; all these were features of the journey little calculated to make it more easy to the foot traveller.

The Hermit, however, seemed to make but little of them; his strong arm brushed the obstacles aside with apparent ease; his well-sandaled feet resisted the insidious attacks of the thorn; his sinewy legs bore him bravely up the hills, and his keen eye warned him in due time from the precipices, and so he pushed his way forward more rapidly than a man of less strength and determination could have done.

For several hours he proceeded through the forest without interruption of any kind, and indeed without encountering anything or anybody at all likely to interrupt him. Now and then a deer, startled from its lair by the unwonted intruder, sprang to its feet, regarded him for an instant with astonishment, and then darted away into the recesses of the forest; anon a big bird, scared by his passage through the branches, burst out into the open air and sought safety in flight from the danger which its instinct taught it to expect, and here and there a snake, roused by the passing tread of the traveller, reared its head, fixed its basilisk eye upon him for a second, and then glided away to its refuge beneath the roots or within the adjacent rocks. But nothing stayed his onward course, and he pushed forward for some hours with the perseverance of a man who, having an object to accomplish, sets himself to the accomplishment thereof with the steady resolution which is the only sure method to obtain success.

The sun rose higher, the light grew stronger, animal creation throughout the whole forest began to stir and awaken into life, and still steadily onward strode the Hermit, never flagging, never wearying, never turning from his course, but always tending in the same direction and walking with the same vigorous stride.

At length he reached the mouth of a deep ravine, which appeared to divide the forest into two parts, beginning at a narrow outlet, and rapidly widening out on each side. As the traveller paused for a moment, he could see that the ground fell rapidly before him, that instead of huge trees, low and stunted bushes occupied the space upon which he was about to enter for some two or three hundred yards, whilst on each side the ground sloped upwards again, forming a kind of vast gorge down which, if he advanced and kept on his straight track, he must immediately descend.

He paused, I say, for a moment, as if undecided whether to proceed or to turn aside, and gazed into the ravine before him.

At that instant the silence and solitude of the scene was suddenly changed. Wild figures rose as if by magic from the brushwood and stunted trees, as if disposed to bar his passage. One of these immediately confronted him, having sprung from behind a large bush where he had lain concealed. It was a man, scantily clad in garments made of the skins of animals, and armed with a staff sharpened at the end into a spear. He was apparently of about middle height, and of no inconsiderable strength, whilst his eyes, gleaming brightly from the dark and bronzed countenance which they adorned, had a wild fierceness of expression which boded no good to the traveller. His hair was matted upon his head, and surmounted by a rough cap of fur, and altogether his appearance, quite as uncouth as that of the Hermit himself, was anything but agreeable in the eyes of the latter. Had the other been alone, indeed, the Hermit would have cared but little for him or his appearance, but he could hardly help doing so when the bushes and brushwood disclosed at least half-a-dozen figures of a similarly strange appearance, armed

The Hermit Attacked by Robbers

with sticks and clubs, if with no more deadly weapon, and evidently disposed to dispute the passage.

Our Hermit was no coward; great as was his physical strength, it was equalled by the high courage with which his heart was possessed, and though the latter probably beat somewhat quicker for the moment, it never quailed, nor did he show aught of doubt or fear for a single instant.

There was no mistaking the intentions of those who thus interrupted his journey, for without parley of any kind they rushed upon him, the first man making a determined thrust with his spear, which, had it taken effect as it was intended, would have deprived the Hermit of his life and the world of this story without any possible doubt. Fortunately for both parties, however, it did no such thing. Our Hermit, without the slightest hesitation, but with no inconsiderable skill, parried the blow with his staff, and immediately brought the same implement down with a mighty thwack upon his adversary's head.

Neither man nor beast could have withstood the force of that blow. He went down like a bullock before the deadly stroke of the butcher's axe, and fell like a log upon the ground.

Whirling the staff round his head, the victor turned to meet his other enemies, and gallantly struck right and left as they closed in upon him. For an instant it really seemed as if he would prevail. So vast was the sweep of that mighty arm, so powerful the weapon which it wielded, and so dauntless the spirit of the man, that it seemed as if, like one of the champions of olden time, he was endowed with the miraculous gift of conquering any number of foes, natural or supernatural, whom fate might bring against him. The heavy blows which he dealt as he swung his staff to and fro, and the unexpectedly resolute character of his defence, might indeed, and probably would, have gained him the victory, had his enemies been less brave and less numerous.

But however brave and strong a man may be, it is heavy

odds against him when he is confronted and attacked by a dozen others, and the bushes presently disclosed fully as many enemies closing in around him, and fiercely striking at him with their clubs and bludgeons.

No aid was near, and only one result was possible. Down they went, right and left, but one struck as another fell, and no man can resist his fate. It must moreover be remembered that our unfortunate friend was by no means so fresh as when he had started that morning : he had journeyed for hours through thick woods and tangled brakes, and was indeed beginning to think of a temporary pause and rest at the very moment when he was thus savagely attacked. His resistance, therefore, could only be prolonged for a certain period, and the more certainly was this the case, since his enemies were able, from their number, and the open nature of the spot upon which he stood, to attack him on all sides at once, nor could he ward off the blows of six or eight strong arms striking at him at one and the same moment.

So presently he got a nasty knock on the head from a rascal who came treacherously behind him, then another from two or three blows aimed at the same time, and in the scrimmage that followed upon their coming to close quarters, he got so knocked about that before many seconds had passed he lay mute and insensible upon the ground.

And now comes what has always appeared to me the most incomprehensible and extraordinary part of the whole story. One would have thought that men, be they who they might, who had thought it worth their while to stop another man upon the highway—or rather in a place where there was no highway at all, but where each man had to make a path for himself—must have had some definite object in view, especially when the person stopped was tall, strong, and likely to resist.

If that object had been revenge, or the gratification of personal animosity towards their victim, one would have supposed that, having mastered and knocked him down, they would certainly have either made an end of him then and there, and, if employed by some rich enemy of the traveller, would have taken his head back to their employer as a proof of the fidelity with which they had discharged the duty they had undertaken, or would have carried him off bodily as a prisoner, and delivered him to those who had appointed to them their work.

If, on the other hand, the attacking party was composed of mere vulgar robbers, with no aristocratic revenge in question, but simply actuated by the desire of plunder, one would have imagined that they would either have destroyed the person they had attacked in pure disgust at finding upon him nothing valuable, or that if they had thought it worth while, they would have carried him off to their mountain fastnesses or forest caves, and held him captive in the hope of ransom, perhaps occasionally, in playful mood, sending a finger or two, or one of his ears, to his sorrowing relatives, in the hope of touching their hearts and opening their purses by this pleasing and simple plan.

The Hermit, for his part, certainly expected no mercy, and when he fell to the ground, had no sort of expectation that he should ever again rise from it as a living man. But in this marvellous world of ours, the wisest and most scientific of us are frequently mistaken, whether we prophesy about the weather, or concerning public events which may happen to be passing around us, or with regard to something more directly relating to our own lives and actions.

In this instance, as an example of the same thing, our friend the Hermit was agreeably—well, not disappointed exactly—but mistaken in his expectation of ending his life under the bludgeon-blows of those who had assailed him.

To this hour I can never make out how or why it was that they did not effectually and for ever knock him on the head, and secure his silence with regard to a transaction which, even in that half-civilised country, might, if a one-sided statement should be made about it, entail unpleasant consequences upon themselves. Perhaps they did not think him worth the trouble; perhaps they had still some mercy left at the far corner of their hearts, or perhaps (which seems to me most likely of all suppositions) they thought he was already dead, and required no more killing.

They might well have thought so, certainly, for the poor man had received blows enough, on head and body, to have killed half-a-dozen ordinary men, and lay there in his own blood, apparently as dead as Julius Cæsar.

It was remarkably lucky, moreover, that the robbers did not think it necessary to bury him, which would have been extremely awkward for him, and have silenced him with equal certainty. However, they did no such thing, partly, I presume, because they thought it a needless ceremony, and partly because they were occupied in attending to their own wounded, inasmuch as, besides the leader, four or five of their number had suffered more or less from the violent resistance of the traveller.

They searched him, and found nothing that they thought worth taking, except his staff and his empty tobacco-pouch; the former they carried off, but ere long threw away in the bushes as being too heavy for use save by a man taller than any of them happened to be; the latter they thought might be useful, and so appropriated, and shortly afterwards left the spot.

It is impossible to say how long the Hermit remained insensible. It must have been for a considerable time, for when at length he opened his eyes, the sun was fast declining, and the shades of evening descending upon the forest.

For several moments our friend could not imagine where he was, or what had happened to him. He lay perfectly still, looking up at the skies, and trying to collect his ideas. Gradually, memory regained her powers, and the whole scene came back to him. His first thought was one of extreme surprise at being alive, mingled, let us hope, with gratitude to a Higher Power, which had spared his life in that hour of danger. His next thought was for his pipe.

Instinctively he felt for it, and as he raised his left arm to do so, the pain was so intense that he nearly fainted, and he became aware that it was either broken, or so bruised as to be but of little use to him. Under these circumstances, he not unnaturally tried the other arm, and to his great delight found that his faithful and beloved pipe was in its accustomed hiding-place, close to his heart.

Joy once more welled up within his breast, although the next moment came the rebound, as the miserable thought came across him that he had no tobacco, and a pipe without tobacco can be of little practical use, although indeed it may recall sweet memories of the past, and suggest pleasant anticipations for the future.

Having ascertained the safety of this valuable implement, he now began to turn his attention to matters which many people would have thought of bef re their pipe.

His condition was the reverse of agreeable, and could hardly be called safe. He was faint and weak—very weak. His head was bruised and beaten, so that if it had not been a remarkably thick one, he must certainly have been killed. He ached all over, and his limbs felt as if they could never again perform their duties towards his unfortunate body. More. over, he did not know exactly where he was, and his journey forward, difficult even to a hale and strong man, had become positively impossible to one in his enfeebled and crippled condition. He tried to raise himself up to a sitting posture, but fell back directly with a low groan. He endeavoured to creep to some better shelter, but the attempt gave him such pain, that he instantly desisted.

Then the terrible thought came over him that he should never leave that place alive. A horrid thought it was, enough to make the bravest heart shrink, for what kind of death had he to apprehend ? Not the death of a brave warrior struck down in open fight by a fair foe, and breathing out his last sigh for the cause for which he had fought, conscious that to the last he had done his duty, and had at length fallen in its discharge. Not the death, either, which a hermit might naturally have expected, when his frame, attenuated with fasting and penance, had gradually worn out, and he lay upon his bed of leaves, peacefully and painlessly breathing out his soul.

Both these kinds of deaths our Hermit pictured to himself as he lay there, and fancied that either would have been easy to encounter.

But neither of these appeared likely to fall to his share. Felled by the blows of cowardly robbers, he had been left there in a position from which it seemed that death alone could release him, and that death would in all probability come either after many hours of suffering from starvation and thirst, or from the wild beasts of the forest, whose fangs he already fancied in his imagination fastened upon his helpless carcase, whilst the brutes snarled and snapped and worried over his still living self.

The idea was horrible, and his bodily weakness contributed to make it more so. He heartily wished that the robbers had done their work more completely, and that he had never waked from that sleep in which they had left him, for surely it would have been better thus than that he should have to meet such a fate as that for which he seemed destined. And as he lay and thought, the shades of evening began to close in, slowly but surely, and new sounds arose in the forest, whose animal life woke with the setting of the sun.

Far, far away, he fancied he heard a sound--a long, low sound, for which he listened again with a tension of nerves of which he had hardly been capable when in full strength. Again it sounded—and then again —and he knew but too well that it was the sound of the terrible panther of the forest, beginning his night-hunt for prey. He was answered by his mate, still in the far distance, and then came other sounds, little less alarming to the unhappy man.

The short bark of the wolf fell upon his ear, and as time passed on this sound came nearer and nearer, and other cries, of strange and wild animals, awoke the echoes of the forest. At last he felt as if he could bear it no longer: the suspense was too terrible—and he shouted aloud in desperation.

Weak as was his voice, from wounds and fatigue, it sounded loudly and strangely in that lonely place, and immediately afterwards the woodland cries seemed to increase, as if the wild beasts, recognising the voice of their enemy, man, were closing in around him with a view to his destruction.

Nearer and still nearer they seemed to come, and to the Hermit's excited imagination the leaves seemed to rustle and the dry sticks to crack before the advancing creatures. His head reeled again ; his brain was on fire; his heart grew sick within him; strange, fantastically-shaped reptiles seemed to crawl around, and over him ; enormous snakes seemed to enfold him in endless coils; cruel faces seemed to peer out at him from the bushes on every side ; bright, fierce, gleaming eyes seemed to glare upon him with ferocious expression, and he felt that a few moments more must end his existence, and blot him out from the earth. One more effort he would make—one more, and then sink back and die: with enormous exertion he raised himself upon his right arm, and once more shouted aloud.

Oh heavens! He was answered. A voice came back to him—no echo—no delusion, but an actual, undoubted, human voice, and it seemed near enough, too, to make it very certain that it was nothing else.

I cannot write for you in the language in which the voice spoke; at least I cannot carry on the conversation which ensued—if conversation you call it—in the language, because it was Spanish, if I am not mistaken, and I don't know a word of Spanish, my ancestors having taken an active part in repelling the Spanish Armada, and having been so indignant at the invasion that they never allowed the children of their family to be taught the language, which did nobody any harm but themselves, and need not therefore be made a matter of accusation against them. However, in consequence of this, no doubt, I cannot speak or write Spanish, and so I prefer to pretend the people in this veracious history were all English, and in the English tongue I shall make them speak.

But all this time I am keeping the Hermit—and my readers also—waiting to hear what the voice said, which was really very little.

"What cheer, comrade?" was what an Englishman would have said, and the owner of the voice said the equivalent to that in Spanish.

The Hermit, exhausted by the effort he had just made, could say no more, and the next moment the person who had answered him stepped forth out of the bushes.

He was a man somewhat above the middle height, with black hair cropped short round his head, handsome features, marvellous white teeth, swarthy complexion, a large gold earring in each ear, a curiously coloured shawl thrown carelessly over his shoulders and round his body after the fashion in which a Highlander wears his plaid, and the butts of several pistols appearing in the belt which it partially concealed.

He was a much smarter-looking fellow than any of the party who had first assaulted the Hermit, who were indeed a beggarly-looking lot in comparison with the newcomer. Nor were his intentions unfriendly, as was immediately evident by his actions. He strode forward to the spot where the Hermit lay, and placing against a tree the gun which he carried in his hand, knelt down on the ground and began to examine his condition.

When he had satisfied himself as to the extent of the

injuries which the other had received, he raised him gently in his arms and propped him up against an adjoining bush. Then he produced a small bag, from which he took a species of ointment, with which he began to touch the various bruises from which the Hermit had been suffering. He very carefully examined his head, and let fall upon it some drops from a small bottle which he produced from his bag—the relief was enormous.

The Hermit felt new life come into him as the stranger applied his remedies, and with freedom from pain and returning strength came, I am glad to say, a deep feeling of gratitude to the man who had indeed preserved him from a certain and horrible death.

CHAPTER II.

At that moment, however, the danger did not seem entirely over. The sounds in the forest had continually drawn nearer, and there seemed a possibility that the beasts might devour both the travellers together. This, however, was by no means the intention of the new comer. He hastily collected a quantity of dried leaves and sticks, laid them in a circle round himself and his patient, and presently set them on fire by rubbing two sticks together in a manner which he appeared perfectly to understand. The fire quickly blazed up, and the beasts which approached, as quickly beat a retreat when they perceived it.

There was danger, however, that other beings might perceive it too, and as soon as the Hermit found voice enough to speak, he felt it his duty to tell his new friend how and by whom he had been struck down, and that, for aught he knew, the robbers were still in the neighbourhood.

At this the other only smiled, but as soon as he had

sufficiently doctored the Hermit's wounds, he assisted him to his legs and asked if he could walk. . To his great surprise he found that he could do so, though weakly, and besides this, that his arm was not only less painful, but stronger than he could have expected. His new friend then told him to lean upon him and follow, which he accordingly did.

They went but a few steps before they reached an enormous tree, spreading out its branches on all sides. It was evidently a very old tree, as not only did its enormous bulk and vast roots testify, but the great hollow within it, as if Time had found it useless to work at it outside, and had therefore concentrated all his efforts to make it decay internally,

There was space enough inside that tree for a dozen people to have sat down to tea comfortably and without crowding, and the Hermit was not surprised when his companion stepped quickly into the hollow and assisted him to do the same.

What followed, however, did surprise him considerably, and so it would have surprised any one who had seen it, even if his intellect had not been previously confused and his perception dazzled by many knocks upon the head.

The Hermit's new friend proceeded to one side of the hollow, and clearing away some of the leaves which lay therein, disclosed a rope, at which he gave a pull, and immediately a large trap-door opened. He motioned the Hermit to descend a ladder which he now saw, and of course he instantly obeyed. Then his companion slowly followed him, having first made some arrangement by which the rope fell, so that it should not be perceived upon the closing of the trapdoor behind them.

They descended a few steps and found themselves again standing upon the ground, in a sort of passage which sloped rapidly downwards, and along which the Hermit followed his companion until it suddenly terminated in a large cave, which, at some time or other, had been either made, or inore probably enlarged, by the hand of man. It was apparently not very far from the surface of the earth, for a faint light (as the Hermit afterwards found, for it was too dark then for him to make the discovery) streamed in from above at one corner, but this was the only communication with the outer air.

As soon as they had entered the cave, the Hermit's new friend felt about on one side of him and presently found what he was looking for, which was something (perhaps a lucifer match box) which enabled him forthwith to strike a light. This he did, and proceeded to light a curious, old-fashioned lamp which stood upon a roughly-made table in the centre of the cave.

By its light the Hermit was soon able to discover different objects around him. In fact, they were not very difficult to discover, being but few in number. There were a few dried skins of animals upon the ground, a couple of chairs manufactured in a primitive manner, and evidently by some hand little skilled in the trade of a carpenter, and a long-barrelled gun leaning against the side of the cave.

This was all the Hermit saw as he glanced around him, and it must be owned that there was nothing very remarkable in the sight. A second glance, however, showed our friend that there was something more in the cave—something that moved in the far corner, and which presently came creeping forward, and disclosed to his astonished gaze the figure of an old—a very old woman.

Her appearance was not altogether inviting. She seemed to be composed of nothing more than skin and bones, bent nearly double with age, and with garments upon her which were, so to say, in tatters, kept together by a large wolf-skin wrapped around her in such a manner as to make it doubtful at first sight whether it was a wolf or a woman you beheld.

It was the latter, however, as you discovered when you saw her head, upon which was a small cap of faded red colour, fitting close, but from beneath which some straggling grey locks appeared. Her face was wrinkled, her teeth few, but prominent, whilst her nose and chin appeared, the one hooking down over her mouth and the other turning up, as if engaged in a continual effort to meet each other, in which they had nearly succeeded. But what struck the Hermit most was the fire which still sparkled in the eyes of the old dame, as if therein was concentrated all the life which remained to that venerable frame. They were very remarkable luminaries, and shone like a cat's eyes in the dark as she came scrambling and stumbling, creeping and crawling, forward from the corner of the cave.

The Hermit's friend accosted her at once with great deference.

"Mother Breenwole," he said, "I've brought you a wounded man, knocked over by the Forest Robbers and nearly made an end of."

At these words the old woman emitted a sound which partook of the several natures of a groan, a sob, and a squeak, and answered, somewhat to the Hermit's disgust—

"Better so, son Pedro, better so than have shown the secret of the cave to a stranger," and she looked on the Hermit with an eye which made him feel glad that it was not she who had come upon him when lying wounded and helpless on the ground.

But Pedro, as we will. henceforth call the Hermit's preserver, replied in cheery tones to the old hag—

"No harm done, Mother Breenwole; one more may know the secret without hurt, and this poor chap was a gone coon if I hadn't come along. We must set him upon his legs again now though, and who can do that better than you, mother?"

The old woman mumbled and muttered to herself as Pedro spoke thus, but raised no further objection; but when the Hermit, at his friend's request, had stretched himself

down upon a huge skin which lay near, she shuffled up close
to him and began to examine his wounds.

The Hermit experienced a queer sensation as he felt
those scraggy, bony old fingers moving about his throat, but
judged it best to show no distrust, especially as it was impossible to believe that the man who had taken the trouble to
save him would now permit him to be killed in cold blood.

After a short examination the old woman told Pedro
that he had already administered the best remedies to the
wounded man, and that the ointment—which was of her own
making—could not be surpassed by any medicine in its effi-
cacy in curing bruises and wounds. All the man now wanted
was food and rest, but the former he must take sparingly lest
the wounds should inflame.

With these words she shuffled back to her corner, and
in a short time produced a wooden dish which contained
some cold meat, apparently venison, which she placed on
the table along with a loaf of bread, and invited Pedro to
partake. A small slice she cut off and brought to the Hermit,
bidding him remain where he was, and when he had eaten
she shuffled off again, and presently returned with a pot of
ointment.

She gave him water to drink from a spring which
seemed to rise in one corner of the cave, and he thought
he had never tasted anything more delicious. Then she put
some more ointment upon his wounds and bruises, chanting
to herself in a low weird tone as she did so, in a language
perfectly unintelligible to the Hermit. Presently she passed
her lean skinny hands to and fro close over his face, several
times, and gradually he felt a heavy, drowsy feeling steal over
him, until little by little the scene seemed to fade before him,
everything became indistinct, and he sank into a deep sleep.

How long he remained in that condition I cannot
say, but probably it was the very best condition in which
he could have been. No man, however strong his frame and

The Hermit in the Cave with Mother Breenwole

vigorous his constitution, can stand such a knocking about
as our friend had that day received, and but for Pedro and
the old woman's ointment, together with the rest afterwards,
it would certainly have gone hard with him.

The Hermit slept, as I have said, but it was not altogether a quiet sleep. Knocks on the head, if administered with
sufficient force by a thick stick and a strong arm, are apt to
produce a confusion in the brain, and a strange jumbling up
of ideas in the mind of the person who has received them,
which no ointment, however powerful, can entirely prevent.
So as our friend slept, wonderful thoughts crowded upon
his brain, the imagination was active although the body
was still, and extraordinary dreams took the opportunity of
paying him a visit.

The days of his childhood came back to him as vividly
as if he was really living them over again; people who had
long been dead talked with him as familiarly as when they
were alive, without exciting in him the least surprise at their
being present, and things of the most curious kind happened
without seeming otherwise than perfectly natural to him. He
dreamed that he was seated upon a footstool at his mother's
knee—that beloved mother whose pure spirit had long fled
to a brighter and better world—and he seemed once more
to hear, teaching her boy the first lessons of gospel truth
and heavenly love, the tender accents of the voice that was
hushed forever. Then again he played upon the terrace and
in the shrubberies of the old place which had once been his
home-he played, and not alone—there were three sisters and
a brother—the playmates of his happy youth—alas! where
were they now?

But in his dream they all lived, joyous and loving as in
the old days, and he laughed and talked with them as then.
Again, he was a soldier, fighting gallantly for his country,
beloved by his comrades and honoured by all who knew him
; and then came a change, a dark, troubled dream in which

everything seemed confused and mixed, and whispers seemed to fall upon his ear, whispers of shame, disgrace, degradation, and a horrible time from which his mind recoiled as if it would shut and blot out that part of his life altogether. And then he fancied himself once more in his cave, with solitude for his comforter, with only the birds and wild animals to talk to, free from the wiles and hypocrisy, the schemes and plots of man, free from the restraints and unreality of what men distinguish by the name of Civilization, from which it seemed to him was banished much of that which most ennobled and most blessed man, and into which much was imported which most enslaved and degraded him.

So dreamed our Hermit as he slept, and tossed uneasily in his sleep as he did so, until at last consciousness gradually came back to him, and he remembered, little by little, the events of the past day, and knew where he was and all that had happened to him.

When he first half opened his eyes, he was scarcely quite awake, and before he was so, the sound of voices fell upon his ear, and with the habitual caution of one who had lived so long in the woods, he shut his eyes again and listened attentively without giving the least sign that his slumbers had come to an end.

The voices he heard were those of Pedro and the old woman, but to these was added another, which somehow or other seemed to chill the listener's blood, and to awaken within him feelings of bitterness and hatred which he had thought were extinct. It was the voice of a man, not a harsh or angry voice, but on the contrary smooth and soft, but it had a peculiar kind of lisp in it not easily to be forgotten. To be sure the words it uttered were neither smooth, soft, nor at all reassuring to the Hermit, for the first which he could distinctly hear had reference to himself, and were spoken in no friendly spirit.

"The old woman is right," said the speaker. "Better

to have knifed the fellow where he lay, or left him to the wild beasts, than run the risk of the secret of the cave being betrayed. But since you have saved him, Captain Pedro, the mischief is done and cannot be helped, unless indeed—" and here the man paused, significantly touched his dagger with one hand, and with the other pointed to the sleeper.

Then came the voice of Pedro in reply—

"No, no, Baron," said he, "none of that—the poor fellow will do no harm, and if there is gratitude in man, will never betray those who saved his life. I could not leave a human being to the wolves and panthers, being human myself, and he who would harm him now must harm me too. Besides, he may be useful some day, who knows?"

The other muttered something between his teeth which the Hermit could not catch, and then the old woman chimed in, recommending the stranger to be off, and not to remain until the sleeper awoke, as it might be better that he should not be seen. Thereupon the man who had been addressed by Pedro as "Baron" arose, and stealthily crept to the side of the cavern opposite that on which the Hermit and his preserver had entered on the previous evening.

As he did so, our friend took the opportunity of peeping at him from beneath his eyelids, for the voice had sorely perplexed him, recalling memories of the past which it had been his constant endeavour to stifle, and reminding him forcibly of one whom he not only believed to be dead, but in whose welldeserved death he had himself borne a share.

As the man passed along, the Hermit could see him, though but imperfectly, by the faint light of the lamp. He was about the middle height, and limped slightly on his left leg. He had on a large slouched hat which half concealed his face, but enough of it was seen to show a large, long gash upon one side, extending from forehead to chin, and entirely disfiguring what might otherwise have been hand-some features. A heavy drooping moustache, a chin closely shaven, and eyes that flashed beneath over-hanging eyebrows, completed the picture, as far as the face of the stranger was concerned, and his figure was so entirely enveloped in a dark cloak, that the Hermit could only obtain, in his momentary glance, the sight of a belt in which several pistols and daggers seemed to be sticking, ready for immediate action if occasion should require.

The Hermit was a brave man, but an involuntary shiver ran through him as he looked at the figure which passed before him. It was that of a man to whom he owed the greatest misfortune of his life the worst—the deadliest—the bitterest enemy he had ever known. But surely that man was not alive. His own right arm had struck him to the ground in fair. fight, and he had seen the warm life-blood welling up from the fatal wound, and the ashen pallor of death creeping over the face which, even so, scowled upon him with savage and bitter malignity.

What did it all mean? Was he awake, or was this still some horrible dream—some strange production of his still heated brain? With a mighty effort he recovered his calmness, but before he had resolved on any definite course of action, the figure had passed from his sight. It had disappeared upon the other side of the cave—disappeared so suddenly and completely that he began to think that it was certainly only in a vision that he had seen once more, that hateful face. Still, it was strange—passing strange—and all the more so as he now. felt perfectly awake, and, in spite of the feverish nature of his sleep, very much the better for his rest.

He therefore began to yawn and stretch himself, as if he had just opened his eyes, and thus very soon attracted the attention of Pedro and the old woman. They invited him to arise and join them in their morning meal, for it was now past the break of day, and Pedro informed our friend that if he meant to journey in their company, he must be ready to start in an hour's time. The Hermit therefore arose, and felt much fresher and stronger than the night before. He thanked his entertainers warmly for their care of him, and assured them of his desire to make any return that should hereafter be in his power.

In answer to his inquiries, Pedro informed him that he was bound for the seacoast, and that he expected to find a vessel there which would convey him to a port not many miles distant from the forest, from whence he could make his way where he would. This seemed to the Hermit as good a way as he was likely to find of supplying the want which had caused him to leave his cave, and he therefore consented with readiness to accompany his companions.

They advanced to the other side of the cave, and then for the first time our hero was able to account for the sudden and mysterious disappearance of the figure which he had seen in the early morning. At one place the rock projected into the cave, and on rounding the angle thus formed a narrow opening became perceptible, through which a man could easily pass, and immediately this was left behind there appeared a passage similar to that by which the Hermit and Pedro had entered on the previous day. This ran on in a straight line for some little way, and then turned suddenly to the left. Then the passage was no longer smooth, and fashioned into a pathway which might be easily trodden. Stones lay upon the ground, and these became more numerous and larger for some twenty yards or so, and then the passage seemed almost blocked up by them. Still, it was just possible to squeeze one's self between the large stones and the main rock, and having done this for the space of two or three more yards, a faint light began to glimmer from above, the ground sloped upwards, and presently the three travellers crept out into a deep, dense thicket, in and round which lay scattered enormous masses of stone and rock, of such a mixed and curious character, that the casual observer might well doubt whether he stood upon the ruins of some mighty fortress or palace of ancient times, or whether some freak or strange convulsion of nature had cast about and left in that spot the vast boulders of rock and massive blocks of stone with which the place was choked.

When they had emerged, the Hermit perceived that the entrance to the cave from that side, though open, was extremely difficult of discovery, owing to the thickness of the brushwood around it, in the first place, and in the second, to the narrowness of the mouth, and the extreme probability that, even if any one discovered it at all, they would never guess that a regular passage lay behind the scattered fragments of rock which I have described.

His companions halted as soon as they were out of the passage, and indeed it was time that the old woman should do so, for she had come so far with difficulty, and was quite out of breath. It was not, however, as Pedro soon informed the Hermit, her intention to accompany them any further. In the neighbourhood of the spot upon which they stood there were other caves and hiding-places, in one of which she expected to find friends with whom she would be welcome. This was all that the Hermit was told, and as he had neither seen nor heard anything of Mother Breenwole to induce him to desire her further acquaintance, he was by no means sorry to be quit of her company.

He and his companion now pursued their way for a short distance through the thicket until they suddenly came out upon a sort of cart-track, down which Pedro turned, and which was easier walking than the brushwood which they had just left. They followed this for half a mile or so, and then the trees began to be thinner, vegetation less luxuriant, and in a short space of time they came out upon the edge of the forest full in sight of the sea.

From the large pine-trees which skirted the forest there was a space of a few hundred yards only, of broken ground and sand-hills, interspersed with brambles and thickets here and there, and then came the gentle slope down to the beach, on which the sea was gently rippling with a faint, pleasant murmur as if trying to keep itself awake on that warm, long day.

The two travellers paused for a moment to gaze upon the scene before them, and then Pedro spoke. "The ship is not here," he said. "We are before our time—let us sit and talk a while under the shade of this pine-tree." The Hermit readily consented, and the two sat down side by side.

At first they did not find much to say to each other, but it was different when, after a few moments, Pedro lugged out from his pocket that which proved to be neither more nor less than a huge pouch of tobacco..

Not having been able to make use of his pipe for more than two whole days, the Hermit, as you may well suppose, was transported with joy at the sight, nor did his pleasure diminish when, having filled his pipe at the invitation of his companion, who speedily followed his example, he found the mixture to be one of which he thoroughly approved. The two men sat and smoked there for some time in silence, until the charms and soothing influence of the fragrant weed unlocked the secret caverns of their hearts, and made each inclined to be somewhat communicative towards the other. The Hermit was the first to speak, feeling indeed a remarkable sensation of gratitude towards the man who had first saved his life, and then ministered to the principal pleasure which made that life endurable. He asked his companion to tell him, if he had no reason to the contrary, how it was that he happened to be alone in the forest on the previous night, and what was his object and pursuit in life.

"To tell you the honest truth," replied the other, "I have for some time been thinking whether or no I should put a somewhat similar question to you. I cannot imagine what could have brought you into the middle of the forest where I found you—where you were going, and what pathway you

The Hermit and Captain Pedro under the Pine tree

meant to follow—you were heading for the sea, but no regular boat comes here—you could not know of my ship—and in short I don't understand it."

The Hermit took his pipe out of his mouth, emitted a whole volume of smoke, and answered his companion at once.

"I am a hermit," he said. "I live in a cave some miles further in the forest than where you met me, and where I should be at this moment if it had not been that I cannot exist without my pipe, and I had exhausted my supply of that precious herb which makes it so delightful."

"That may be all very well," returned the other. "But why are you a hermit? I have always understood that hermits are people who, worn out with the vanities and struggles of the world, retire to pass their time in prayer and meditation, and think of nothing else, banishing altogether such trifles as pipes from their consideration."

"Possibly," observed our friend, "this inay have been the case with hermits in ancient times, but the world grows wiser as it grows older."

"True," responded Pedro, "but somehow or other you do not look to me the sort of fellow that should be a hermit. You look more like a soldier. Tell me if I have not guessed right?"

The Hermit heaved a deep sigh as his companion spoke, and after a short pause replied to him in the following manner.

"I had almost vowed that I would tell my tale and open my heart to no one. I have suffered—suffered deeply—and I have left the world behind me just as much as many of those old hermits of whom you were speaking just now. But you have saved my life, and if you really desire to know anything of my past history, I do not think I should be right in refusing to tell you, provided always that you solemnly engage not to disclose it to anyone else without my consent."

Pedro having readily given the desired promise, the Hermit proceeded to tell him his story.

"I was born," he said, "of noble parents in a distant country. I had a happy home, and a joyous boyhood. My father and mother were devoted to their children, of whom I was the eldest. I had one brother and three sisters, and a more attached family can never have existed. We were together whenever it was possible, and loved each other with the truest affection.

"My mother died when I was about seventeen, and my eldest sister two years younger. A profound grief seized upon my father. He shut himself up in a country villa which he possessed, refused all consolation, would see none of his friends, join in no amusements, and follow none of his usual occupations. The result was that he died within the year, and we were left orphans.

"It was about this time that we became acquainted with Count Benjanisi—who or what he was I hardly know, but he apparently had great command of money, of the value of which I myself knew little or nothing. He professed the greatest admiration for my sister Angelina, and at the same time threw himself as much as possible into my society, apparently as a means whereby he might obtain access to her he loved. He encouraged to the utmost extent of his power an unhappy propensity for gambling which I had somehow acquired, and endeavoured in every way to poison my young mind, and corrupt my morals. Meanwhile he had effectually succeeded in gaining my sister's affections, and she, poor girl, loved him devotedly, and believed him to be little short of perfection.

"Somehow or other, however, I obtained a knowledge of some conduct of his which gave me warning in good time, so far as my finances were concerned, and I cautiously held aloof from the Count. He saw that I avoided him, suspected or ascertained the cause, and became from that moment my deadly enemy.

"At that time a war had recently broken out, our country having been invaded by a neighbouring monarch. A military ardour seized me, and although I might have escaped the service on account of my wealth and rank, I joined the army, and became an officer in the king's guards. In a skirmish which shortly took place, I was fortunate enough to distinguish myself, and to attract the notice of our general. All seemed to prosper with me, and to add to my good fortune, I fell deeply in love with Bianca, the general's daughter, who returned my affection with all the impulsive love of a young heart.

"Bianca! my soul bleeds as I pronounce thy name, and my tongue refuses to continue the narration of the misery which followed. Would to heaven I had died when first I saw thy sweet face!"

Here the Hermit paused, seemingly quite overcome by the depth of his feelings. Large tears forced their way from his eyes and ran down his bronzed cheeks, and his whole frame quivered visibly from the internal emotion he experienced.

"Cheer up, mate!" interposed his companion, with rude good-nature; "cheer up, unburden your soul, and hap 'twill relieve you after all."

The Hermit gulped down his rising feelings, took a long pull at his pipe, and continued in the following words—

"My Bianca was beautiful as a flower in early spring, and pure as the dew that kisses the rose-buds at dawn of day. She was promised to me, and our future apparently lay before us as safe, and smooth, and happy as the life of mortals may be. But listen to the melancholy sequel.

"The traitor Count Benjanisi belonged to my regiment. Envy at my success in love as well as war added to the bitter hatred he already felt for me, and deepened his resolve for vengeance. He first strove to detach from me the affection of my betrothed. In this he signally failed, but his neglect and cruelty to my sister, whom he openly abandoned, broke the poor girl's heart, and she died, the victim of his heartlessness.

"I had, I thought, a right to revenge my poor Angelina, but it was pointed out to me that the faithlessness of lovers was but too common, and that any measure which I took against the villain could only expose my sister's memory to unjust reproaches, since she, poor child, had perhaps built too much on his attentions, and he could excuse himself in the eyes of the world by saying that he had meant no more than ordinary civility and was not to blame if a girl chose to break her heart on his account. Therefore I could do nothing but trust that Providence would in good time repay the villain for his perfidy. But worse was to come.

"Enraged at the unsuccessful issue of his attempt to wean my Bianca from me, he laid his plans to ruin me with diabolical craft. I still played high, and was always rather fortunate in my dealings with Fortune. But all at once, I perceived—or thought I perceived—a certain unwillingness on the part of my comrades to play with me. Little did I know that the demon Benjanisi, paving the way for his great attempt to destroy me, had set afloat, but so craftily that I could not detect it, a report of malpractices on my part, which had created, almost insensibly, a prejudice against me. Yet my character stood so fair, and I was so popular with my comrades, that his machinations would have been of no avail had he not resorted to a still more diabolical expedient. I afterwards discovered that he had bribed my servant, and it was with the connivance and assistance of the latter that he carried out his nefarious plot.

"One day we were playing cards, some of my brother officers and I, when Count Benjanisi lounged in. I took but little notice of him, but afterwards recollected that he stood for some little time near the door on which our overcoats hung. There was good deal of smoking going on, and, owing to this and the excitement of our play, he might have easily tampered with my coat, as he doubtless did, without my detecting him in the operation.

"Presently he came forward and stood behind me. Fortune had as usual favoured me throughout the evening, and I was in high spirits. At that moment I was dealing, and the atmosphere was tolerably thick, as you may imagine. I turned up a king. At the same instant another king dropped upon the table, and the hand of the Court Benjanisi seized my wrist with a grip of iron; naturally I shook it off in fury, but in the confusion the cards got mixed, every one rose, and there was a violent altercation. The Count swore vehemently that he had seen me drop a king from my sleeve and pretend to have fairly turned it up.

"I knew well enough that the card had dropped from his hand and not from mine, and loudly declared this to be the case. Who was to decide between us? The base villain avowed his belief that if I was searched then and there, proofs would be found of my guilt. Of course I submitted willingly, when in one of the pockets of the coat I had on, two marked cards were found, and a whole pack in the pocket of my overcoat."

CHAPTER III.

"Now came into play the fiendish machinations of my enemy: the reports which he had sedulously spread were remembered and believed, and when, on searching my quarters, another pack of marked cards, and also some loaded dice, were found, nothing could save me.

"I need hardly tell you that it was through the villainy of my servant that all this had occurred. Believe me or not, but before you refuse to do so think what object I can have in telling you the story at all, if my version is not true. It was in vain that I protested and swore; even the previous high character which I had borne could not stand against proof so apparently strong.

"I was turned ignominiously out of the regiment, and my career in life ruined forever. At once I challenged my vile traducer and offered to decide the matter by fair fight. He replied, with a sardonic smile upon his, sallow features, that 'he did not fight with card-sharpers,' and even to this I had to submit.

"Great heaven! what agony did I endure. My brother and young sisters alone believed in my innocence. It maddens me to think of that which happened next. Without my knowledge, my brave young brother picked a quarrel with the demon Benjamin, to avenge the insult which had been offered to his family. My first intelligence of the matter was that the boy—for he was little more—had been brought in, run through the chest, and dying from the effects of the wound inflicted by the superior strength and skill of his adversary. One of my remaining sisters, delicate from her youth, soon followed to the grave the brother to whom she had been devotedly attached. The other—my last relation—entered a convent, and sought in the consolations of religion that comfort which the world denied.

"I was alone, and had but one object in life—revenge upon the author of misery and the destruction of my family. I watched for an opportunity—days, weeks, months—but none occurred. The wary villain avoided me, and I discovered moreover that he had actually formed a plot to have me assassinated, and thus removed from his path forever.

"I have not yet mentioned the deadliest blow of all. My Bianca was lost to me. Poor girl! I hope—I know—I feel that she loved and trusted me still. But her father was inexorable. Himself the soul of honour, he could not tolerate the bare suspicion of its ·absence in the heart of another. As soon as my disgrace had been accomplished, he forbade me his house and refused me permission to see or to approach his daughter.

"I was in despair. Count Benjamin took the opportunity of eagerly urging his pretensions to Bianca's hand. Her father supported his pretensions. My brave girl resisted all pressure, and at length took refuge in the same convent as my last remaining sister. Nothing daunted, the villain now formed the project of carrying her off from the convent. He laid his plans well, but happily I discovered them. My resolution was soon taken. This should serve to supply the opportunity for which I had so long waited.

"I had money—for the demon who had ruined my honour had not been able to deprive me of the poor dross which is valueless without it; nay, I am wrong, not wholly valueless; at least it was not so in my case, for, by a liberal use of my wealth, I hired a small band of men to waylay the count and his party upon their expedition. You need not shudder: murder had no place in my thoughts—all I wanted was to compel him to the combat which he had declined. I succeeded. The party with him were well-armed, but they were engaged in a nefarious deed, and had probably no great heart in their enterprise. They fled upon the first attack of my men, which was made not far from the walls of the convent, which their leader had intended to scale.

"I took good care that my enemy did not join in their flight. He was left alone with only two companions, whilst I, with a dozen men at my back, could have had him surrounded and slain at a word from my lips. I scorned such a proceeding. Nay, more; I told my people that I was about to engage in single combat with that man, and I charged them to let him depart without injury if he should overcome me. Murder was ever abhorrent to my feelings, and it was not his death but my revenge that I craved. Traitor to the last, he fired a pistol at me whilst I was actually giving my men these directions, but fortunately his coward heart made his hand tremble, and he missed me. Then I called on his two friends to stand back as mine had done, and I attacked him.

"It was a fair fight; he had a sword and so had I, but I had right on my side and the deep sense of bitter injury, whilst he had a bad, black heart, and the knowledge that he was face to face with the man whom he had bitterly and cruelly wronged. Could there be a doubt as to the issue of such a combat? After a very few passes, I broke through his guard, and, having him momentarily at my mercy, I slashed his face from ear to chin and gave him a mark which he will carry to his grave."

At this point of the Hermit's story Pedro gave a sudden start, but immediately resumed his former attitude of earnest attention to the recital.

"Furious with pain and rage," continued the Hermit, "the count redoubled his efforts, and rushed upon me with the fury of a madman. But I parried his blows without difficulty, and he almost ran of his own accord upon the point of my sword, which passed clean through his body. He fell upon the ground and lay at my feet covered with his own od. I stood by, and soon saw that no more was necessary. I was rid of my enemy forever.

"For a few moments I stood over him hoping that he might speak, and perhaps say some words of repentance for his crime, and give me some clue by which even then I might have re-established my position and regained the honour of which he had so basely robbed me. But as I gazed upon the dying wretch, no sign of repentance or softness came over his features, over which the ashy pallor of death was already spreading. On the contrary, a look of unextinguishable hatred seemed to disfigure still more his wounded face, as he passed away from a world which his crimes had disgraced. He lay dead at my feet, and the sight was not one which I cared longer to look upon.

"I left his body where it lay and departed with my

companions. But I had nothing left to live for, and life seemed to me a weary burden. I determined to quit for ever the haunts of men, and bury myself in the solitude of some wilderness or forest, where the sin and misery of man might cease to torment me. I roamed listlessly at first from place to place, until at last I heard of this forest which we have just quitted together. Therein I wandered, caring little whether the robbers who frequent, or the ghostly creatures who are said to inhabit it, should dispute my right to do so. Neither the one nor the other, however, troubled me until the occasion which has led to our acquaintance.

"I found a cave in the middle of the forest, wherein I took refuge, and which has been my home for many months. One companion alone I had-my pipe; one solace remained to ine-tobacco. By the aid of this soothing weed I have often been able to forget my sorrows—so far as such sorrows can ever be forgotten. Seated in or near my cave, with my pipe in my mouth, I have mused on the past with a bitterness rendered less intense as the sweet influence of the charm stole over me, and ever and anon has seemed even to inspire me with some faint hope for the future.

"Fancy then my sadness when I found that the large stock of tobacco which I had brought with me to the forest began visibly to decline. I eked it out as long as I could, but at last it vanished, and I was without my only consolation.

"I tried to bear it; but man is only man after all, and it was impossible that I could do so. Therefore I resolved to make one more visit to the haunts of men, in order to supply myself with that which had become for me a necessity. Unfortunately, my wanderings had been quite desultory on first entering the forest; I had gone hither and thither for some miles before I stumbled upon the cave, and consequently I had no idea which was the shortest way out into the open country again. So I could only march straight on, and hope for the best.

"I need tell you no more; you know the sequel of my story, and how that, but for your kind assistance, I must certainly have perished. Now you know all that I have to tell, and the woes and misfortunes which have made me what I am."

Whilst the Hermit was speaking, his companion listened with the utmost attention, and when he had ceased, remained silent for a few moments, as if buried in thought. Presently he lifted his head which he had allowed to sink forward into his hands, which rested upon his knees, and looked steadily at the other.

"I believe you," he said at length; "I believe every word which you have told me. But there is one question which I desire to ask you, and I beseech you to answer me truly. Have you ever had any reason to believe that this precious Count Benjamin of yours was not dead after all—or is there any person of your acquaintance who at all resembled him in appearance?"

"Friend," returned the Hermit, speaking with the solemnity of one who felt he was touching upon subjects of a deep, if not sacred nature, "I will even answer you as freely and fairly as you ask me. I never knew any person who resembled that fiend, and I vow to you that, twenty-four hours ago, I would have sworn that he was not only dead, but that these eyes witnessed his death. Even now I know not how to doubt it. The gulf which separates the living from the dead may be deep or shallow—wide or narrow. No mortal man can say that it is impossible for one who has once left this world to reappear therein. I may have seen a spirit; I may have been under some strange delusion, but I do truly say and swear to you that the first doubt of the count's death which ever crossed my mind arose this very morning in the early twilight, before I joined you at your breakfast.

"Awakened by the sound of voices, I fancied that I heard that voice, whose tones I remembered but too well, and when, shortly afterwards, a figure crossed the cave, the height, the general appearance, the manner of walking, all reminded me forcibly of the man. Still I was so firmly convinced of his death that I should have thought it a strange but passing fancy of my brain, had I not had a glimpse of his face, and of a scar so exactly like that which must have resulted from the wound which I myself inflicted, that I confess my mind to have ever since been filled with doubts and misgivings."

"You do well to speak thus frankly," remarked the other, "and in return for this and your story I will in a few words relate to you my own. I am of an ancient but decayed family, and have knocked about the world since the age of fourteen, when my father's death turned us young ones adrift. It is not necessary to tell you of my adventures since then, both by sea and land. Suffice it to say that they have been many and perilous. At last, some three years ago, I became the captain of a small ship, with as gallant a crew as ever sailed on the blue sea. Why should I hesitate to tell you the whole truth? I am a rover—a pirate, if you like the name better. I love the ocean. I love the excitement of the wild, free life I lead; but I vow to you that, save in fair fight, no man has ever fallen by my hand, and no such cruel actions as those of which you sometimes hear in old stories of buccaneers, have been perpetrated by my crew.

Some time since, we discovered the caves and recesses with which this forest abounds—or at least those which lie within easy distance of the shore. We determined to make use of these as hiding-places, wherein our plunder might be secure until we gave up our roving life, or went off to some other part of the world. There are several caves more or less like that which we quitted this morning, and a large treasure, belonging to me and my crew, is deposited in these.

"I came on shore three days ago, to tell you the truth, in order to give a meeting to that very person whose presence has filled you with such strange emotion. I will tell you at once that he is no old acquaintance of mine. I met him first at a masquerade ball in a sea-coast city not far from this shore, about two years ago. He gave the name of the Baron Ferdinando, and seemed anxious to make my acquaintance, and that of two of my officers who were with me. In this he succeeded: we sailor-men are not hard to know, or difficult to get on with when you know us. Since that time he has given us information of booty to be captured, which has been accurate and useful, and on one occasion he made a short expedition with us. Now that I think of it, he advised killing the prisoners, after we had captured a small vessel, and was not much pleased at the manner in which I at once negatived the proposal.

"To cut a long story short, he gradually made himself friends among my crew, among whom, by the by, he entered a fellow of his own—a sullen dog, whom I like but little, and whom they call Philippo. By this means he became acquainted with our course of life, our plans, our ways of living, and even of the position of those caves in which our treasure is hid. I have had my doubts about him once or twice, but when he appointed a meeting with me yesterday, I did not like to decline, especially as he stated that he had something of importance to communicate. That something was that a large merchant vessel, with a very valuable cargo, will pass off this coast some time tomorrow. The Baron's information has hitherto always been so correct, that I have no reason to doubt its accuracy on the present occasion. Yet I did not quite like the bearing of several questions he put to me as to the treasure—which cave held the most? of what did it exactly consist ? had we thought of the difficulty of moving it when we wished to do so ? The questions were asked in a simple and natural manner, but experience has made me suspicious.

"Now if this man turned out to be your confounded Count come to life again, I should be more suspicious still. Suppose he is treacherous—he might bring us into trouble easily enough, and who but he would get the treasure afterwards ? He did not recognise you, certainly, or he would probably have tried to pay off old scores, and verily he would have had a good opportunity. As it was, he suggested putting a knife into you, and if he and the old hag you saw (who lives in these caves and looks after them a bit for us) had been alone, I would not have given much for your chance. But it was not likely that I had saved a fellow's life to let him be butchered by an ugly, illconditioned son of a gun like that. He excused himself from joining us in this expedition, but said he would not be far off, and could be of more use on shore. I want no unwilling hands in my vessel, and he may come or go just as he pleases. But if he means treachery—"

Here Captain Pedro clenched his fist and shook it, softly and silently, before him, in a manner which betokened no good to the individual of whom he spoke, if he should bring himself within its reach after having given occasion of offence to its owner.

Both men sat silent for a short time, and then the Hermit said—

"Whether he be Ferdinando the Baron, or the Count Benjamin come back to life, is more than you and I can tell. But if there be treachery in the world, it is written on that man's face. It is your duty—and it will be your wisdom—to guard against it."

"True," replied the other, "but how is this to be done? Every minute I expect to see my vessel rounding the bay. I invite you to come on board. Close to the shore we must await the arrival of the merchant vessel. I see now what treachery Ferdinando can practice upon us, since he will not be with us. My crew are faithful and brave. Suppose that he is really villain enough to intend to carry off our treasure from the caves, he will find himself terribly mistaken if he thinks to escape our vengeance. We should follow him to his death—and it would be but justice to slay him."

As the two conversed, a small vessel was seeb rounding the bay from the direction in which Pedro had told the Hermit he expected his ship to come, and the captain soon recognized it as his own. They descended to the shore, and a boat was presently sent off, in which they rowed back to the ship.

The crew appeared to be a reckless, merry set of fellows, but treated their captain with respect, and evidently regarded him with affection. He invited the Hermit to come down into his cabin, and when there, suggested to him a plan which had come into his head.

"It is possible," he said, "that if Ferdinando and Benjamin are one and the same person, you may recognize the man he has put aboard this ship as one of my crew. He is but a poor sailor, anyhow, but may be a good man for all that. Now do you stand at my cabin door, or rather just behind it, so that you can see well, and I will call this man with several others, from the end of the passage, so that they must pass the door in coming to me. Note them well, and see if you remember the face of any one of them."

Accordingly, the captain went a little way from his cabin, and (using nautical phrases which I forbear to repeat, for fear of making a mistake in them) called several of the crew by name, whilst the Hermit stood in such a position as enabled him to see them without being seen.

Captain Pedro then returned to his cabin and found the Hermit pale with emotion. In the man Philippo he had recognized the servant who had betrayed him to Count Benjamin, and enabled the latter to carry his abominable designs against him to a successful issue. He no longer doubted that the villain Count intended treachery also in the present instance. What was to be done? They might seize Philippo and endeavour to wring from him a confession of his master's schemes. But to this there were two objections.

First, that he might not know them, and secondly,

that the crew might dislike the arrest of one of their number upon the mere word and suspicion of a stranger. This notion, therefore, was at once discarded.

Captain Pedro's chief apprehension was for the concealed treasure. After hearing the Hermit's story, he had come to the conclusion that Count Benjamin—for he no longer doubted the identity of Baron Ferdinando with the villain—had a design upon the contents of the various caves, and that he might possibly have confederates in the forest at that moment, and intend to carry off the treasure whilst he knew that the pirates were engaged upon their present scheme. The more he thought it over, the more likely did this appear, and he expressed to the Hermit his doubt whether it would not be better to land a portion at least of his crew in order to visit and guard the caves.

To this, however, there were also weighty objections. The crew barely numbered seventy men all told. If the Count had really concealed friends in the wood—and how could they tell but that the very people who had attacked and left the Hermit for dead might belong to his party?—was it not probable that they would be in sufficient numbers to be able to overcome any such small detachment as could be well spared from the crew ? It would be useless to send less than twenty-five or thirty men to make the thing tolerably certain, and the caution of the pirate captain forbade him to attack any vessel with such a reduced number of sailors as would then be left in his vessel. This plan, therefore, was also ultimately abandoned, and none other seemed to suggest itself.

At last it occurred at the same time to both the Hermit and Captain Pedro that there would be great advantage in the adoption of a middle course. The Hermit was of little use on board ship, nor indeed was he by any means anxious to join in a piratical attack upon peaceful traders. At the same time, he felt bound to render any service he could legitimately afford to the man who had saved his life. He was therefore quite willing to land again upon the shore, accompanied by three of Captain Pedro's most trustworthy men, who knew every corner of the caves in which the treasure was hid, and could conduct him safely thither. It was settled that they should at once proceed to the nearest cave for the purpose of discovering whether there was anything suspicious, or whether things were all right, after which they were to return to the shore and signal the vessel by means of a white handkerchief if the latter, a red if the former should turn out to be the case.

Accordingly, without the crew being generally informed of what was going to be done, the Hermit and his three companions were quietly sent off in a boat and landed upon the shore, the former being much gratified by the present of a quantity of the best tobacco sufficient to last for a couple of days even if he should make a continuous use of his pipe.

The small party advanced to the edge of the forest, which they cautiously entered, and proceeded by a narrow pathway which the pirates were able to discover by marks made by them on former visits to the same place. When they had gone some distance, they stopped, and the eldest of the three, a wary old sailor named Stefano, told the Hermit that they were now within a few hundred yards of the entrance to one of the caves, wherein a large quantity of their valuables was hidden. He proposed, with the Hermit's permission, to go forward alone from the point at which they then stood, in order to see whether they might safely enter the cave. Presently he returned, and told them that all seemed safe, but that he could perceive that some one had visited the spot since they were last there.

The four men advanced, and presently arrived at a small opening in the side of a large rock, much overhung with branches of trees, which had to be pushed aside before it could be well discovered. Here they paused, and Stefano pointed to the ground, whereupon were impressed the marks of footsteps, evidently of tolerably recent date. They listened attentively, but could hear no sound, so they crept quietly forward into the cave.

All was still and silent as death. The passage into this cave was but short, and the cave itself appeared to have no other egress than the aperture by which they had entered. One of the pirates now struck a light, and for a moment the sudden change from darkness to light dazzled them all.

As soon as they were able to see more clearly, an exclamation of surprise and wrath burst from the three pirates. Their treasures had been buried on either side of the cave, or thrust away in various recesses around it. But the place was not as they had left it. The hand of the spoiler had been there. Many things of little value appeared to have been contemptuously tossed aside, but the best part of their treasure seemed to have disappeared. Nor did it seem as if the robbery had been perpetrated in a hurry. The earth had been carefully dug up, bags and boxes of coin and other valuables abstracted, and a thorough search made over the whole cave. Who, then, were the robbers?

Stefano, who had been informed by Captain Pedro of his suspicions concerning the individual whom the pirates knew as Baron Ferdinando, had no doubt at all in the matter, and at once informed his comrades of the same. Loud and deep were their threats and curses upon the head of the supposed robber. He had certainly, however, not been alone, nor could the robbery have been perpetrated by one person only. The question was, how many assistants had he with him ? Then, how had they conveyed away their booty, and in what direction had they gone?

Further examination answered the second of those questions.

Although no other opening appeared at first sight, by which men could enter the cave, it seemed that at the far end there was an aperture leading into another place of the same kind, wherein the ground sloped upwards at the further end, and allowed of the easy passage of more than one man into a wider and larger excavation, from which it was not difficult to pass out into the forest. The footprints here showed the Hermit's party that it was by this means their treasure had been carried away, and also that some half-dozen persons at least must have been concerned in its abstraction. Outside the cavern, moreover, they perceived the footprints of some beasts of burden, and the mystery was so far solved. Whoever it was who had visited their hiding-place and taken away their goods, had doubtless provided himself with horses or mules, which he had laden with the proceeds of his expedition.

What were they to do? If they pursued the robbers, they would probably overtake them, but the result of their doing so might not be entirely advantageous, as, considering the probable number of the party, they would run no inconsiderable risk of losing their lives as well as their property.

Meanwhile time had been slipping away. I do not think I have clearly stated that which was the fact, namely, that the Hermit had passed an afternoon and night on board Captain Pedro's vessel, and that it was in the early morning that he had again been put on shore. Since that time several hours had elapsed, and the captain would doubtless soon expect news of their expedition. As they could evidently do nothing by themselves, they judged it best to return to the shore without further delay, and communicate with the vessel.

In a very different frame of mind, therefore, from that in which they had landed a few hours before, they began rapidly to retrace their steps to the shore. They had accomplished something more than half the distance when the loud sound of cannon broke upon their ears. The pirates looked at each other with a smile, and remarked that the captain was speaking to the merchant ship, and that they should just be in time for a share in the plunder, which might help to make up for that which the crew had lost by the treachery which had despoiled their cave. The firing continued as they hastily pushed their way through the forest, and the men remarked to each other that the ship which they had attacked must be making a better fight than common, but that it would be of no avail against Captain Pedro.

Presently they came out upon the beach, and approached near to the water's edge. An unlooked-for and no less unwelcome sight met their eyes. Instead of seeing their own ship proudly clinging as it were to the side of her enemy, and the flag of the latter hauled down, as her crew fled before the pirate boarders, a totally different state of things seemed to exist. Captain Pedro's vessel appeared to be sheering off from the merchant ship (which was much the larger of the two) as well as she could, whilst the deck of the latter seemed to be thronged with men, who were keeping up a heavy and continuous fire of musketry upon the baffled pirates, whilst every now and then came a puff of smoke from the side of the larger ship, followed by a flash, and then a deep, rolling sound as of distant thunder rolling up the bay.

It was evident that Captain Pedro had "caught a Tartar," and the Hermit's companions cast looks of blank dismay upon the scene before them. It was not of very long dura-tion. They could distinctly hear the cheers and shouts of the enemy as they maintained their fire upon the pirate vessel, and it became soon apparent that she could only escape by a miracle. As miracles do not generally occur on behalf of respectable people, much less in aid of those who live by plundering others, it was hardly to be expected that this channel of escape would open before Captain Pedro and his crew. Nor indeed did it do so.

They returned a feeble fire for some time, but grad-ually it slackened, and after a tremendous volley from the merchantman's defenders, and a few more discharges from her heavy guns, the pirate vessel slowly toppled over on one side, and appeared to be about to settle down and disappear. No white flag had been shown—no signs of surrender given—perhaps because it was known to be useless, but more probably because those who manned that vessel knew not what yielding meant. But as soon as the fate of their beloved ship appeared to be beyond all doubt, the two younger of the Hermit's companions threw themselves on the ground and fairly wept with shame and rage. Old Stefano roused them from this condition.

"Up! men," he cried, "there is something yet to be done! see, some of our men have escaped from the ship, they may yet be saved! Courage! do not give way to despair which can help nobody!"

With these words he encouraged his two mates, and at the same instant the Hermit perceived that which the more experienced eyes of the old sailor had discovered before, namely, that from amid the smoke and spray which surrounded the sinking vessel, a boat was emerging, rapidly pulled by strong arms towards the shore. The same causes prevented her being seen by the crew of the larger vessel until she was halfway between the ship and the beach. Then they raised a loud shout, and directed their fire upon those who were evidently the only survivors of the pirates.

But the boat kept on her way until within some forty or fifty yards of the shore, when a lucky shot seemed to strike her, and with a loud shriek from some of those on board, she broke up, and her crew were in another instant struggling in the water.

Up to this moment the Hermit and his companions had remained stationary, silent, but deeply interested spectators of what was going on. But when they saw the boat thus swamped they could restrain themselves no longer, and, leaving their posts, they rushed down eagerly into the sea, as if to meet and save any of their comrades who might yet be alive.

It was a moment of suspense, of excitement, even of

agony. At that particular spot the trees and shrubs came more nearly down to the water's edge than at any other point, since the boat's crew had naturally steered for the landing-place where they might most quickly find shelter from the enemy's bullets. It was soon evident to those on shore that some at least of their friends would reach them in safety. The merchantman was too far to render it probable that many men, if any, would be hit whilst swimming singly in the water, and before long one after another landed and joined the Hermit's party.

Their attention, however, was specially directed to one man who was gallantly supporting another as he made his way to the safety of the shore, and as they rushed to relieve him of his burden they discovered that it was none other than Captain Pedro himself, supporting the almost lifeless body of Philippo. The latter had escaped all the previous dangers of the fight, and was among the crew of the boat who seemed so nearly free from further peril, when the shot which capsized the boat drove a splinter into his body, inflicting a wound which utterly prevented his attempting to swim to shore.

His was the shriek which had reached the ears of the Hermit's party when the shot struck the boat, and without any doubt he must have perished then and there, but for the resolution and bravery of Captain Pedro. The latter, seizing the wounded man, plunged with him into the sea, and by dint of almost superhuman exertions, succeeded in bringing him to land.

Out of twenty men who had manned the boat, ten were saved besides these two, the others perished either from injuries received before or after the shot struck the boat, or else because, being unfortunately unable to swim, they had nothing for it but to be drowned.

No sooner were the survivors on shore, than they hastened to seek the friendly shelter of the trees already mentioned, carrying Philippo with them. Before anything else was said or done, they watched with deep anxiety the conduct of their foes, who, they apprehended, might follow them on shore. They were, however, soon relieved from this fear. The pirate vessel had settled and gone down like a log. The boat which had attempted to reach the shore had also been destroyed, and although the victors might have seen, or at least might have expected, that some of her crew must in all probability reach the shore, they did not feel inclined to follow them into the depths of a forest wherein the risks they would possibly encounter would be greater than any advantage to be derived from the capture or destruction of the few survivors of their enemies. So they made no sign of pursuit, or even of approaching any nearer to the shore, and as soon as this had been satisfactorily entertained, the Hermit began to inquire anxiously into the causes of the disaster.

It was soon explained. The merchantman had been no merchantman at all. Disguised as such, she carried guns far superior in weight to those of the pirate, and was manned by a crew at least four or five times as numerous as that of Captain Pedro, and had soldiers, well armed and ready for action, on board. She allowed the pirate to come quite close to her and showed no signs of resistance.

Had her crew waited until Captain Pedro had given the signal to his boarders, nothing could have prevented the capture or destruction of him and his whole crew. Fortunately for these, or for those few, at least, who now survived—by some mistake the merchantman disclosed her real character before the captain's ship had actually thrown her grappling-irons and sent on her boarders. It was too late, indeed, for the vessel to escape, and many of the crew had been killed at the first discharge from the decks of her opponent, but the result had been that which have seen.

None of those who had been saved with Captain Pedro were seriously hurt, except Philippo, the men who had been badly wounded among the boat's crew having naturally enough been those who had failed to reach the shore. It did not take many words for the captain to tell his tale to the Hermit, who in return informed him of what they had seen at the cave. Pedro stamped in fury upon the ground.

"That vile Ferdinando!" he cried, "would that he stood here before me!"

CHAPTER IV.

At that moment a deep groan broke from Philippo, whom the pirates had placed upon the ground, and around whom they were standing whilst the above conversation passed.

"Poor fellow," said the Hermit, "his course is run, I fear: there can be little hope for him with that deep wound in his side."

So saying, he stooped over the wounded man, who at that moment opened his eyes and gazed upon the person whose voice he had heard.

Scarcely had he done so, when he gave a kind of a shriek and fainted away immediately. They dashed water in his face, and one of them gave him a sip of brandy from a flask which he had about him. Presently the man opened his eyes.

"Where is he?" he said, "where is he? where is my dear old master? Surely it was his face I saw. Oh how cruelly I wronged him? I am punished now though. If he would but forgive me before I die."

The Hermit stepped forward.

"Pietro Manti," he said, and the wretch started again when he heard the tone of the voice which pronounced his real name instead of that by which he had been known among the pirates. "Pietro Manti, I am not one to bear malice against a dying man. Grievous is the wrong you have done me. May Heaven forgive you as I do."

"Ah, Marchese!" groaned the man. "It is but too true that which you say. Yet before I die I can do something to restore to you that of which I helped to rob you. Witness all to what I now say;" he gasped for breath, but recovered himself by a mighty effort, and as Captain Pedro and the surviving pirates stood around, he said, slowly, but very clearly and with great earnestness, "I swear by all sacred things, and by all which good men hold to be sacred, that I tell the truth now, when I know I am close to death. The Marchese Cellano here—my kind old master of old days—is as innocent as the babe unborn of anything of which he was charged by the Count Benjamin, and for which he was driven from his regiment. The Count gave me much money, I hid the cards and loaded dice where he told me, I was his slave. He wished, I know not why, to ruin the Marchese, and I, oh wretch that I am, I helped him to do it!"

As the wretched man spoke these words, the pirates looked at each other in astonishment, Captain Pedro being the only one of them who understood what they meant. The Hermit then spoke—

"You hear, my friends," he said, "what this man declares, and it is useless for me any longer to conceal my rank, though I had wished that it, together with much of my past life, might have been forgotten. I am indeed that unhappy Marchese Cellano, who was, years ago, ruined by the machinations and treachery of him whom you have known as Baron Ferdinando. But perchance this is not all ye have to hear, and there may be something more closely affecting yourselves." Then bending over the dying man,

"Pietro Manti, I have already assured you of my forgiveness, but if you would be forgiven elsewhere, make what atonement you can—Have you no more to tell? How came you on board the ship which has just been destroyed? What was your object, and what your intention?"

The man groaned again heavily.

"Ali me," he cried, "I die of thirst, and this pain which racks me through and through. For the love of heaven, water!"

They poured water down his throat again, and once more gave him some brandy, after which he spoke, though still with difficulty.

"The truth of what I have told you may easily be proved," he said. "Sewn tightly within my doublet is a paper which contains a statement which I drew up some time since, intending to extort money from Count Benjamin, if need should be, by placing it in the hands of a friend who should threaten him with exposure. It tells the whole story of the plot against the Marchese, and contains besides some notes from the Count to me, with directions which will help to show the truth, and some private memoranda of his besides with which I made free, in order to have proofs of what I should disclose if it became necessary. They will help my lord to establish his innocency. For me, the villain Count has deceived me with the rest of you—you are all betrayed!"

The pirates started, but at a gesture from Captain Pedro remained silent, whilst, after a gasp which seemed likely to be his last, the unhappy man continued—

"He sent me on board your vessel as a spy, to glean and impart to him all information respecting your proceedings, and the secret of your buried treasure. This last, however, he discovered for the most part without my aid, thanks to the open-heartedness with which you treated him, and which might have softened the heart of a man less base than he is, and turned him from his purpose. That purpose was to get rid of you all, and appropriate your treasure to his own purpose. This was the plan:—

"He was to give information of your being in this bay to the authorities of the neighbouring country, and counsel them to send a ship, disguised as a merchant ship, but supplied with guns, and having, besides her crew, a number of soldiers sufficient to overwhelm you.

"Confident in the certainty of your destruction, I know he had planned to carry away your treasure yesterday or today—about the time at which he thought you would be watching for your supposed prey or actually attacking her. I was to have left you two days since, and he promised to ask the captain that I might go with him for a short time, in order to give me an excuse for leaving the vessel which I had joined by his orders. But he never made the request, but left me on board, unable to get away, doubtless believing and hoping that I should be killed with the rest of you, and thus the man who knew more of his crimes than any other man would be removed from his path forever."

Here the poor wretch paused and gasped again— again they gave him water, but it was of no avail—he groaned again, then tried to speak once more, and then having raised his head a few inches from the ground, with a sudden convulsive movement fell back, dead.

For a moment the whole party remained silent, their hearts filled with mingled surprise and anger. Then the captain directed that the body of the dead man should be searched, and there indeed was found a packet such as that which he had described, which was immediately handed to the Hermit.

They forthwith deliberated as to what would be their best course to pursue. There they were, fourteen men besides the Hermit, but only the latter and the three who had gone on shore with him had any serviceable weapons except daggers, inasmuch as most of them had thrown away all that they could in their struggle to swim to the shore. It was evident, however, that there was but one chance of that which at this moment they valued almost more than their lives—namely, revenge.

From the account given by the Hermit and his party, and judging by the short time which had elapsed since the Baron Ferdinando had been with Captain Pedro in the cave wherein the Hermit had been carried, it seemed most probable that the outer cave, which Stefano had visited, had been the first which the robbers had plundered. The question then arose, whether they would have been satisfied with the booty obtained there, or have gone on to empty the other caves also.

Pedro strongly inclined to the latter belief, and if so, it was scarcely possible that they could have accomplished their object within so short a period. He therefore determined that they should all go at once to the cave which they knew to have been plundered, and thence track the footsteps of the robbers, in order to find out which direction the latter had taken.

Accordingly, they advanced without delay upon the cave in question, and of course found things as the Hermit's party had told them. They found, however, something more. A good many articles of clothing had been among the concealed property, and these came in exceedingly well to supply the pirates with dry garments in place of those they wore, which had been thoroughly drenched in their involuntary swimming-match. There was a better find still in store.

The robbers, having secured what they considered the most valuable part of their prey, had not searched every hole and corner, and had chanced to overlook a recess in which Captain Pedro had concealed a quantity of arms. This was the very thing they wanted, and when, in addition to this, they found a certain quantity of dried provisions which had not been removed from the place where they were hidden, they really began to feel quite cheerful again. Their captain gave them a few minutes for refreshment, and then, every man being armed and ready, they set out in pursuit of the robbers.

It did not require the sagacity of Red Indians to follow the trail, which lay before them without any attempt at concealment. The plunderers of the cave, whoever they were, had evidently loaded several mules with their booty, and had pushed on through places where the brushwood allowed them to do so, for some forty or fifty yards, until they had come into an old and almost disused track, along which they had turned and could be traced for several hundred yards further.

Here the tracks became somewhat confusing, but after a short investigation they came to the conclusion that the party must have separated, and Captain Pedro was not long in guessing what had happened.

"Those tracks," he said, "lead out of the forest, and in all probability the villain who has plundered our cave has sent some of his party with the beasts laden with the spoil, to carry it off, safe from our pursuit. But this smaller pathway, up which we can see that some of the fellows have gone, leads to another of our caves, and in all likelihood they have had it in their minds to go there and perform the same feat. They can hardly have had time to get away, and we shall catch them red-handed; we will therefore follow at once."

So saying, the captain led the way, and the fifteen men advanced upon the track of the robbers. Ere long they arrived at the entrance of another of their hiding-places, but this appeared to have been entirely undisturbed, which puzzled the captain for a moment. Presently, however, he exclaimed, addressing the Hermit—

"I think I know what is the meaning of this. do not think that I ever told that rascal of this cave, and I remember very well telling him that most of our treasures were hid in the cave near the sea and in that to which I first took you. This shows me that it must certainly be by him that this robbery has been committed, although indeed we have little cause to doubt it after what Philippo has said. He has probably gone on to the further cave, thinking that he would make a clean sweep of all our goods while he was about it."

Captain Pedro gnashed his teeth as he spoke, and

again they pushed forward. In a little while they arrived
at the very spot at which the captain, the Hermit, and the
old woman had come out from the cave into the forest. The
Hermit recognised it at once by the huge blocks of stone
and rock already mentioned, and perceived from the time
they had been walking that they had come by a somewhat
roundabout way from the shore.

The party now began to advance very cautiously, for
Captain Pedro knew that as no animals such as horses or
mules could be taken into the cave on account of the narrowness of the passage, the party before them could not be
far off, unless indeed they had passed by the cave altogether.
Presently he directed the party to stop, and creeping forward
with the greatest care, proceeded to investigate the matter
alone.

Almost immediately he returned with triumph upon
his countenance. Some twenty yards from the mouth of the
cave, where the trees and brushwood became thicker, and
the passage of a beast of burden almost impossible, he found
three mules tethered to a tree, and apparently left alone.
From this the captain came at once to the conclusion that
the robbers, whosoever they might be, were few in number
and could therefore be the more easily overpowered. Had
they been numerous, he said, they would most likely have
left one of their party with the mules, and also to act as a
scout. As it was, he judged that they had all entered the cave
in order to bring out the valuables therein as soon as they
could, and start at once upon the homeward track.

There was but one opinion as to the course to be pursued. The passage must be entered and the matter followed
up at once. They might of course have waited until the robbers re-appeared with their booty, and have attacked them
as they emerged from the cave, but the impatience of the
pirates was too great, and these men, who had acquired the
whole of their treasure by plundering other people, were just

as indignant at being made the victims of a similar process as if it had all been gained by honest labour.

Each prepared himself for a struggle, and it was evident that there would be little mercy shown if they overcame the spoilers. Captain Pedro himself first entered the passage, but stumbled immediately over something which lay at the entrance. It was the body of old mother Breenwole, with a red handkerchief twisted round her venerable neck, which plainly denoted the method of her death. Not particularly lovely in life, the old woman's countenance was very much the reverse in sher present state, and her features were distorted by the last agony. She had evidently been only killed a short time, for she was still warm, and the captain had no doubt that she must either have met the robbers accidentally or perchance had been in league with Count Benjamin or Ferdinando, had helped to guide the party to the mouth of the cave, and had then and there met the due reward of her perfidy at the hands of the very people who were about to profit thereby.

Speculation upon the matter was idle, however, for it was evident that the hour for action had arrived. Having laid the body of the old woman aside, the pirates followed their captain, and one by one entered the narrow passage. Very quietly they crept along, stepping noiselessly over the rough stones, and taking every precaution that their approach might not be discovered by those they sought. After some little time they came very near the cave, and distinctly heard voices speaking in a low tone.

Captain Pedro looked round to see that his men were all following, crept on and on until he got to the rock round which the cave was entered, and then suddenly rushed forward. In an instant the state of things was apparent.

Five men were employed in rifling the contents of the cave. Four of these were engaged in pulling from their hiding-places the various articles of value which formed the treasure of the pirates, whilst the fifth was receiving them from the hands of his companions and arranging them on the table in such manner as to enable them to be the more easily carried away.

The first-mentioned individuals were all unknown to the Hermit, and appeared to be of an inferior grade, but in the fifth he instantly recognized his enemy, the treacherous Count Benjamin. The robbers leaped to their feet as soon as they found they were discovered, and seized their arms. But Captain Pedro shouted in a voice of thunder—

"Back, dogs, ye are taken like rats in a trap, but your lives shall be spared if ye surrender—all but one."

As he spoke, his followers came rushing after him into the cave, and the robbers saw at once that resistance was useless. Count Benjamin, however, knowing well enough that for him the game was up, determined to make an effort. Ever crafty, his cunning did not desert him even at this critical moment, and he resolved to play a desperate card. He addressed the pirates as coolly as if he were in command of a victorious force and they his captives, instead of the position being exactly the reverse.

"My men," he said, "your lives are all forfeit to the state. I, whom you see before you, can aloe save you. I desire to do so. Do not be deceived: to take my life could help none of you, but aid me, and I not only promise you a free pardon, which my interest can obtain for you, but also an amount of riches greater than all that you have in this cave. I vow it on the honour of a gentleman."

He spoke boldly, and even the pirates who had been most incensed against him were struck by the calmness of his bearing in that hour of danger. But Pedro left no time for hesitation.

"Friends!" he cried, "you hear a traitor's voice. Who sold us to the ship of war? Who has lost to us our own vessel?

The Robbers Attacked in the Cave

Who has plundered our caves? Is a traitor ever to be trusted? Believe this villain, and you put your necks in a halter."

The manner in which the pirates received these words at once showed the Count that he had nothing to expect from them. A glance at his companions told the same tale. They had already laid down their arms at the command of Pedro, seeing at once that this was their only chance of life. One hope only remained.

The ascent by way of the ladder through the tree was close behind the spot where the Count stood; he took his resolution immediately; with a rapid movement he overset the lamp, and at the same instant darted to the ladder. If, in the darkness, he could manage to accomplish the ascent, he might yet escape from his enemies. The result of his attempt threw the occupants of the cave into the greatest possible confusion. No one at first seemed to understand the position of affairs, and everybody ran here and there, stumbling over everybody else, and not knowing what had really happened.

Count Benjamin, however, never lost sight of his object, and made straight for the short passage behind him which led to the ladder—this once gained, and he felt that it would be like a new life given to him. He had no difficulty in finding the passage, having kept his eye on it as he threw over the lamp: he entered it, and cautiously, though as quickly as he could, crept up to the ladder: three more seconds and he would be safe! But at the very instant that he placed his foot upon the lowest round of the ladder, a powerful hand was laid upon his shoulder, and a deep voice thundered in his ear—

"Turn, traitor, and face Carlo Cellano!"

The unhappy wretch collapsed as if struck by a thunderbolt. His teeth chattered in his head; he trembled in every limb like one with the palsy, and with a groan of despair and horror, sank in a heap upon the ground.

The pirates after a short interval obtained a light, and were able to ascertain more exactly the position of affairs.

As the robbers had been interrupted before they had been able to carry off any of the booty within the cave, and as this was the largest depository of their treasures, they were rather pleased than otherwise.

Matters might have fared much worse with them but for the avaricious nature of Count Benjamin, who, fearful of having too many associates to share the spoils with him, and relying upon the absence of Pedro's band and their probable destruction, had only taken with him seven companions in all, and had sent away three of them with the mules bearing the treasure captured in the first cave. Had he had the seven all with him in the last cave, they might have given some trouble to the pirates, and had he taken a larger body of men, and posted scouts outside, the position of Captain Pedro's party might have been awkward. As it was, however, all had turned out as the latter could have wished, save in the matter of the plunder of the smaller cave.

It now remained to be determined what should be done with the prisoners. The four men captured with the Count had been promised their lives Captain Pedro, and although some of the pirates were rather inclined to grumble at this, yet they held, even in their rough life, that the word so given was sacred. Moreover, their chief reason for destroying these men would have been their knowledge of the secret of the caves, and the captain pointed out to them that now they had lost their vessel, the latter would no longer be of the same service to them. So they agreed to spare the men's lives, and only bargained for being permitted to give them a sound flogging which was duly administered under the superintendence of old Stefano, and was not soon forgotten by those who underwent it.

There remained Count Benjamin, alias Baron Ferdinando, to be dealt with. The Hermit, whom we may as well call by his real name, the Marchese Carlo Cellano, declared his desire that the wretch should be given up to the authorities, so that his own fair fame might be cleared before the world, and a punishment inflicted upon his enemy according to the due forms of law. But to this Captain Pedro stoutly demurred.

In the first place, he said, law was so uncertain, and lawyers such curious customers, that this Count or Baron, being rich and influential, might get off altogether. In the next place, although it might suit the Marchese to have the trial conducted before a court of justice, neither the captain nor his followers particularly desired to appear as witnesses in a place where inconvenient remarks might be made about themselves, and added to these reasons was the fact that they had a very substantial grievance of their own against the prisoner, with whom they were resolved to deal upon their own account.

The request of the Marchese, therefore, was of no avail, and all that .Captain Pedro would grant was that the accused should have a fair trial then and there. Confronted with his accusers, the miserable man lost all the former courage of his bearing. A ghastly pallor overspread his countenance, and he trembled in every limb.

Captain Pedro acted as judge, and directed twelve of his men to serve as the jury, whilst old Stefano. and the Hermit stated their several charges against the prisoner. The four robbers who had been taken with him, and who scarcely felt themselves safe yet, willingly gave evidence as to his having hired them to assist him in plundering the caves, to which he had shown them the way.

He attempted no defence, and indeed appeared paralysed with affright, and utterly unable to speak. The jury took but a very short time to consider, having resolved to find the poor wretch guilty before they had heard half that was to be brought against him. Then it became the duty of the judge to pass sentence, about which his only doubt was whether to yield to the loudly expressed wish of some of the pirates that the prisoner, having committed such crimes of treachery as to constitute him a worse criminal than was often found, should be put to death with such tortures as would aggravate the punishment to the greatest degree.

Here, however, the entreaties of the Hermit prevailed, and the wretched man was quietly strangled with the same handkerchief as that with which he had put an end to old mother Breenwole.

The pirates then prepared to quit the cave, carrying with them such of their valuables as they deemed it best to remove.

As the events of the last few days had changed the whole current of our friend the Hermit's thoughts, he desired them to accompany him out of the forest, and promised that, if they would give up the trade of piracy (to which respectable people had considerable objections), he would use his influence to obtain for them a free pardon, and such suitable employment as they might desire.

As they had lost their vessel, and the greater part of their comrades, the men, after some consultation, resolved to accept the offer. They accordingly conducted the Hermit out of the forest, accompanied him to the chief city of the country, and acted under his advice.

Everything turned out as well as could possibly have been expected. As soon as it had been found out who the Hermit was, and what had been his story, people could not make too much of him.

Not only were his friends the pirates pardoned, but people of position and consequence vied with each other in procuring employment for them. Captain Pedro was appointed to the command of one of the finest men-of-war in the service, and old Stefano became head butler to an affluent nobleman.

The Marchese Carlo Cellano became the rage. His innocency having been completely established by the documents found on Philippo and by the latter's dying confession, everybody at once discovered that they had always believed him innocent, and it was astonishing to think that he could ever have been deemed otherwise by anybody. But although he found himself able to re-occupy his estates, and again enjoy his title and the privileges of his rank, he never attempted to re-enter his regiment, or mingle with those who, say what they would, had treated him as if they thought him guilty.

He held aloof to a great extent from all society, and clung with faithful tenacity to that pipe which had so comforted him in his solitude. Seated beneath a shady tree upon the lawn of his beautiful villa, or upon a couch at the window which commanded the most magnificent view over the surrounding country, he would smoke as if it was his greatest pleasure, and dream over the past with a feeling curiously commingled of joy and sorrow.

He had conquered in the struggle—but at what a terrible cost. His enemy had indeed fallen, but together with him had fled the hope of his own youth, the dear ones who had made that youth so happy—above all, the affianced bride whom he had so long and so faithfully mourned. She, indeed, lived, but, immured within the convent wall in which she had taken refuge from the base Count Benjamin, she seemed as much lost to him as if the grave had actually closed over her.

One day as he was musing over this, the one sorrow of his life which time seemed unable to allevi. ate or remove, a note was put into his hand, which he read, carelessly at first, but afterwards with more interest. It was couched in these words:—

"One who knew the Marchese Carlo Cellano in earlier and happier days would fain congratulate him on his return to life and fame. If the Marchese is in the orange grove of the Celli gardens at sunset tomorrow he may see the writer."

Our friend laid down the note and pondered upon the question—not whether he should accept the invitation, for to that he made up his mind at once, but as to who the writer

THE MOUNTAIN SPRITE'S KINGDOM

could possibly be. Having no clue whatever, he soon came to the wise conclusion that he had better not guess when he should probably know without doing so in a few hours.

Accordingly, having fretted himself meanwhile as little as he could, he was at the appointed place at sunset on the following day. Several persons passed and repassed him, without speaking or taking any notice of him, until at last he observed that two figures, much concealed by long black veils, had done so more than once, and still did not seem to leave the place. He fixed his eyes upon them as they approached again, and as they came close to him, he saw the one grasp the arm of the other and distinctly heard the words—"It is he!"

The Marchese took off his hat, and bowing to the ladies, for such they evidently were, asked if they were expecting any one.

"Yes," replied the one who had not yet spoken. "We await a very old and very dear friend—but fear he has forgotten us."

At the sound of that voice the Marchese started as if he had been shot.

"That voice!" he cried— "Bianca? Is it indeed you?"

The lady threw back her veil and disclosed the features of his former betrothed.

"It is I, indeed, Carlo," she replied, "I who have never ceased to think of you, but who am, alas! forgotten."

"Forgotten," exclaimed he. "Never, dearest lady; but are you not a nun, whom it were a crime to think of? So I was told, and deemed that my misfortunes had separated us forever."

"No action of mine has done so," replied the lady. "I have vowed no vow and taken no veil. I took refuge in the convent, as you know, and there have I stayed for these long years; but never whilst I believed you to be alive would I become a nun. The unhappy man who is dead spread reports of your death after his recovery from a wound which he said he had received whilst defending the convent from some robbers who were about to attack it. He was found upon the ground, run through the body with a grievous wound, and was long in recovering. But I never believed those reports, and I am as I was when I entered the convent."

This was not strictly true, as the lady must have been several years older, but it was sufficiently near the truth to satisfy our friend, especially when the story was confirmed by the lady's companion, who turned out to be none other than his own sister.

The rest of the story may be told in a very few words. The Marchese `Carlo Cellano and Bianca were married as soon as the wedding clothes could be made and proper arrangements carried out. They lived very happily all their lives, and had strong sons and beautiful daughters to cheer their declining years, And for the good of all married ladies I may record it as a true and undoubted fact, that Bianca never once interfered with her husband's smoking. Now and then, it is true (but not often), she said that it kept him up a little too late at night, but on the other hand its soothing influences were very great, and during the whole course of their long and happy life as a married couple, Bianca always declared that, in her solemn judgment and opinion, a pipe of good tobacco was as desirable a thing for a Marchese as for a Hermit.

4

THE RHINE CASTLE

CHAPTER I.

IT WAS a very old castle on the banks of the Rhine, and of course it was haunted. Indeed, on that noble river nobody thinks anything of castles which are not haunted. In most of them there is a good, oldfashioned, respectable family ghost, with which is connected some wondrous legend of the past, the recital of which in the dusk of a winter's evening, when a party of relations are sitting round the smouldering embers of a wood fire, sends most of them to bed in a remarkably nervous frame of mind. This castle was not a whit behind others in the antiquity and respectability of its ghost, although the legend attaching to the worthy spirit was less tragic and terrible than was sometimes the case.

The castle stood on the very banks of the river, and from its terraces a shrubbery or rather a wood, stretched down to the very edge of the water. Formerly (so ran the tale), the owner of this territory had a beautiful daughter, who (as is occasionally the case with rich people) had numerous lovers among whom she found it difficult to make a choice. The lover whom she secretly preferred, and who on his part was entirely devoted to her, received at her hands no very civil treatment, and at length, being probably somewhat badly off for common sense, he gave way to despair. Having done this for a sufficiently long time, he proceeded to drown himself, which was a useless and ridiculous, not to say wicked, course of proceeding; and having satisfactorily accomplished his absurd object, his body floated down the stream and greeted the eyes of the young lady as she was standing in the wood close to the edge of the river, having just been indulging in her favourite pastime of playing on her harp, which stood by her side as she pensively mused, leaning her head on her hand and gazing down upon the water.

The effect her nerves was, as might have been expected, the reverse of soothing. She screamed, tried to drown herself with her lover, and, having been prevented from doing so by attendants who were fortunately near at hand, went mad as soon as she conveniently could, died shortly afterwards, and ever after, harp in hand, haunted the spot at which she had thus encountered the body of her unhappy lover.

It was rather a convenient legend, this, for lovers who happened to have the run of the castle woods, for every one took them for the ghosts of the aforesaid legend, and they were thus secure from the interruption of mortal intruders.

At the time of which I speak, the castle was inhabited by an individual of strange and fantastic character, who claimed to be, and for all I know was, the descendant in a direct line from barons who had possessed that castle for any number of years you please to name.

They had been queer characters, by all accounts. The best of them had been rough soldiers, rather brutal than not in their manner of warfare, and not over particular against whom they fought or how they carried on the strife. Some, however, had been much worse. Robbers, rebels, leaders of roving bands of marauders, and even a few acknowledged murderers, went to make up the roll of the illustrious ancestors of the present Baron. Latterly, however, there had been no remarkable criminals of his race. Perhaps it was because the times had been less stirring, perhaps there was greater vigilance on the part of the authorities in looking after evildoers, or perhaps (to be as charitable as we can), the breed had really improved, and the more modern of the barons, repenting and regretting the deeds of their forefathers, had really become reformed characters, and set themselves down to lead regular and respectable lives.

Be this how it may, nobody had ever accused the baron of whom I speak of being anything more than eccentric; or, to speak more plainly, mad. No one exactly knew why they thought he was mad, but this made very little difference in the general opinion. There could not, indeed, be much evidence upon the question, because nobody ever saw him. He scarcely ever ventured beyond the spacious grounds of his castle, and when he did so, turned back immediately upon seeing anybody, and hastily regained the privacy of his own domain. He kept no servants except an old man and his wife who had been born and bred upon his estates, and who made it a solemn rule never to speak of their master and his family. They obtained such additional help as they required from some of the cottages near, but of those there were few, for the population of that country was thin and scattered, and there was no busy neighbourhood through which gossip about the castle and its inhabitants could circulate.

So time passed on, and but for the events which I am about to relate, the Baron and his castle might have passed on too, and faded away in good time without any record of them having become known to the world. There seemed no reason, indeed, why anybody should concern himself about either the one or the other. That country was full of castles and barons; most of the former were said to be haunted, and many of the latter were known to be eccentric, if nothing more, so that on looking back, one cannot form any accurate guess why this particular baron and this particular castle should have required a story all to themselves. So it is, however, and the story is like the Baron, of a somewhat remarkable character, if, indeed, a story can be properly said to have any character at all.

The Baron's character as not a good one among other barons, for when a man holds himself aloof from the class to which he belongs, they are pretty sure to think and speak ill of him, and the present case was no exception to this general rule. Our friend had as bad a name among barons as anywhere else, and was never invited or received as a visitor in any of the other castles which were inhabited by persons of his own rank. In fact, for any reason to the contrary that I have been able to discover, he might have lived and died in the utter seclusion which he seemed to prefer, had it not been for one special circumstance which prevented such a result. That circumstance was the fact of his having no heir to inherit the broad lands which lay around the castle of his ancestors, and being able, so the world. understood, to dispose of the same according to his own will and pleasure.

Now when a person, be he baron or peasant, simple or gentle, occupies this particular position, he sooner or later becomes an object of interest to the neighbourhood, in which his lot happens to be cast. Had our hero been a poor' man, with nothing to leave behind him, he might have left it when and how he pleased, and nobody would have troubled his head about the matter. It was different, however, when his retiring from the world would leave a castle and landed estates without an owner. So after the lapse of a certain time the circumstances and condition of the Baron de Grumpelhausen became the common subject of discussion in more than one household, and principally in those which were fortunate enough to contain unmarried members of the fairer portion of humanity.

Among these it was, strange to say, the prevalent, nay almost universal, opinion that the Baron ought to marry, and as time passed on without his taking any step in this direction, the opinion of his madness became more than ever firmly established among the ladies. It was undoubtedly sad, if not mad and bad, most likely all three, that such a Baron should be without a wife, and such a castle without a mistress. Such, however, seemed but too likely to be the case at the time our story begins, nor did any of the fair creatures who lamented the probability feel able to avert so melancholy an occurrence.

Among those who took it most to heart was a respectable, I should rather say noble dame, who lived in another castle not many miles distant from that of the Baron. She was a lady of rank, and thought a good deal of it too, in which she was doubtless justified, as the Counts of Stuttenguttenheim had been counts ever since there were such things as counts at all, and everybody knows that the farther back you can trace your family and the more ancestors of rank you can reckon upon your fingers, the nobler, the wiser, the better, and the happier must you be. There is no doubt, therefore, that the Countess of Stuttenguttenheim must have been noble, wise, good, and happy to a very great degree, since she could count back the ancestors of her house to a time more remote than I dare mention, for fear I should not be believed.

She was all this, I do not doubt, in spite of the trifling disadvantages of having a husband who was old, deaf, cross, very disagreeable, and as poor as a church mouse, though why a church mouse should be poorer than any other mouse I never could see, and I don't believe it.

You could not, with any approach to accuracy, have called the Count of Stuttenguttenheim a church mouse, for the old heathen had never entered a church in his life; but you could make no mistake in calling him poor, and that in every sense of the word, for he had neither money, brains, nor friends, which are three things without some one or more of which a man may be called poor indeed.

How he and his wife had managed to exist so long, I cannot say, but they did so, and moreover possessed olive branches in the shape of three daughters, by either of whom, had they been guided by the opinions of their parents, the name of Grumpelhausen would have been readily substituted for their own. But the daughters of an ancient house must not be dismissed in this summary manner. The respect due to their exalted rank compels a somewhat more detailed description.

Albertina, Gertrude, and Margaret von Stuttenguttenheim were maidens worthy of their race, and more than worthy of their parents, who were as frightful an old couple as you would come across in a long day's journey.

Their mother, indeed, tall, angular, and scraggy, had a sort of natural dignity about her, doubtless derived from an innate consciousness of the grandeur of her position in society, which carried off, to a certain extent at least, or at all events went far to moderate, the first impression made by her extreme ugliness. But their little, short, podgy father had no redeeming quality apparent to the eye of the beholder, and looked very much more like a broken-down tallow-chandler than a man of family and position. But the daughters were somehow or other of an entirely different model.

It is very odd that this should be, as it sometimes is, the case, and that remarkably ugly parents should have children of ravishing beauty. In the instance of which we are now speaking there could be no doubt at all upon the subject, one way or the other. The father and mother were as ugly as sin, and the daughters as beautiful as the contrary of sin, whatever is the best word to express it.

Albertina was tall and fair, with light blue eyes, clear transparent skin, finely moulded limbs, graceful action, pleasant manner, and agreeable conversation, Gertrude was shorter and plumper than her sister, but equally fair, with an expression of countenance which spoke of a nature essentially good-humoured, and a frank liveliness about her which was extremely taking. Margaret was the dark one of the party, with masses of raven hair, rich brown complexion, beautiful figure, and fit to be an empress, if there had happened to be a place of that kind vacant at the time of which we write.

Such were the three daughters of this ancient house, and it was on their account that the old dame, their mother, took so strong an interest in the case of our Baron.

Why indeed should she not do so ? Here were three charming girls, there an unmarried man rich and titled. What mother could sit still and see time gliding by without an attempt made to bring together elements which seemed intended to be combined, but which accident or fate had hitherto kept asunder ? But whether the old Countess sat still to see this or not, the facts remained the same, and the difficulty before her was one which she did not perceive the way to overcome.

In our day the matter would have been comparatively easy. She would have managed to bring the Baron over to a croquet or lawn-tennis party, prepared a picnic or even given a ball, and at all events worried him with invitations till he had been forced out of his shell, and been brought in contact with those three charmers, of whom one or the other would certainly have enslaved him; or she would have made an expedition to see his castle, pretending to have been informed that he was away from home and by clever management have brought him suddenly face to face with the beauties.

But these were not things which could be done in the days of which we write. Croquet and lawn tennis were not known in that part of the world, picnics in secluded places would have been dangerous, as liable to interruption from bears, wolves, and robbers, whilst a ball would have been an event utterly unheard of, and in fact, from badness of roads and scarcity of neighbours, quite impossible to accomplish. No: if the thing was to be done at all, some other means must be found; some scheme planned which should be promptly and vigorously carried out, and to this the fertile brain of the old Countess again and again reverted.

For some time the only thing that occurred to her was the good old-fashioned plan of attacking and plundering the castle, carrying off its owner as a captive, and releasing him only as the husband of one of his vanquisher's children. The only, or at least the principal, objection to this scheme was to be found in the fact that the Baron's castle was strong, and that his means of defence were so much greater than the Count's means of attack, that any attempt of the sort would probably meet with failure as complete as ignominious.

This idea, therefore, had to be abandoned, and the old lady racked her brain for another to no purpose. At last she bethought her of having recourse to magic, which was an art much held in esteem in those days, although very imperfectly understood. If any one has a turn for the thing in our days, it is well known that the best, if not the only way to proceed, is by spirit-rapping or table-turning, both of which are said to be healthy and innocent recreations, if not always as efficacious as might be desired. But in those old days spirits had other things to do than to rap their knuckles against walls or wainscots, and tables were in the habit of standing still in their proper places and doing the duties for which they had been made, without indulging in gymnastic exercises which had never been expected of them.

Those who wished to employ magic for any purpose in those days, generally did so in a regular and straight-forward way, going off to consult a witch or a warlock, or a respectable demon of some kind or other, of whom there were always plenty to be found, as there probably are still if we only looked for them in the right places.

These creatures being regular dealers in the commodity of magic, were of course ready to supply any quantity of it upon the shortest notice, and it was in this direction that the Countess of Stuttenguttenheim at length determined to turn for assistance.

The Rhine has always had plenty of spirits on its banks and in its waters, and there could therefore be no difficulty about the matter. Goblins, water-sprites, and merry little devilets were always as plentiful as blackberries in the locality of which we are now speaking, and the only question was as to the best way of getting hold of one of the best of them, without his getting hold of you. For, of course, any one who wanted some great deed accomplished by the aid of one of these gentlemen, whether it was the removal of some enemy or the acquisition of riches, or any trifle of the kind, was very likely to have to sign some awful bond-possibly with his own blood, which might be inconvenient as well as alarming and find himself engaged in some consequent disagreeable entanglement at a future period of his existence.

Now, this was not at all what the old Countess wanted ; in fact, she altogether objected to the kind of thing, and had no intention of signing anything except, if she could manage it, the register of the marriage of one or other of her three daughters. All she wanted from the dealers in magic was a little information as to the best way of getting access to the Baron, for if this could once be accomplished, she had unbounded confidence in her own resources and the charms of her children.

In order to obtain the desired boon she determined to inquire of the very best demon who could be had for money, for although the latter article was very scarce in the family, yet any which might be forthcoming could surely be expended in no more legitimate way than by forwarding the fortunes of a daughter of the house.

With this object in view the old Countess had her bathchair drawn up and down the banks of the river for several consecutive days, anxiously looking out for demons, but with a total want of success.

When this had gone on for the best part of a week, one of the under-housemaids, who had once had an aunt in the witch business, and therefore knew something about it, told the upper-housemaid, who told the cook, who mentioned it to the lady's-maid, that there was a cave further down the river, and not far from the Baron de Grumpelhausen's castle, where people went to consult a spirit who dwelt there, and who was most obliging in the way of telling them a number of things they wanted to know, and who had consequently a great reputation.

The lady's-maid, of course, mentioned this to her mistress that very evening whilst doing her hair, and the Countess immediately sent for the girl, and having heard all she knew, and scolded her as in duty bound, for knowing anything about such matters, seeing that her knowledge ought to be entirely confined to dusters, broomsticks, and slop-pails, determined forthwith to visit the cave and consult the oracle.

Accordingly, the very next day she disguised herself in an old bonnet and a dark gray cloak which entirely enveloped her, and set out for the cave, attended only by her faithful maid Dorothy. This damsel was much younger than her mistress, and a comely lass withal, and to say the truth, she was not particularly delighted with the expedition. These kind of things always have to be done in the evening, when all kinds of disagreeable people are about, let alone demons, and the banks of the river were not in those days (whatever they may be now), the place upon which a respectable young woman would prefer to take her walk at that period of the day. However, the Countess so settled it, and mistress and maid set off together, starting sufficiently early in the afternoon to arrive at their destination shortly before sunset, which they did without any interruption or adventure of any kind.

The cave to which they had been directed was situate but a short distance from the river banks, and was very easy to discover, from the circumstance of there being no other cave near it. There was a path which led to it from the river, from which people used to land upon the shore and proceed by the said path to the cave. The entrance was also not difficult to find. You had only to walk straight on, and presently you saw immediately before you a gully, into which you entered (unless you happened to be frightened at this point and consequently turned back), and at the end of the gully was the entrance into the cave, just for all the world as if a railway tunnel had been bored into the mountain, only that it stopped when you had gone a few yards, and the faint glimmer of light from the outside showed you rough and rugged rocks and great masses of stone cast here and there, which showed very clearly that no railway engineer had constructed the place, and no railway train could go far without very fatal results to all concerned.

At this place the mistress and maid duly arrived, and (rather to the disgust of the latter) walked straight into the cave. Before they had proceeded many yards, however, they came to a rock which barred their advance, unless they could manage to climb over it, which would have been a trouble-some and unpleasant operation.

According to the housemaid's instructions, this was fortunately unnecessary, for she had told them that when they were well in the cave they had only to ask, and they would be answered by the being who dwelt there. They must ask in rhyme, she had been told, or at least those who did so always got the quickest and best answers. It was certain that they were "well in the cave" now, or at all events they were in it, though Dorothy had her doubts whether it was "well" to have come at all. So the old Countess prepared herself for the coming interview with great deliberation. She coughed, drew herself up to her full height, looked carefully forward (which was perfectly useless, as it was too dark to see anything a yard in front of you), cleared her throat again, coughed once more, and then gave utterance to the following lines which she had, after much thought and labour, composed on the previous day, and of which she was not a little proud—

> "Whoe'er thou art, oh mighty one! that dwellest in this cave,
> Thine be the will and thine the strength, to grant me what I crave.
> Three daughters have I—lovely (though by mother this is said),
> And charming: but by some ill luck, they none of them are wed.
> My Albertina holds herself as well as any queen—
> My Gertrude is the dearest duck that ever yet was seen.
> These two are blonde—then Margaret, the only one that's dark,
> Has charms to raise in ev'ry heart love's instantaneous spark.
> Yet they've no chance of finding mates, for, living where we do,
> The eligible men, alas! are very, very few.
> Yet one there is. Hard by the stream, amid his woods and dells,
> Spouseless and lonely in his life, the Grumpelhausen dwells.
> How can I get him for my girls? that is, for one or t'other,
> That one may win a loving spouse, and two may gain a brother!"

She spoke, and for a moment nothing was to be heard save the water slowly trickling along the sides of the cave from the mountain, finding its way out to the river, and having nothing at all to do with magic. Then presently there came a low voice from the interior of the cave. It seemed to come from some place very near the two women, as if the speaker was just behind the rock opposite to which they had. stopped. There was nothing very remarkable about the voice, save that it was rather like some whispering very loudly. And it replied to the demand of the Countess in such a manner as to make its meaning easily understood.

"Secrets of import dire can I reveal
To those who at my shrine subm'ssive kneel,
And hidden mysteries can I disclose,
And call dead mortals back from death's repose.
But 'tis a task unsanctioned by the Fates,
To find for three young maidens fitting mates ;
And they must act like fairies, nymphs, and elves,
Keep good look-out, and find them for themselves !
Yet, to a mother's feelings am I kind,
And willingly some remedy would find ;
And could I but myself three people be,
I'd rid you of your girls, and wed the three !
But, failing this, I would not that to-day,
Unanswered and repulsed you went away ;
So listen to my words : to-morrow morn,
Bid thy retainers come with hound and horn,
The wolf through all these woodland glades to chase,
And they shall meet the Baron face to face.
Let thy three daughters come and boldly ride,
I cannot talk of bridegroom or of bride,
But they shall meet the Baron in the dell,
And then, the consequences who can tell?"

The Countess listened to these words with the deepest attention, and, upon the whole, was not dissatisfied with what she heard. It was true that the retainers of her husband were but few in number, they had no hounds worth much, and their performance in the hunting line was therefore not likely to be remarkable for its success. This, however, was a matter of very small importance, for as she understood the words of the voice, the hunting was to be a mere pretext, by means of which her daughters were to obtain the Baron's acquaintance. She therefore began to express, in such rhymes as she could manufacture on the spur of the moment, her cordial thanks to the Being, whoever or whatever he was, who had responded to her demand in a manner so prompt and courteous.

Scarcely, however, had she got out more than a line or two, when a frightful roaring proceeded from behind the rock in front of the old lady, which so terrified her that she immediately seized Dorothy's arm, and beat as hasty a retreat as possible, fully persu ded that she was about to be devoured that very instant. She need not have been in the least degree alarmed, first because no wild beast, whether in the flesh or in the spirit, could possibly have desired to touch so old, tough, and skinny a creature as she was, and secondly, because, had she considered for a moment, she would have remembered that the housemaid had told her that the spirit of the cave always intimated by roaring his desire to put an end to an interview which he thought had lasted sufficiently long. At any rate, he was successful in getting rid of his visitors on the present occasion, and the Countess made the best of her way home and related what had happened with great satisfaction.

Of course there was no doubt as to obeying the commands of the spirit of the cave, for as commands they were considered by her to whom they were addressed. Every retainer, therefore, was summoned to attend on the morrow, and every hound that could be produced was to be pressed into the service. Owing to the poverty of the Count, his band of retainers had dwindled down to a very small number, and neither in dress, arms, nor discipline were they such as befitted a nobleman of his rank and position. But, after all, a hunting expedition was not quite the same thing as an advance to battle, and neither discipline, arms, nor dress were deemed of much importance on the present occasion. A motley crew assembled at the Count's, or rather at the Countess's, commands, and the dogs were of as mixed and curious a character as the men, various breeds, from the large boarhound down to the snapping little mongrel, being represented in that strange pack.

But men and hounds mattered but little, so that the three young ladies could be furnished with the excuse for the ride which was to bring them into contact with the head of the House of Grumpelhausen. They were all dressed alike, and each was mounted upon her own steed, for no poverty had prevented the Count from keeping horses for his daughters, though they were not such as he might have preferred had his means been sufficient to enable him to exercise a wider choice. Albertina's sorrel was very old, Gertrude's chestnut was blind of one eye, and Margaret's bay mare was generally lame. This day, however, they were all put in requisition, and the old Countess herself would have mounted a horse too it she could, in order to have seen the result of the under-taking. This, however, was impossible, partly on account of her having long given up riding, and partly because there was no fourth horse at her disposal. The only equipage was a gigantic bath-chair, in which she was occasionally drawn about, but rather for appearance than for any other reason, since she could walk as well as most persons of her age, as had recently been shown by her expedition to the cave. However, to put the best possible face upon it, she went out in her bath-chair to see the party start, under the direction of old Karl the huntsman, and having wished them all possible good luck, returned to the castle to await the result of her scheme.

The morning was fine, the scenery beautiful, and the three young ladies remarkably cheerful as they rode forth.

The old Man with the Faggot on his back

I regret to inform my sporting friends that I am unable to give them any such accurate account of the hunting as I could wish to have done. No authentic record of the event has come down to us, and being personally unacquainted with the nature and habits of the wolf, and the particular method adopted in that country for hunting him down, I am unable to invent any details upon the subject. I only know that the hunting party found one wolf, if not more, and, for all I know, a bear or two.

At all events, the hunt went on, and the usual train of circumstances followed, namely, that the young ladies got separated from their retainers, and found themselves riding in the woods, they knew not exactly where. Being bold, high-spirited girls, this accident did not much distress them, but when Albertina's girths broke, Gertrude's chestnut got into a bog from which it could not get out again, and Margaret's bay mare fell so lame that it could not be made to move another inch, things began to look rather serious. The sisters all dismounted and held a serious consultation together.

What was to be done? They could hardly pass the night in the forest, for besides the cold and general unpleasantness which would be consequent on such an arrangement, it was possible that some of the hunted wolves might take an unhandsome advantage of their situation, and turn the tables upon them by an evening maiden-hunt, which might amuse them as much as a wolf-hunt had amused the maidens in the morning. But if they did not intend to be the objects of such a pastime for the wolves, it was evident that they must take some immediate action in order to save themselves from such a contingency.

Where should they turn, and what should they do? For a few moments they looked at each other in sad perplexity, and no idea suggested itself to any of the three. They looked first one way and then another, up at the sky (so far as they could see it through the tops of the high trees), and down on the ground, and could see or imagine no way of escape from the fate with which they were threatened.

Suddenly they perceived some object moving among the trees, and in another instant discovered that it was an old, a very old man. The weight of years upon his back, together with a faggot he was carrying, bent him almost double; a long white beard fell forward over his breast, scarcely could he drag one aged limb after the other, and his whole appearance indicated extreme age and poverty combined. As, however, he seemed to be the only living being near them, the sisters lost no time in accosting him, which they did all at once, one asking where they were, another if there was any house at hand, and the third which was the best way out of the forest?

The old man stared from one to another, doubtless surprised at the sight of so much beauty in such a strange and wild place. Then he replied in the feeble and tremulous tones of old age that he could not direct them, but that he was going home, and if they liked to follow him they could do so. As this appeared to be their only chance of escape from the dangerous situation in which they found themselves, the young ladies thankfully accepted the offer, and followed the slow steps of the old peasant through the trees and brushwood as well as they were able.

During their walk he asked them who they were, and how it was they came there, and they, seeing no object in concealment, told him the truth, so far, at least, as concerned their names and rank, and the fact of their having come out to hunt the wolves, for it was unnecessary to let him know that they were hunting a husband also. The old fellow asked them several questions about their family and themselves, all of which they answered with good nature and affability as became noble ladies, and he seemed to be much impressed with their rank and dignity. At last, after having passed for some way through the forest, they suddenly came upon a small cottage built into and forming part of a wall which seemed to be the boundary of some park or pleasure-ground. The old man opened the door of this place and bid them enter, which they accordingly did, and found themselves in a small passage passing quite through the cottage; at the other end of the passage was another door, which stood open, and disclosed a magnificent view beyond.

The sisters all hastened forward immediately, and found that they were looking upon the castle and domain of Baron de Grumpelhausen, which they recognized at once from having seen it at a distance from the river, although the view from thence was so intercepted by thick foliage and large trees, that they had formed little idea of its size and grandeur. It was very large, very finely situated, very grand altogether, bearing the unmistakable signs of great antiquity, and an involuntary cry of surprise and pleasure broke from the three sisters as they gazed upon it. The view was indeed lovely, for they had ascended through the woods by an almost imperceptible rise in the ground until they were now nearly on a level with the castle, from which the ground fell away to the river which they saw below, although the trees of course intercepted their view to such an extent that they could only here and there catch the silvery glitter of the water in the distance.

It was, indeed, a beautiful sight, and the view from the castle itself must be still finer. The young ladies turned round to speak to their conductor and guide, but found to their surprise that he had disappeared ; not knowing his name, they called him frequently by various different appellations, none of which produced the slightest effect. They searched the cottage to no purpose. It was a very ordinary cottage, with very common furniture, but seemed to contain no living creature of any kind. They went back through the door by which they had entered from the forest, but he was not there, and they stared at each other in the greatest surprise, wondering what the old man's motive could be for deserting them, and that, too, when he might reasonably have expected some reward for the service he had already rendered.

CHAPTER II.

HOWEVER, it was useless to speculate and guess on such a subject, and they soon turned themselves to the more practical consideration of what they should do next. The cottage, it was true, was better than the forest as far as shelter was concerned, but, for all that they could see, it contained not a scrap of food of any description, and they all three began to feel hungry. It was already long past their usual luncheon hour, and their long ride and subsequent walk through the woods, had given all three a good appetite which ought certainly to be satisfied as soon as possible. The question was how this was to be managed, and it was not long before they all three came to the same conclusion.

Why not go boldly up to the castle? Of course they had heard of its being haunted, but that was not enough to stop three high-born ladies, especially when they had had no luncheon. Besides, it was still broad daylight, when no ghosts would be likely to be about. Moreover, this was the castle of the very man whose acquaintance their mother was so anxious they should make, and it really seemed as if the Fates had purposely arranged the matter in order that her wish should be gratified. So, gathering up their riding apparel as well as they could, the three young daughters of the House of Stuttenguttenheim tripped lightly over the park, and made the best of their way to the castle of the Grumpelhausen.

As they approached it, they were struck with the

grandeur of its position and general appearance, but each girl thought within herself that if she were the mistress of the place, it would be smartened up and repaired within a very short time. It certainly required some such process, for it would be no exaggeration to say that in some parts it was positively ruinous. The ivy with which it was covered had grown to an enormous size, and had eaten into and weighed down the wall at many points, whilst the neglect of all repairs during a long series of years had told upon the ancient fabric, and reduced it at certain points to a lamentable state of decay.

Still, there was a good deal of it in sufficiently fair condition, and perhaps, after all, things were worse to the eye than in reality, for the walls were so massive that the crumbling away of some of the outside stones still left a good barrier against wind and weather.

The sisters marched boldly up until they came to the drawbridge, over which they passed, and without more ado pulled the handle of the bell which they saw immediately before them. They had scarcely done so when the door was thrown open, and an aged domestic stood before them, clad in faded livery, but evidently in his best dress, prepared to wait at dinner or perform any other similar function which might be required of him. He appeared in no degree astonished at the sight of the three ladies, although one would have imagined that it was about as unexpected a sight as he could well have seen. He showed, however, no signs of being taken by surprise, but on the contrary, bowed in the most polite and deferential manner, and asked whether they would be pleased to take luncheon at once. As nothing could have been more agreeable to their feelings than this proposal, the sisters readily accepted the invitation, and forthwith entered the castle.

The old servant led the way to the spacious banqueting hall, in the centre of which stood a table, loaded with food of a substantial nature, which was exceedingly tempting to them at that particular moment. Two other servants appeared at the summons of the first, and if they were not quite as polished and handy as pattern London footmen might have been, they performed the duties before them with a cheerful alacrity which atoned for other deficiencies. The three girls were somewhat astonished at finding everything ready for them, but their astonishment did not perceptibly affect their appetites, and they made a hearty meal without the least hesitation or bashfulness, doubtless feeling that either of these would have been entirely out of place.

When they had concluded their repast, the old servant who had first received them respectfully opened a door on one side of the banqueting hall, and held it open for them to pass through, which they accordingly did, and found themselves in a large, rather dark drawing-room, somewhat scantily furnished with heavy, old-fashioned furniture, but possessing as its greatest attraction three windows which commanded the most superb view toward the river. From the middle of these windows the sisters looked out upon the scene with delight, and again the same thought crossed the mind of each, and each fancied herself the happy mistress of that magnificent place. As, however, the master had not appeared, and, as far as matters had yet gone, gave no sign of any intention of appearing, the chance of winning him for a husband was still somewhat remote.

The young ladies began indeed to reflect that they were in a very curious, not to say awkward, position. They had left their father's house with no means that they knew of by which to return, and had entered the house of a stranger without having ever seen him, partaken of his hospitality with great readiness, and up to that moment had no idea whether he was at home or knew of their coming, or whether when he came home (supposing him to be absent) he would not be excessively annoyed at their intrusion.

As these considerations passed through their heads,

they began to feel rather uncomfortable, for the situation was one in which none of them had ever been before, and might at any moment become exceedingly unpleasant. They consulted together as to what they had better do, and at last settled that it would be best to ring the bell and ask whether the master of the house was at home, and if not, when he was expected.

They were on the point of carrying this intention into effect, when the door opened and in walked a respectably dressed old woman, who came up to them, dropped a low curtsey, and asked whether they would like to see their rooms. The sisters were much surprised at the inquiry, which, like the circumstance of their having found luncheon ready for them, seemed to show that they or some other guests had been expected.

Albertina, therefore, as the eldest, thought herself bound to prevent any possible mistake by asking the old woman a few questions concerning the matter. The servant listened with great respect, but replied that she really knew nothing except that she was directed to prepare for three young ladies that day, and had accordingly done so. No other answer of any sort or description would she give, and all attempts to discover anything about the owner of the castle utterly failed.

The rosy Gertrude tried her hand' next, but with no better success, and the lovely Margaret fared no better in the attempt. As, however, they had no means of getting home, and must evidently remain where they were for the present, the sisters thought that they could do no better than allow the old woman to show them their rooms as she had offered to do.

They accordingly followed her up a grand flight of stairs and along several passages until they came to a gallery, into which opened a number of bedrooms. Into one of these she conducted the young ladies, and they found everything prepared in that and in two adjoining rooms, as if they were expected to occupy them as a matter of course.

The sisters looked at each other in astonishment, and the same thought crossed the mind of each at the same moment. They had no clothes but those they were then wearing! How could they possibly manage? What could they possibly do? Should the Baron suddenly return, all might depend upon his first impressions. A chance which, once taken and properly improved, might lead to the most fortunate and desirable of results, might on the other hand be lost forever, should the Baron first. see them in the costume in which they had traversed the woods, and walked through brake and briar for so long a time.

Never were three young 'ladies in a more extraordinary position, or one more difficult to extricate themselves from in a manner which should be: satisfactory to themselves. However, as the old woman, after respectfully asking them whether they wanted anything, stood waiting for a reply, they thought they could not do better than explain their difficulties to her, and ask her counsel and advice.

She listened with respectful attention, and at once generously placed the whole of her wardrobe at the disposal of the sisters. Unfortunately, however, the aforesaid wardrobe was both limited in its extent, and what there was of it was hardly suitable to the quality of the daughters of the House of Stuttenguttenheim. The garments, in fact, were scanty, and their material coarse, not to mention the trifling inconvenience of their none of them fitting any one of the young ladies, in consequence of having been made for a much smaller person.

They were therefore compelled to reject the proffered kindness of the old domestic, which they did as gracefully as they could, and determined to make the best of it without change of raiment. Fortunately they were dry, so that they ran no risk of cold or rheumatism from damp garments.

Moreover, brushes and combs were in their room, by the aid of which, and by assisting each other in tidying their hair, a very few minutes enabled them to present an appearance which, if it was not all that they themselves could have wished, would have been considered eminently satisfactory by the great majority of beholders, especially if the latter had belonged to the male portion of humanity.

Having thus completed their toilet, the sisters thought that it was foolish to remain in their bedrooms, as it was a fine autumn afternoon, and they had some little curiosity to see the castle and its grounds.

They therefore descended to the drawing-room in which they had previously been, and seeing nobody to either direct or interrupt them, passed thence into a large room adjoining, which appeared to have served, if indeed it did not still do so, as a kind of armoury for the Barons of Grumpelhausen. Upon its oaken walls were hung numerous old-fashioned implements of warfare, helmets, swords, coats of mail, pikes, spears, and a variety of unpleasant weapons of that description. Over the mantelpiece, however, which was a curious specimen of old marble, was the huge picture of an armed man, inclosed in a magnificent and elaborate frame, which was fashioned also of oak most fantastically carved into the heads of men, horses, and dogs, which ornamented the wall and gave it a somewhat grotesque appearance.

The picture itself was remarkable for nothing but its size, for the subject of it was neither beautiful nor prepossessing, while as a work of art it was below mediocrity. However, when the girls had glanced at the armour which hung upon the walls, and made the natural observation of young ladies in a large room, namely, that if all the rubbish and furniture were cleared out, it would make a capital room for a dance, they approached the mantelpiece and began to examine the picture.

"What a curious old frame," remarked Albertina.

The Old Fellow in the Picture

"Yes," chirped Gertrude, "and do look at the heads of the men and animals all round it. How funny they are."

"And how well carved," observed Margaret.

"There is not much beauty in any of them, however," said the elder sister. "I think I never saw such a collection of frights in my life."

"Not more frightful than the old fellow in the picture, though," laughed Gertrude. "He is the ugliest old thing—"

"Thank you!" suddenly said a deep voice which apparently proceeded from the picture which they were thus criticizing. The sisters all uttered a slight scream of affright, and hastily retreated several paces from the mantelpiece. "Thank you!" repeated the voice gruffly; "you are rather cool hands, though, to come into a fellow's house and abuse him before his face in this manner."

This remark astonished the girls almost as much as the voice, for they saw nobody, and had certainly abused nobody and nothing but the picture, which could scarcely represent the owner of the castle, as it was evidently that of a man who had lived at least a century before, and was clad in the warlike costume of a period long past. Being richly endowed with the courage of their race, and feeling moreover that politeness required some observation upon their part, they looked at each other for a moment, and then Albertina spoke.

"Sir," she said ("for your voice leads us to believe that you are a gentleman, although we have not the advantage of seeing you), my sisters and I intended no disrespect to the owner of this beautiful castle, nor were we aware that he was present in the room."

"Well, I didn't say he was," responded the picture. "I'm his great-great-grandfather, though, which comes to the same thing, and you insult him when you abuse me."

The girls were more than ever astonished at this speech, and began to feel rather uncomfortable, as was perhaps not unnatural under the circumstances of the case, which were somewhat peculiar. Things were come to a pretty pass, if you might not express an opinion unfavourable to the personal beauty of a man's great-great-grandfather without being thought to have insulted the man himself, and if the picture of the aforesaid relative resented such a criticism, it was evidently the beginning of a state of things which would render visits to picture galleries extremely delicate undertakings, and prevent a great deal of innocent enjoyment and pleasant conversation about the merits of the pictures. They were at once distressed and alarmed at the occurrence, and Albertina, having regained courage, again addressed the invisible speaker in extenuation of the fault which they seemed to have committed.

"Sir," said she, "believe me when I tell you that we were quite unaware either of your relationship to the owner of the castle, or of your power to understand what we were saying. Had it been otherwise, we should certainly have refrained from making any observations which could by any possibility have wounded the feelings of such a respectable old gentleman."

"Old!" shouted the voice in a tone of anger, as she concluded. "What the plague do you mean by calling me old? I died, or rather was killed, before I was fifty, and you don't call that old? Time don't count after one's dead, you know, and this happened less than two hundred years ago. And then to call a Baron 'respectable!' 'Respectable" indeed, as if one was a master tailor! Really you ought to know better—you have no manners at all!"

The sisters listened to these words with increased awe and astonishment; they had evidently come into a strange place, but they had never read or heard of ghost who spoke in so extraordinary a manner, or who made such little mystery about himself, and seemed to be possessed of all the feelings of an ordinary mortal. They began to think that they had better escape from his presence as soon as they could, but did not like to do so whilst he was so angry, nor did Albertina quite relish the idea of his having the last word, which, as is well known, it is the woman's right to have in every controversy. So, in spite of her growing alarm, she once more addressed the picture in these words—

"Really, sir, I sincerely beg your pardon, in my own name and in that of my sisters. We intended no harm and meant no disrespect. If we have done the one, and apparently implied the other, pray forgive us, and attribute our having done so to our ignorance, and not to our design."

"Now you speak well," immediately returned the picture, "and in consequence thereof I will give you some information. The next room is the tapestried chamber; a visit to it will repay you. Spend ten minutes there, and then go out on the terrace-walk. Proceed to the end thereof, and you will see the whispering grotto. No one comes here without going to see that, and you may probably find it useful to do so."

Delighted at the change of tone in which these words were uttered, the three girls all joined in a chorus of thanks to the picture, who, however, said no more, but looked as ugly as ever as he seemed to glare at them out of his frame. They deemed it best to follow his advice as soon as possible, and were not sorry to get away from him, which they did as soon as possible. Opening a door which they supposed to lead to the chamber which he had told them to visit, they judged that they had made no mistake when they found themselves in a spacious apartment, entirely hung round with tapestry of a character marvellous and an appearance richly beautiful.

This they vastly admired, and would probably have stayed much longer than ten minutes in the room, had it not been for the words of the picture, which they feared to disregard, lest he should say or do something disagreeable in consequence. So, having observed glass doors opening from a corridor close to the drawing-room, and evidently leading into the garden, they returned thither, casting furtive looks round at the picture as they hurried through the armoury, not without some apprehension that they might again be accosted by that ghostly voice. The Baron's great-great-grand-father, however, said nothing this time, and the sisters passed through the room, and came to the corridor of which I have spoken.

Sure enough, the glass doors opened on to a short flight of broad stone steps, after descending which, a few steps brought them to the terrace-walk, which was a promenade in front of the castle, commanding a grand view, and terminated at one end by a stone wall which separated it from the park, and at the other by large trees, the commencement of the forest, which approached close to the castle grounds at that part.

But among the trees, which cast their dark shadows over it, was a kind of natural cave or grotto formed in the rock, which at that particular point rose somewhat abruptly for the space of fifty or sixty yards right and left, jutting upon the one side close to the castle walls which were there built upon it. This was doubtless the whispering grotto of which the picture had spoken, and which of course the sisters felt bound to visit, though with a somewhat vague idea of how they might find it useful. However, as they walked on the terrace-walk, they discussed again the nature of their present position.

It was getting late in the afternoon, and they must before this have been missed at home. What steps would their mother take? I do not think they gave their father a thought; he would do nothing if left to himself, but wait till they came back of themselves, and perhaps be rather sorry if they never came back at all. But their mother would be anxious. If she knew where they were, she would probably send after them. Unfortunately, however, there was no one whom she could very well send; every possible retainer and every available horse had been taking part in the hunt that day, and fresh men and horses were not to be had for the wishing.

They felt sure that no one could or would look for them until the next day, so that they would certainly have to pass the night in the castle. And even when next day came, how was their mother to discover where they were ? This was the subject of their discourse as they slowly advanced towards the grotto, which was an ordinary place enough, with a little fountain at the back, over which a stone nymph presided, holding in her hand a huge stone shell into which the water lazily trickled from the spring in the side of the cave. The floor was paved with small stones, but the whole place had evidently been neglected for many years, and the first thought of the girls was, that it had in it the making of a charming summerhouse, if properly set to rights, but that at present it bore a somewhat damp and uncomfortable appearance.

They entered it, however, and standing before the fountain, looked around them. As it was rather dark, and there was nothing to see, it is not surprising that they saw nothing. Then they took some of the water in the palms of their hands, and tasted it. It was cold and pure, as is not unfrequently the case with water taken fresh from a spring in the rock. They bathed their foreheads with it and felt it refreshing, which is also not an uncommon attribute with fluid of this kind. Up to this time they had not spoken since they entered the grotto, but now Gertrude observed with a laugh—

"What a quaint old place! I wonder who made it, and when it was made, or whether it came here naturally, without being made at all!"

Scarcely were the words out of her mouth, before a voice came from the nymph, or from some one close to her, speaking in tones which, though low, vibrated through the whole grotto and startled the girls not a little, although they had made up their minds to be startled at nothing else after their extraordinary interview with the picture. And these were the words which the voice spoke, or rather sung to a peculiar tune—

" Three sisters came roaming out into the wood,
　　Out into the wood with the hound and horn,
They thought they would catch if they possibly could,
　　A wolf and a husband the very same morn.
　　　For girls are fair, and lovely, I ween,
　　　And oftentimes men are uncommonly green,
　　　And a mother is always crafty!

"The wolves they were wild and ran howling away,
　　Ran howling away from the hound and horn,
And the sisters were forced in the castle to stay,
　　In the very same clothes that all day they'd worn.
　　　For girls are fair, and lovely, I ween,
　　　And oftentimes men are uncommonly green,
　　　And a mother is always crafty!

"Three bodies were floating a-down on the Rhine,
　　A-down on the Rhine without hound or horn,
And the father is drowning his sorrow in wine,
　　And the mother she wishes she'd never been born!
　　　For girls are fair, and lovely, I ween,
　　　But men are not always uncommonly green,
　　　And a mother may be too crafty!"

As the voice sang these verses, the unhappy girls exchanged looks of horror. Here, in verse sang by some mysterious being, was their mother's plan openly disclosed; a plan in which they had joined, and which really looked contemptible when thus plainly stated by another. Not only so, but if there was any meaning in words, the prophet, or spirit, or wizard, or whatever it was that spoke, clearly intended to state that the result of their attempt to secure the Baron as a member of their family would be their own destruction and the ruin of their parents' happiness. For the "three bodies" evidently referred to themselves, and they began to feel as if they were already in the river.

The prospect before them was certainly not reassuring, and, so far, their visit to the "whispering grotto" appeared to be anything but useful to them, and thus distinctly to belie the words of the picture. Trembling they stood before the fountain after they had heard the verses which the voice recited, but they had sufficient sense to know that to stand there trembling was of no use whatever. So Margaret, who was supposed to be rather a poet in her way, plucked up courage and thus replied to the invisible speaker of the grotto—

> "Three sisters are we : 'tis a true indictment,
> Yet what you say we hope, Sir, isn't quite meant!
> To hunt down wolves, and other forest vermin,
> Is what no judge will as a crime determine,
> Nor will the law with angry eyes behold us:
> We've only acted as our mother told us!
> If we are wrong, forgive! and in forgiving
> Say how may we remain among the living.
> You frighten us—tho' perhaps you don't intend to,
> And drowning is so very sad an end, too!"

She spoke, and after a very brief interval of suspense the same voice replied to her appeal in the following words,

> "For life, your one remaining hope and chance is
> Dependent on the Grumpelhausen's fancies.
> By forest-law you're his—and must obey him—
> Here none can interfere—no band can stay him.

Unless he speaks the word and bids them spare you,
The castle goblins will in pieces tear you,
Or, since you've ventured to come here so madly,
You'll starve, or drown, or somehow perish sadly.
If quite submissive to his will and pleasure,
Of mercy you may perhaps obtain a measure.
Some folk he cannot spare, but then he can some,
Provided they afford sufficient ransom;
And if you're good and reasonable creatures,
Your case is not without redeeming features—
The Baron's short of servants—wilt annoy you
In scullery or kitchen to employ you ?
Or would you think it better, and a higher place,
To dust the furniture and clean the fireplace?
To do a little wholesome household duty
Will neither hurt your health nor spoil your beauty;
And if content with work that's thus assigned you,
What matter if your parents never find you?"

It may be easily supposed that these words were not
calculated to restore confidence to the young ladies, to
whom there was nothing attractive in the idea either of being
drowned, or of becoming household servants to the Baron.
What were they to do? The night was now approaching, no
assistance was to be procured and they saw nothing for it
but to return to the castle and make the best of it. Before
doing so, however, Margaret fired one parting shot at the
spirit of the grotto who had made such unpleasant proposals.
With pouting lips and eyes full of tears, she thus made her
protest against the treatment with which she and her sisters
were threatened—

"Sir Spirit, or by whatsoever name
They call you when at home (it's all the same),

We high-born damsels deem it only right
To tell you that you're very unpolite.
We lost our way, and here for shelter ran,
Thinking your Baron was a gentleman—
And, as I tell you boldly in your grotto
'Noblesse oblige'— a very famous motto.
But if he acts as you suggest he will,
Don't fancy that we then shall think so still;
His conduct will be infamous and low,
And I, for one, won't fail to tell him so!"

As soon as she had pronounced these words (which she did with some emphasis), the indignant girl turned round, and the three sisters left the grotto together. With no very pleasant feelings they retraced their steps to the castle, and although they found a repast set out for them in the banqueting hall, none of them felt at all able to do it justice. Their hearts were heavy, and full of direful and sad forebodings. And in this state we must unfortunately leave them, whilst we return to the home which they had quitted on the morning of this eventful day.

The old Countess had awaited with much anxiety the result of the hunting excursion, fully relying upon the promise given to her in the cave, and thinking it far from improbable that the Baron de Grumpelhausen, having been captivated at first sight by the charms of one or other of her daughters, might return with them to a family repast after the chase. As the day wore away, she began to wonder why they did not return, and when some of the hunting-party came in, then some more, and gradually most of the retainers found their way home, and none of them could give any intelligence of the young ladies, her anxiety began to take a different turn.

They must have fallen from their horses and been hurt, or they had been seized by robbers, or devoured by wolves, or drowned in the Rhine. Certainly some terrible accident had befallen them, or they must have returned long since. The old lady was in a great state of alarm, and when they went to dinner without their daughters, for the first time for many years, the Count was forced to take three extra bottles of Rhine wine to get rid of the low spirits which such a circumstance produced.

Dinner past—still no daughters—the few people about the house were sent out in every direction, but nobody liked to go far, and nobody found anything. In fact, no news arrived until near sunset, when the three horses came in covered with mire, all more or less lame, and bearing evident marks of having had a rough journey. Then the mother gave way to despair and went at once into hysterics, on partially recovering from which, she clutched her husband's wig from his head, scratched him severely down one side of his face, and said it was all his fault, which the unhappy man did not attempt to deny, although there was not the shadow of a foundation for the charge. Then she wanted everybody to go everywhere at once, and do everything directly, the natural result being that nobody went anywhere or did anything. All was bustle and confusion, however, and nobody had any sleep in the castle that night.

Next morning the same sort of thing went on, the count hiding from his wife in abject terror, whilst she gave all kinds of contradictory orders, and really seemed to be half beside herself with alarm and distress. The only cool head about the place was the maid Dorothy, who was not only comely, as has been said, but had a great deal of common sense about her. Being moreover very fond of the three sisters, she was sincerely distressed at the thought that some evil might have befallen them, and most anxious that nothing should be left undone in order to obtain news of them.

She advised her mistress to send scouts in every direction (though, alas! there were but few to send), and further suggested that she should again consult the spirit of the cave from whom she had previously sought advice. Now this was the more good of Dorothy, inasmuch as she had not at all liked the former expedition, and had no wish to repeat it. But she saw the absolute necessity of doing something, and of employing the superfluous energies of the old Countess during this time of trial, and she therefore urged her to the step.

The old lady, however, flew into a passion at the suggestion, declaring that their misfortune was all because of their taking the spirit's advice, for he it was who had suggested the hunting-party, hinting at "consequences," indeed, but in such a way as naturally led her to suppose they would be such as she should desire, whereas, so far as she could see, they had probably been utterly disastrous.

She abused the spirit in no measured language, loudly declaring that he was no better than an old rascal, who had intentionally misled her, and vowing that she would have no more to do with him. After a while, however, as Dorothy reminded her that they did not actually know that evil had happened to the young ladies, and that it might possibly turn out for the best after all, and the spirit of the cave be less guilty than she supposed, the Countess began to soften down. She could not, however, bring herself to pay a second visit to the cave, and it ended by her requesting Dorothy to go alone, which the damsel did not much fancy, but eventually undertook to do.

That very same afternoon, therefore, the good girl set out, unattended by any one, and unprotected by anything save those invisible beings which always watch over youth, innocence, and beauty, and thus she walked along the banks of the river, and reached the cave in due time without encountering any adventure. She approached the dread spot in the same manner as she had done before when in company with the Countess, entered the cave, walked up to the big rock, and having been carefully instructed by her mistress how to address the being whom she had come to consult, pronounced these words in a low but firm tone—

"Great sir! the Countess very much afraid is
Some evil has befallen our young ladies;
They hunted, yesterday, as you desired,
But were not with us when the day expired;
And tho' we've searched o'er forest, hill, and plain,
Alas! they have not yet been found again!
Wherefore I've come to humbly ask for aid,
And pray that succour may not be delayed."

As soon as Dorothy had spoken thus, she paused for a reply, for which she had not long to wait. The same voice, proceeding from the same place, and speaking in the same tone as before, thus answered her inquiries—

" 'Tis not for man to penetrate
The hidden mysteries of fate,
And yet, fair maid, to thee I'd fain
Thy wishes grant and all explain.
Then listen, maiden, whilst I speak
True words of those for whom you seek.
The sisters, hunting yesterday,
Became the Baron's lawful prey,
And in his castle now abide
Upon the lofty mountain side.
The captives of his bow and spear
With whom durst no man interfere."

Dorothy listened to this statement with equal surprise and regret. She could not help feeling that the spirit of the cave, though doubtless an excellent fellow in his own way, had dealt rather hardly with the family of Stuttenguttenheim in the present instance. It was distinctly by his advice that the hunt had been arranged, and he now seemed to take it quite as a matter of course that it should have turned out in the disagreeable manner which it had done. She was, of course, not aware of the extreme inaccuracy of the statement that the sisters were the captives of the Baron's bow and spear, neither of which articles, as we have seen, had been employed in the matter, but even if it had really been so, this would not have absolved the spirit from the grave charge of having deceived the old Countess to the destruction of her daughters.

Dorothy felt, therefore, rather indignant at the cool way in which the invisible being seemed to take it, and although she was well aware that individuals of the spirit class have a code of law and morality peculiarly their own, and are not amenable to the laws by which the proceedings of ordinary beings are regulated, she could not help feeling that this was rather a special and exceptional case, and that she was bound to make some sort of protest against the course which the dread inhabitant of the cave seemed inclined to follow. So she thought for a few seconds after the voice ceased, in order to be sure of her rhymes, and then resumed the conversation as follows—

"Dread Sir, when here my Lady came with me,
You told us both, as plain as plain could be,
That the young ladies, if they hunting went
Should meet the Baron; and whate'er you meant,
No man, or woman either, in their senses,
Could doubt your meaning as to consequences.'
'Twas not that they his captives 'should be led,
But one of them should capture him instead;
And if the contrary has fallen out,
The fairness of the act I more than doubt.

What can I tell my mistress? that she err'd
In acting on th' advice which here she heard—
That she, in fact, in your good words believer,
Was only trusting to a gay deceiver?
It cannot be! I'm sure you cannot mean
So far the spirit office to bemean,
As thus t'entrap a dame of her position,
And bring her into such a sad condition!
Pray tell her what to do and how recover
Her daughters—even tho' they get no lover!"

CHAPTER III.

She spoke in an earnest tone, and with a courage which deserved great praise, since she knew that she ran great risk of offending the spirit of the cave in accusing him of having deceived the old countess, as he certainly had done, and if he should become really angry, there was no knowing whether he might not inflict upon her some disagreeable punishment then and there. But, being both courageous and faithful, the fair Dorothy spoke as I have said, and having done so, awaited the reply with heightened colour and beating heart, but quite prepared to take the consequences of her boldness, whatever they might be.

In a very short time the voice replied, and that in no angry manner, but in rather a melancholy tone, as that of one who grieved at having offended the person he addressed; these were his words—

"The secrets of the spirit-world are grave;
In open air or in the sacred cave
They cannot be revealed—yet they exist,

Believe me, maid—and to my counsel list.
Be not too rash the spirits to reprove
(Tho' courage they respect, and beauty love),
But think and know, since thou canst understand,
They hold not fate's decrees within their hand;
They but interpret things which may be known,
And show what is permitted to be shown.
What chanced on yesterday you know not yet,
And when you know—perchance may not regret—
Then judge not harshly, ere you know the end;
But would you the imprison'd girls befriend—
There is a way—safe, certain, sure, and true,
And their release, fair maid, depends on you.
Hie to the Baron's castle in the morn
(You need no aid from men with hound and horn),
Demand their ransom boldly, and forsooth,
You'll see I'm only telling you the truth;
And if the damsels thus you nobly save,
Come here and thank the spirit of the cave!"

Dorothy paid great attention to this speech, but was rather alarmed at the advice which it contained. She was very ready to do anything in her power to help the Countess to recover her daughters, but at the same time she did not particularly desire to be destroyed in the attempt. She could not but feel, moreover, that if the Baron had really carried off and imprisoned three damsels in his castle, another more or less would probably make no difference to him, and the result of her obeying the directions of the spirit might be that she would share the captivity of the sisters without being of the smallest use to them.

She hesitated for a moment, therefore, as to whether she should not ask whether there was no other way by which their release could be equally well effected, without her being called upon to run what she felt to be a great risk. Remembering, however, that spirits are queer customers to deal with, and that she had certainly obtained direct, positive, and definite information from this one, she deemed it better, on the whole, to be content, and not to go on asking questions, which might possibly arouse him to wrath. Besides, she was nearly at the end of her rhyming powers, and, should she attempt to continue the conversation, and break down in doing so, who could answer for the consequences ? So she murmured a few words of grateful and proper acknowledgment, and forthwith quitted the cave.

It must be confessed that during her homeward walk, sundry doubts arose within the damsel's breast. If the spirit had wilfully misled and deceived the mistress, it was possible that he might be intending to play the same game with the maid. This was not a pleasant reflection, and there was another which she could not help making within herself. Why should she tell the Countess the last advice of the spirit? He had told her where the young ladies were, which was the particular piece of information, to obtain which she had been sent to the cave ; would not the countess be satisfied with this, and was there any occasion to tell her the whole conversation ?

But the thought of concealment was banished as soon as it was entertained, or rather it never was entertained at all, but only flashed across the girl's mind. Dorothy was too honest and truthful to hide anything of the sort, and the very first thing she did when she got back was to seek the presence of her mistress, and give her a full, true, and particular report of everything which had taken place in the cave.

The old lady listened with feelings of a varied character. She was very angry that things had not turned out exactly as she had expected. Still, she could not feel sorry that the Baron's acquaintance had at all events been made, and being of a sanguine temperament, hoped that all would eventually turn out for the best. She would rather that the Baron had himself sent, as a gentleman should have done, to inform the Count and herself of the fact that their daughters were in his castle, and invited them to come there too, and reclaim them in a proper manner.

But as the Baron had taken no step of the kind, it seemed certainly desirable to follow the advice of the spirit, and let Dorothy proceed to the castle in which the poor girls were immured. In fact, there was nothing else to be done, unless the Countess went herself, and in her own opinion this would have been the better and more desirable course, if the spirit had given directions less positive and definite. But if, after having designated one person to perform certain duties, they were undertaken by another, there would be an excuse for the adviser if things went wrong, and it was evidently better to follow implicitly, if at all, the advice which had been given. There was, moreover, something appropriate in the idea of sending a maid to imprisoned young ladies, although indeed the fair Dorothy could hardly be called an ordinary servant, being rather more of a companion to the Countess, and altogether a superior sort of person.

It was very soon settled that she should obey the directions which had been given, and accordingly the next morning she set forth. It had occurred to the mother of the lost damsels that the messenger charged with such an important mission as the recovery of her daughters should go in proper state, and therefore the family coach of the Stuttenguttenheim's was ordered to be got ready. Unfortunately, however, it was so long since this had been used, that there were considerable difficulties in obeying the order. The wheels refused to act, and the body seemed inclined to come to pieces. So at last they brought out an old cart, into which they yoked an older horse, and in this vehicle Dorothy was driven to the gates of the castle of the Baron de Grumpelhausen, where she alighted and rang the bell, not without some little beating of the heart at a faster rate than usual.

During the interval for which we have left the three sisters to their fate, their adventures had doubtless been of an exceedingly interesting character. But, unluckily, there has never been an account given of them upon which the veracious historian could positively rely. I confess that I have always wondered how they managed without any change of dress, and with no clean things, and can only imagine that the wardrobe of the old woman who had shown them their rooms proved, on closer investigation, to be more ample than had at first appeared to be the case, or that some other female inhabitant of the castle must have turned up to help them.

Certain it is, at any rate, that they contrived to get on, somehow or other, and that their imprisonment was not one of a very dreadful character. They were neither starved, drowned, nor tortured, and in some respects had no cause to regret the change from the paternal mansion, since the food was better and more plentiful in their present abode. What little there is to tell, being entirely derived from the gossip of the country afterwards, may or may not be entirely correct, and must be accordingly received with caution.

It is rumoured that the castle nobly vindicated its reputation for being haunted. Strange noises sounded at the most unexpected times and places; white figures peeped round corners suddenly, the rustling of stiff brocade dresses was distinctly heard in passages where nothing was to be seen, and the distant clanking of chains, and groans which were scarcely human, were only too plainly audible in the dead hours of the weary night. But somehow or other the sisters survived it all, and the second morning of their sojourn in the castle found them still alive, and as cheerful as could have been expected under the circumstances.

The odd thing was that the master of the castle had so far never appeared. Save the old retainer who had at first received them, and the venerable dame, who turned out to be his wife, they had seen none but domestics of an inferior grade, and no great number of these.

It may be asked why, under these circumstances, they did not attempt to quit the castle. It must be obvious, however, to any one who takes the trouble to think about the matter, that there were evident objections to such a course. Even if no one had offered opposition to such a step, it was not very safe or very pleasant for three young ladies again to traverse the forest unattended, and was a step not to be taken if it could be avoided. Besides this, the words they had heard in the "whispering grotto" had so distinctly informed them that they were prisoners, that it never entered their heads to doubt the fact, and they would probably have waited some days longer before they had become sufficiently desperate to attempt an escape.

They were rather pleased, however, to find that in spite of the alarming words which had fallen upon their ears, nobody endeavoured to impose upon them the performance of those household duties or menial employments with which they had been threatened. They had, in short, been allowed to do pretty much as they pleased, subject always to those ghostly visits of which I have been unable to obtain an account which I could conscientiously present to the public as undoubtedly accurate.

Upon the morning of Dorothy's arrival the three sisters had breakfasted in the banqueting hall, and were standing at the bow window of the adjoining room, looking out over the river, when the loud peal sounded at the gate, and their hearts beat high in the hope of deliverance from a situation which was worse from its uncertainty than from anything else. Presently the door opened, and the same old domestic introduced Dorothy into the apartment. With a cry of joy the girls rushed to meet her, and after tenderly embracing her in the delight of seeing a home face again, eagerly asked after the welfare of their parents, whom they naturally imagined to be overwhelmed with grief at their loss.

Having reassured them as far as she was able, damsel began to question the sisters as to their own condition, and the conference would doubtless have continued for some time, had it not been interrupted by the sudden opening of the door which led into the armoury, and the unexpected appearance of a personage whom they had not yet seen.

It was a tall man who entered, clad in armour from head to foot, as if immediately about to enter battle instead of walking into a room which contained nothing but members of the softer sex, although it may be that he feared an encounter with such more than with mailed warriors.

His head alone was unprotected by warlike or any other covering, so that it could at once be seen that he was a man of middle age, not unprepossessing in appearance, though withal of a somewhat grave and stern aspect, as one who had known trouble and felt something of the cares and troubles of life. His beard cut into a point, hung as beards not unfrequently do, down upon his breast, adding much to the dignity of his appearance, and the eagle glance that shot from his proud eye betokened one of noble birth and high position.

He strode forward into the room for several paces, and then halting, looked upon the four damsels who stood before him, marvelling who or what he was. For some moments he regarded them without a word, and then haughtily waving his hand, he thus addressed them.

"I hope, fair dames, that ye find the castle to your liking. In me you behold its owner. But how comes it there are four of you? I fancied I had but three captives."

At this Albertina immediately interposed.

"We be no captives, Sir Baron," she said, "if that you be Baron, but three maidens who have lost our way in the woods, and taken refuge in your castle. We pray you send us home to our parents therefore, without delay. This is our mother's handmaid, Dorothy, who has come to fetch us, and is no captive either."

The Baron smiled grimly, but answered in a sportive tone—

"Dorothy, Dorothy, my mother's maid,
She stole oranges, I am afraid,
Some in her apron, and some in her sleeve,
She stole oranges, I do believe."

"Sir!" cried Dorothy, indignantly stepping forward at this supposed imputation upon her honesty. "I never stole anything in my life, and it's a shame for any one calling himself a gentleman to say so!"

"I never called myself a gentleman," replied the Baron, "inasmuch as a man's own testimony in such a case goes but for little; but, fair maid, I did but quote from an ancient song, and if you ever stole anything it was more likely to be a heart than an orange, and that you could not help. No, mistress Dorothy, you are no captive, having come here on a lawful errand. But for these young ladies, who had no business to be hunting in my woods at all, they are certainly my captives, and belong to me absolutely, unless I choose to let them be ransomed."

Margaret's dark eyes flashed fire at these words.

"It is no such thing !" she said. " Are we in a civilised country, that such claims should be made ? What have we done wrong? What right has any man to capture free-born damsels, and require ransom before he lets them go?"

The Baron again smiled.

"Might, sweet child," he remarked in a sarcastic tone, "has ever prevailed over right in this land ; and the will of the Grumpelhausen must not be questioned here.

You and your sisters are mine. Ye cannot escape me, and
had better submit with patience to the power which you are
unable to resist."

"I never heard of such a thing!" cried Albertina
indignantly.

"Probably not," rejoined the Baron; "but we live and
learn, you know."

Then little Gertrude took up the discourse.

"Sir," she said, "it is really a great shame for you to
treat us thus—"

"Have you been treated badly?" interrupted the Baron.

"No, sir, it is not that," replied the girl; "but it is too
bad for you to call us captives when you know quite well we
are no such thing. Why can't you send us home quietly, like
a good, respectable baron?"

"But," gravely returned the other, "I never pretended
to be a good, respectable baron. Who can have told you such
nonsense about me? Good and respectable, indeed! I am the
very reverse. A bad, loose-lived, robber-baron if you please,
doing what I please and when I please it, restrained by no law,
a dealer in unlawful things with unlawful people, a regular
demon, if you like to call me so; but good and respectable!
not that if you please!" and a sardonic smile sat upon his
countenance.

The sisters knew neither what to say nor do as they
listened to these strange observations of their host. They
therefore remained silent, and looked one at the other in dire
dismay. Then Dorothy stepped boldly forward and spoke with
head erect, and eye that sparkled with honest indignation.

"Sir," she said, " you cannot mean what you say. No
true nobleman would capture and detain helpless damsels
in the way you threatened but now. Surely you spoke but in
jest. Suffer me to take back word to the countess that her
daughters will be speedily restored to her."

"I have never had any other intention," observed the

Baron composedly, "as soon as the proper ransom shall be forthcoming. You would not have me give up my prize for nothing?"

And without another word he turned round and re-entered the armoury, closing the door behind him. As soon as he was gone the three sisters fairly broke down and burst into tears: It really seemed as if their hunting expedition would cost them dear, and that their captivity was only at its commencement. What ransom could their father pay? Nothing, as they well knew, which could satisfy the rapacity of the Baron. There seemed to be no way out of the difficulty, and their prospects were as gloomy as well could be the case.

Dorothy, however, did her best to cheer up the poor girls, telling them that when things were at the worst they often mended and took a turn for the better, and exhorting them to keep up their hearts and make the best of it. They dried their tears after a while, being brave damsels, and then held a consultation which lasted several minutes, at the end of which they came to the conclusion that it would be desirable to ascertain what sort of a ransom the Baron would actually take. So they followed him into the armoury, but he was not there, and they knew not where to look for him. Whilst they stood in doubt upon this point, Dorothy walked up to the mantelpiece and began to look at the carving and the picture. As she was contemplating the latter, to her intense surprise a deep voice proceeded from it, and abruptly asked her the question—

"Well, how do you like me?"

Overcome with astonishment (for the sisters had not told her of their conversation with this self-same picture), Dorothy could at first make no reply, upon which the picture, as if impatient of delay, gruffly observed—

"Have not you got a tongue in your head, that you can't answer a civil question? How do you like me?"

"Very much, sir," replied Dorothy, thinking it best to

sacrifice truth to politeness at that moment, and making a curtsey to the picture as she spoke.

"I'm glad of that," remarked the picture quietly, "for I like you, too—very much."

"Thank you, sir," replied Dorothy, still more surprised and confused, whilst Albertina, Gertrude, and Margaret stood listening in amazement.

"Yes, I do," continued the picture. "You are just the sort of girl I do like, to tell the truth."

This repeated assurance of regard on the part of the picture gave Dorothy fresh courage, and she began to think that she might possibly be able to turn it to account in furthering the escape of the three young ladies from the castle. So she looked up at the picture, as if its addressing her had been the most ordinary, every-day occurrence in the world, and making another respectful curtsey, demurely said—

"If you really like me, sir, it would be very kind if you would help me to get my young ladies home, away from this castle and its owner."

"You mean my great-great-grandson," remarked the picture. "Well, that is easy enough to be accomplished, at all events."

"Please tell me how, sir," asked the girl.

"Why," said the picture promptly, "you must take their place, of course. One can see with half an eye that the Baron likes the looks of you, and if you will stay in the castle, there is no doubt but that he will let the three ladies go."

"Oh, sir!" replied Dorothy, "how can you say such a thing? I'm sure the Baron would never want a poor girl like me, or count me equal to three such young ladies as these."

"Just you try him," responded the picture, and at the same moment the three sisters all came forward and cried with one voice—

"Oh, Dorothy, if you could save us so!"

"What?" asked the poor girl, trembling all over, I stay

all alone here with this terrible Baron? Why even if he wanted me, I should be frightened to death, and he couldn't really want me, you know."

"But his great-great-grandfather wouldn't say so if he didn't," observed Margaret.

"Of course I shouldn't," said the picture.

"I never heard of such a thing," sobbed Dorothy.

"But would you do it to save us, dear, kind, good, sweet Dorothy?" said Gertrude eagerly.

"I would do anything for you, dear," answered the girl.

"Then do it!" said the voice in a tone more cheerful than it had hitherto used, and at that moment the picture swung round upon hinges moved by hidden springs, and the Baron himself stood before the astonished girls.

"After Dorothy's last speech," said he, "further concealment is unnecessary. I love her, and if she will consent to remain in my castle, it shall be as its Baroness, a position which I am confident she will adorn, and make happy a home which has too long been desolate and lonely. Young ladies, your hunt in the forest will thus have borne good fruit after all, and your excellent mother will have so far carried out her benevolent intentions in providing the Grumpelhausen with a wife."

The girls were all so much amazed as to be unable to speak for some seconds. When they had sufficiently recovered their presence of mind, Albertina replied with a dignity befitting her rank and family.

"Sir Baron," she said, haughtily regarding him, "so that you forward our return to our parents, it is no concern of ours whether you wed or not; and if you are bent on doing so with one beneath your own rank, you could find no better mate than Dorothy."

"That he couldn't, I'm sure!" cried the good-natured Gertrude, and Margaret likewise gravely nodded her assent to the proposition.

Meanwhile the person chiefly concerned in the proposed domestic arrangements of the Baron was perplexed and amazed beyond measure. How, when, and where the head of the House of Grumpelhausen should have seen and taken such a fancy to her, as he had evidently done, was a thought which puzzled her extremely, and the change in her prospects was so great, so sudden and unexpected, that she felt perfectly bewildered.

Had the three sisters resented the proposition of the Baron as in the slightest degree insulting or annoying to themselves, I really believe that Dorothy would not have entertained it for a moment, so fond was she of the young ladies, and so loyally attached to the ancient house of Stuttenguttenheim. But, since their attitude was entirely different, the damsel could not help seeing the advantages which were offered her in the proposed change of her condition. From being the handmaid of the old Countess, loved and trusted indeed, but still a servant, she would be raised to a rank and position superior to that of her mistress, to whom she might still be a useful friend and valuable neighbour. True it was that she did not know much of the Baron, nor had he encouraged her much by the character which he had given himself, but after all, his acts might belie his words, and his decided preference for her was very flattering, to say the least of it.

Hardly knowing what to say or do, Dorothy did the most natural thing in the world, namely, burst into tears. The sisters comforted her, and the Baron said all he could think of with the same view, and at last, after sundry denials and doubts, she gave her consent to the settlement of the matter in the manner which he proposed. Upon this the Baron embraced her tenderly, and being a just and impartial man, saluted the three sisters also, one after the other, saying that it was the invariable custom of his family on such occasions.

Thinking it useless to resist, the girls submitted without

a murmur, and this ceremony having been completed, the question of their getting home had next to be discussed. The cart which had brought Dorothy was still waiting, and it was agreed that they should all go back in it, Dorothy having stipulated with the Baron that she should accompany them, which he permitted upon her promise being given that their wedding should be very shortly celebrated. The Baron was very anxious to come too, but from this he was dissuaded by Dorothy, who foresaw that his reception by the old Countess might not be exactly what could be wished. In this surmise she was undoubtedly right, as will be seen immediately.

The cart bore its precious burden safely to the abode of the Stuttenguttenheim family, and the parents of the lost damsels were doubtless overjoyed at their return. But no sooner had the old Countess heard the whole story than she flew into a furious passion, calling the Baron every bad name she could lay her tongue to.

What! her peerless Albertina, her sweet Gertrude, her queenly Margaret, were none of these good enough for his high-and-mightiness, but he must take up with a lowborn wench, forsooth, who ought to be their scullery-maid! Then she turned upon Dorothy herself, and gave her what she called "a piece of her mind," and a very disagreeable piece it was, too. She accused her of fraud and deception, of having laid herself out to entrap the Baron, and employed her situation about the young ladies as a means to wheedle them out of the position which one of them had a right to expect.

The girls were quite ashamed of this harsh and unjust language, but poor Dorothy bore it meekly, and after the storm was over the old lady relieved herself by a great gush of tears, and was afterwards quieter and more composed. Then she took to declaring that she should never be able to spare Dorothy, and that she must really tell the Baron that she had changed her mind upon the subject of matrimony, and could not agree to marry him.

Dorothy, however, having once given her promise, was determined to keep it, and gently reminded her mistress that, but for this, she would not have recovered her daughters so easily. The latter, too, joined in the opinion that faith must certainly be kept, especially as a contrary course would raise up a powerful enemy to their house in the person of the justly provoked Baron. So the old lady was forced to give in, and a messenger was sent to inform the Lord of Grumpelhausen that he might visit his intended bride when he pleased.

He pleased very soon, and was received by the old Countess with more urbanity than might have been expected. The fact is, that after giving the matter full consideration, the good lady had come to the conclusion that there was more to be gained by being friends with the Baron than by quarrelling with him, and that if she had failed to secure him as a son-inlaw, the next best thing was that he should wed some one who was attached to her family. So matters being thus set right, all went smoothly and well, and the wedding was duly celebrated within a very short space of time, for people in those days, and in that part of the world, seldom delayed these matters when they were once determined on.

When the nuptials were over, and she had a little time to think about all that had occurred, Dorothy remembered that upon her second visit to the spirit who had directed the hunt, and afterwards the method by which the lost girls should be recovered, he had intimated that if her attempt succeeded, she should "come and thank the spirit of the cave." Accordingly, having asked her husband's leave overnight, she set off in the morning, alone as before, safely reached the cave, and walking up to the same place as before, thanked the spirit in the following appropriate terms—

"Oh dread inhabitant of this dark cave,
Thou aidest me the missing ones to save.

From servant I've become a noble dame,
And thank you very kindly for the same!"

Immediately the voice answered—

"And dost thou thank me, who hast others saved,
Only alas! thyself to be enslaved,
Tied to a robber-baron for thy life,
And doomed to be his miserable wife?"

At these words Dorothy became very angry, and instantly replied—

"I am not miserable—not a bit
And, spirit tho' you be, 'tis most unfit,
This charge against my husband dear to bring ;
He's not a robber, sir, nor: no such thing;
And if he was, in spite of that, or you,
I'd be to him a loving wife and true."

"I am very glad to hear it," replied the Baron in his natural voice, and suddenly stepped from behind the rock and stood before his astonished wife. Having first reassured her by a tender embrace, he then proceeded to explain to her several things which the accomplished reader has already guessed.

He, the worthy Baron de Grumpelhausen, was the spirit of the cave, as well as of the whispering grotto, and had moreover represented the departed soul of his great-great-grand-father in the recess behind the picture of the latter. A secret passage from the castle communicated directly with the grotto, and by means thereof the Lord of Grumpelhausen had often been able to utter prophecies and commands which were more or less useful to his family and himself.

As to the cave, its mysteries were also well known to his illustrious house. It has been said that the Baron was eccentric, and one of his fancies was to act the part of the spirit of the cave, and amuse himself with the visits paid to it from time to time, by the scattered population around. It was by accident that he was there upon the occasion of the first visit of the old Countess, unless indeed he had received secret intelligence of her coming, and of this I am not certain.

At that time he was very much struck with the appearance of Dorothy, and in fact, fell violently in love with her at first sight. Fate placed in his hands the means of making her acquaintance very speedily, and that, as we have seen, under circumstances which enabled him to prosecute his suit to a successful issue without let or hindrance. So the charming handmaid of the old Countess von Stuttenguttenheim became Baroness de Grumpelhausen in the manner we have seen.

She amply realized the fond expectations of the Baron, and made him an excellent wife. Moreover, in her prosperity she did not forget her old friends. In spite of its ghosts and goblins, she made the castle quite gay with the festivities which she introduced into it. Balls, parties, gatherings for croquet and lawn tennis, even football and cricket matches, each in the proper season of the year, were arranged by the indefatigable Baroness, and attended by all people for many miles round who were fortunate enough to be upon her visiting list.

The result was natural. The three sisters of the House of Stuttenguttenheim came to all these entertainments, and not only came, but saw and conquered too.

The adorable Albertina married an officer of high rank, who lived but on her smiles. Gertrude went to cheer the home of a merchant of immense wealth, who lavished it upon her with the generosity of devotion, whilst Margaret became the wife of a nobleman of ancient lineage and vast estates, who worshipped the very ground she trod on.

The Voice behind the Rock

Baroness Dorothy was well satisfied in having promoted these three marriages, and none the less so because the old Countess took the whole credit to herself, and moreover went so far as to state—and that so often that it is charitable to suppose she quite believed it—that to her foresight, advice, and good management was due the marriage of Dorothy herself to the Baron de Grumpelhausen. How she made it out I do not exactly know, but as her doing so satisfied her, and did no harm to anybody else, it did not much matter. At all events, she held and spread abroad this view of the case until the day of her death, which did not occur until she had dandled upon her knees several grandchildren, and told them the adventures of this story with additions and exaggerations which doubtless rendered the narrative attractive beyond measure.

The Count preceded his wife to the family tomb by some years, having eaten unripe pomegranates in larger quantities than prudence would have dictated, and afterwards drank his claret without having the chill taken off. So it took him off, and nobody missed him when he was gone. There is very much more to be told about the castle and its inhabitants, but it is well to leave them at the particular point which we have now reached. When people are happily married they like to be left alone sometimes, and so we will leave the Baron de Grumpelhausen and his Dorothy to themselves.

It was a happy match in every respect, and the Baron never had cause to regret the eccentricity on his part which had led to it. The only difficulty I have in saying good-bye to the happy pair is that of drawing a moral from their story. There is one to be drawn, no doubt, but it cannot be that we should all frequent mysterious caves or whispering grottos, because very few of us are ever likely to have the opportunity of doing so. It cannot be to avoid husband-hunting, because, in the result, those who followed this interesting occupation were as well provided for as she who did not, and therefore no particular lesson can be learned upon this point, nor can it be any of those ordinary morals which are drawn from ordinary stories, because this is in fact one of rather an extraordinary character. So I think the best thing to do is to leave the moral alone, and let people try to find one out for themselves if they want one; and if writers of stories would take this course rather oftener than they do, it is my private opinion that they would please their readers a great deal more than they do, and would at the same time save themselves an infinite amount of trouble which produces no adequate result. And with this sentiment I bid farewell to the Baron and Baroness de Grumpelhausen.

THE END.

"A promising apprentice". Knatchbull-Hugessen M.P. as caricatured by Ape (Carlo Pellegrini) in Vanity Fair, June 1870.

ABOUT THE AUTHOR

Edward Hugessen Knatchbull-Hugessen, first Baron Brabourne, known also as E.H. Knatchbull-Hugessen, was a British politician who began his political career as a Liberal and later became a Conservative. In 1880 he was elevated to the peerage as Baron Brabourne.

He was the younger son of Sir Edward Knatchbull, 9th Baronet, who twice served as Paymaster-General, and his second wife Fanny Catherine night, who was a niece of author Jane Austen. In 1849 his family received a Royal licensee adding the surname of Hugessen to his name. Hugessen had been the maiden surname of his father's mother. He was educated at Eton and Oxford, at Magdalen College, and served as President of the Oxford Union.

In 1857 Knatchbull-Hugessen was elected Member of Parliament for Sandwich (a town in the Dover district of Kent, in southeast England), a seat he would hold until 1880. He served as a Lord of the Treasury under Lord Palmerston, who was Prime Minister at the time, from 1859 to 1860, as Under-Secretary of State for Home Affairs under Lord Russell in 1866 and under Gladstone from 1868 to 1871 and as Under-Secretary of State for the Colonies under Gladstone from 1871 to 1874.

He was admitted to the Privy Council in 1873 and raised to the peerage as Baron Brabourne in 1880. Shortly after becoming a Peer he joined the Conservative party, citing his opposition to the interventionist policies of Radicals such as Joseph Chamberlain. In 1882 he became a founding member of the Liberty and Property Defence League.

Knatchbull-Hugessen wrote many well-known short stories and fairy tales. He produced a book or two of these stories each year from 1869 to about 1894. He wrote a dozen or more such books. These publications were popular at the time, and were illustrated by leading artists of the time. 'The Times' newspaper noted that his stories... "are of a very high order; light and brilliant narrative flow from his pen, and is fed by an invention as graceful as it is inexhaustible." He was widely likened by the reviewers to masters of the fairy-tale such as Grimm and Andersen, and his prolific output of the tales even led a critic at 'The British Quarterly Review' to question his dedication to his job at the Colonial Office... "We should like to know whether Mr. Knatchbull-Hugessen maintains his intercourse with the fairies of the Colonial Office. If so, what department of office duty is specially favourable to them; whether, too, they come when Parliament breaks up, or whether their visits are intermittent all the year round."

In a letter of 1971, J.R.R. Tolkien recalled that, as a small child, his bedtime reading was the fairy stories of Knatchbull-Hugessen. He recalled especially being read one story of an ogre who catches his dinner by disguising himself as a tree.

Brabourne also edited the first edition of the novelist Jane Austen's letters, published in 1884. This edition included about two-thirds of her surviving letters, and was dedicated to Queen Victoria. He had inherited the letters after his mother's death in December 1882.

He died on February 6, 1893 at Smeeth Paddocks, and was buried in St Mary the Virgin Churchyard at Smeeth, Kent, on 9 February.

HISTORICAL CONTEXT

1820 —Marriage of Sir Edward Knatchbull (1871-1849) and Fanny Catherine Knight (1793-1882), his second wife, who was a niece of the deceased romance novelist Jane Austen.

—Arthur Wellesley, 1st Duke of Wellington, serves as Prime Minister of the United Kingdom, 1828 to 1830.

1829 *—April 13: The Catholic Relief Act is passed, repealing the Test Act of 1672 and other punitive laws then in force, and made it legal for Catholics to serve in Parliament.*

—April 29: Birth of Edward Hugessen Knatchbull-Hugessen, at Mersham Hatch in Kent, England, seat of the Knatchbull baronets.

1830 *—June 26: King George IV dies and William IV ascends the throne.*

—November 22: Charles Grey, 2nd Earl Grey, chosen to serve as Prime Minister of the United Kingdom, 1830-1834.

1831 —Birth of his brother, the Rev. Reginald Bridges Knatchbull-Hugessen, later the rector of a church at Mersham.

—Knatchbull's father, Sir Edward Knatchbull (1781-1849), serves steps down after serving in Parliament, representing Kent, since 1819

—Knatchbull's father, Sir Edward Knatchbull (1781-1849) is elected to Parliament representing one of two new eastern divisions of Kent, following a split of the Kent district, a seat he held until resigning in 1845.

1832 —*June 7: The Great Reform Act passes, doubling the franchise. The right to vote is granted to small landowners, tenant farmers, shopkeepers and some householders and lodgers.*

1833 —*August 28: The Slavery Abolition Act gains royal assent, banning slavery throughout the British Empire.*

1834 —*The Conservative party is founded.*
—Knatchbull's father, Sir Edward Knatchbull (1781-1849), serves as Paymaster of the Forces 1834-1835.

—*July 16: William Lamb, 2nd Viscount Melbourne, serves as Prime Minister of the United Kingdom. .*

—*November 17: Arthur Wellesley, 1st Duke of Wellington, serves as Prime Minister of the United Kingdom.*

—*December 10: Robert Peel, MP to Tamworth, serves as Prime Minister of the United Kingdom, to April 8, 1835.*

1835 —Birth of Lord Brabourne's brother, Herbert Thomas Knatchbull-Hugessen.

—*April 18: William Lamb, 2nd Viscount Melbourne, serves as Prime Minister of the United Kingdom, to August 30, 1841.*

1837 —*June 20: Queen Victoria ascends the throne*
—Birth of his brother, William Western Knatchbull-Hugessen (1837-1864)

1838 —*August 1: The Slavery Abolition enters into force, abolishing slavery in the British Empire.*

1841 —Knatchbull's father, Sir Edward Knatchbull (1781-1849), serves as Paymaster General
1841-1845.

*—August 30: Robert Peel, MP to Tamworth,
becomes Prime Minister of the United Kingdom
for the second time, to June 29, 1846.*

1842 *—Summer: The first peacetime income tax is
introduced.*

1846 *—June 30: Lord John Russell, 1st Earl Russell,
MP for the City of London, serves as Prime
Minister of the United Kingdom.*

1848 *—February: The "Communist Manifesto" is
published by Karl Marx and Friedrich Engels.*

1849 —May: Death of Lord Brabourne's father, Sir
Edward Knatchbull (1781-1849) at the family's
Mersham Park estate in Kent, England.

—By royal licence Lord Brabourne assumes the
additional surname of Hugessen, which was the
maiden surname of his father's mother.

1850 —Knatchbull graduates from Magdalen College,
at Oxford.

*—The East Coast Main Line opens, a nearly 400
mile railroad line linking London to Edinburgh,
built by tree railway companies, the North
British Railway, the North Eastern Railway
and the Great Northern Railway.*

1851 *—May 1: Opening of the Great Exhibition of the
Works of Industry of All Nations, also known
as the Crystal Palace Exhibition, referring to
the temporary structure in which it was held,
at Hyde Park, in London, to October. Organiz-
ers included Prince Albert, husband of Queen
Victoria.*

1852   —Knatchbull marries Anna Maria Elizabeth, younger daughter of the Rev. M.R. Southwell, vicar of St. Stephen's, St. Albans.

—February 23: Edward Smith-Stanley, 14th Earl of Derby, serves as Prime Minister of the United Kingdom,

—December 19: George Hamilton-Gordon, 4th Earl of Aberdeen, serves as Prime Minister of the United Kingdom, to January 30, 1855.
1853-1856

1853-56   *—The Crimean War is fought between Russia and a British alliance who feared Russian expansion in the Balkans, resulting in an allied victory.*

1854   *—Doctor John Snow discovers that cholera is caused by contaminated water.*

1855   *—February 6: Henry John Temple, 3rd Viscount Palmerston, MP for Tiverton, serves as Prime Minister of the United Kingdom, to 1858*
—June 29: The "Daily Telegraph" begins publication.

1857   —April: Knatchbull is elected to the House of Commons as M.P. representing Sandwich, a town in the Dover District of Kent, in southeastern England, holding the seat until 1880.

—April 5: Birth of Edward Knatchbull-Hugessen (1857-1909), son and eldest child of Knatchbull and his wife.

1858   *—February 20: Edward Smith-Stanley, 14th Earl of Derby, serves as Prime Minister of the United Kingdom, to June 11, 1859.*

—Birth of Katharine Cecilia Knatchbull-Hugessen, daughter of Knatchbull and his wife.

1859   —June: Knatchbull begins to serve as Lord of

the Treasury of the United Kingdom, under Lord Palmerston.

—June 12: Henry John Temple, 3rd Viscount Palmerston, MP for Tiverton, serves as Prime Minister of the United 185Kingdom for the second time, to October 18, 1865.

1861 —Birth of Eva Mary Knatchbull-Hugessen (1861-1895), daughter of Knatchbull and his wife.

—December 14: Prince Albert, husband of Queen Victoria, dies at the age of 42.

1863 *—January 10: Opening of the world's first underground railway, in downtown London, known as the London Underground or The Tube.*

—Birth of Cecil Marcus Knatchbull-Hugessen (1863-1933).

—Mr. Knatchbull-Hugessen, senior member of Parliament for Sandwich, Deal and Walmer, fixes the first column of a new pier that is being built using stones from the demolished Sandown Castle.

1864 —November 8; A final opening ceremony for the pier is performed by Mr. Knatchbull-Hugessen, although an earlier ceremonial opening of the new pier had been held on July 14, with all the troops of Walmer lining the pier and a procession of workmen and the construction company people, led by the mayor, who declared the pier open to the public, even though it was not yet complete. from "History of Deal," by John Laker)

1865 *—October 29; Lord John Russell, 1st Earl Russell, MP for the City of London, serves as Prime Minister of the United Kingdom for the second time, June 1866.*

1866 —May: End of Knatchbull's service as Lord of the Treasury.

—Knatchbull serves as chairman of the Treasury Committee which sat in Dublin to investigate the problems of the Irish Constabulary, which had at that time 1,500 vacancies. Their proposal for increased pay and improved working conditions helped to restore that force.

—December: Knatchbull begins service as Under-Secretary of State for the Home Department, under Lord (Brabourne) Knatchbull-Hugessen about matters of education and schools.

1873 —Publication of Knatchbull's fifth book, "Queer Folk: Seven Stories."

—Knatchbull becomes a sworn member of the Privy Council.

—Knatchbull grants permission for excavation of a possible Romano-British cemetery on lands belonging to himself at Brabourne, in Kent. (See "Archaeologia Cantiana," volume 9, 1874.)

1874 —Publication of Knatchbull's sixth storybook, "Whispers from Fairyland."

—Publication of Knatchbull's storybook, "River Legends: or, River Thomas and Father Rhine."

—February: End of Knatchbull's service as Under-Secretary for the Colonies.

  —*February 20: Benjamin Disraeli, 1st Earl of Beaconsfield and MP for Buckinghamshire, : serves as Prime Minister of the United Kingdom for the second time, to April 1880.*

1875 —Publication of Knatchbull's storybook, "Higgledy-Piggledy: or, Stories for Everybody and Everybody's Children."

1877   —Publication of Knatchbull's biographical account of Oliver Cromwell, "Life, Times and Character of Oliver Cromwell."

1878   —Publication of Knatchbull's storybook, "Uncle Joe's Stories."

1879   —Publication of Knatchbull's storybook, "Other Stories."

1880   —May: Knatchbull is elevated to the peerage as Lord Baron Brabourne

—*April 23: William E. Gladstone serves second term as Prime Minister of the United Kingdom, to June 9, 1885.*

—*December 20; Start of the First Boer War in South Africa, also known as the First Anglo-Boer War, the Transvaal War or the Transvaal Rebellion.*

1881   —*March 23: Signing of a peace treaty concludes the First Boer War, resulting in a Boer victory, and the eventual independence of the South African Republic. The British agreed to complete Boer self-government in the Transvaal under British suzerainty. The Boers in turn accepted the Queens nominal rule and British control of foreign affairs, African affairs, and native districts.*

—Publication of Knatchbull's storybook, "The Mountain Sprite's Kingdom and Other Stories."

—Publication of Knatchbull's book, "The Truth about the Transvaal," presenting a British view of the Boer conflicts in South Africa and Britain's retreat from the Transvaal area, saying that the Boers' desire to maintain slavery was the reason why they parted ways with the British government.

—August 3: The Pretoria Convention signed and later ratified, October 25, by the Transvaal Volksraad or parliament kept the Transvaal under British suzerainty and British troops withdrew.

—Knatchbull withdraws his support for the Gladstone government.

1882   —Knatchbull becomes a founding member of the Liberty and Property Defence League.

—Death of Knatchbull's mother, Fanny Catherine Knight (1793-1882), who was a niece of famous romance novelist Jane Austen. At this time, Knatchbull inherits the surviving letters of Jane Austen from his mother.

1883   —Publication of Knatchbull's storybook, "Ferdinand's Adventure."

—In South Africa, the London Convention, providing for full independence and self-government, although still with British control of foreign affairs, is enacted, superseding the earlier Pretoria Convention.

1885   —Knatchbull formally joins the Conservative party.

—Publication of the book edited by Knatchbull, "Letters of Jane Austen," presenting surviving correspondence of the romance novelist Jane Austen, who was Knatchbull's great-aunt. The book included about two-thirds of Austen's surviving letters and was dedicated to Queen Victoria.

—June 23: Robert Gascoyne-Cecil, 3rd Marquess of Salisbury, serves as Prime Minister of the United Kingdom, to January 1886.

—The Reform Act of 1885, otherwise known as the Redistribution of Seats Act, was an electoral reform legislation that redistributed the seats

in the House of Commons, introducing the concept of equally populated constituencies. It was associated with the Representation of the People Act of 1884.

1886 —*February 1: William E. Gladstone serves third term as Prime Minister of the United Kingdom, to July.*

—*July 25: Robert Gascoyne-Cecil, 3rd Marquess of Salisbury, serves as Prime Minister of the United Kingdom for the second time, to August 11, 1892.*

—*In South Africa, discovery of the largest deposit of gold-bearing ore, in a large ridge 30 miles south of the Boer capital of Pretoria, reignites British imperial interests in maintaining control of South Africa.*

—Publication of "Facts and Fictions in Irish History: A Reply to Mr. Gladstone," in which the Baron Brabourne attempts a conciliatory view of relations between the Irish and British.

1887 —Knatchbull's short story, "Ella's Fault," appears in a collection of short stories by various authors, "Jack Frost's Little Prisoners: A Collection of Stories for Children from Four to Twelve Years of Age."

—*November: The fictional detective Sherlock Holmes first appears in print, in "A Study in Scarlet," written by Sir Arthur Conan Doyle.*

1889 —May 2: Death of Knatchbull's wife, Lady Brabourne.

—April 16: Knatchbull's eldest son and namesake, the Hon. Edward Knatchbull-Hugessen, was elected to the Parliament representing Rochester, a seat vacated by the resignation of Colonel Hughes-Hallett.

1890 —June 3: Marriage to Ethel Mary Walker, daughter of Colonel Sir George Gustavus Walker (1830-1897)

1891 —Birth of son Adrian Norton Knatchbull-Hugessen (1891-1976), who emigrated to Canada and became a Canadian lawyer and senator.

—Publication of "Catalogue of a portion of the topographical and general library of Lord Brabourne, comprising the chief histories of the various counties of Great Britain and Ireland," in preparation for its being sold by auction, by Sotheby, Wilkinson & Hodge, scheduled for May 11, 1891.

1892 —*August 15: William E. Gladstone serves fourth term as Prime* Minister of the United Kingdom, to 1894.

1893 —February 6: Death of Sir Edward H. Knatchbull-Hugessen at Smeeth Paddocks.

—February 18: Birth of Alicia Mary Dorothea Knatchbull-Hugessen (1893-1974)

Milton Keynes UK
Ingram Content Group UK Ltd.
UKHW022033310823
427750UK00014B/432

9 781628 345063